PLAYING THE BONES

PLAYING THE BONES

A NOVEL

Louise Redd

LITTLE, BROWN AND COMPANY
Boston New York Toronto London

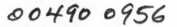

Copyright © 1996 by Louise Redd

First Edition

The characters and events in this book are fictitious. Any similarity to real per-sons, living or dead, is coincidental and not intended by the author.

Library of Congress Cataloging-in-Publication Data

Redd, Louise.
Playing the bones / Louise Redd. — 1st ed.
p.   cm.
ISBN 0-316-73511-6
1. Young women — Texas — Fiction.   2. Man-woman relationships —
Texas — Fiction.   3. Blues musicians — Texas — Fiction.   I. Title.
PS3568.E296P53   1996
813'.54 — dc20   95-47917

10 9 8 7 6 5 4 3 2 1

MV-NY

Published simultaneously in Canada by Little, Brown & Company (Canada) Limited

Printed in the United States of America

For Allan

I need to thank Tom Wissemann, my neighbor and friend, for loaning me a few of his many stories. I'd also like to thank some people for their indispensable encouragement: Lady Margaret, True, and Allan Redd, Rule Brand, Michael Pietsch, Andrew Cohen, Patrick Woodall, Ritu Varma, Lee Gaillard, Emily Hassler, Anne Munch, Dar Craft, Denise Clark, Ellen Sammon, Sid Evans, Michelle and Dave Feller-Kopman, Eileen Nehme, and especially Matthew McEvoy.

PLAYING THE BONES

MEAN GIRL BLUES

On my list of One Hundred Things I Want Out of Life, hearing a certain man say "Hey my baby" is Number 2.

Eva, my therapist, opens every session with the same question. This Tuesday is no different from the others.

"Lacy," she says, "may we fill in the first slot on your list today?"

The list was Eva's idea. I've managed the other ninety-nine, but the list is under constant revision, like everything in my life. To avoid her question I scribble lyrics on a legal pad in my lap. I don't play an instrument, nor do I sing, rap, dance, perform card tricks, or even make love very well. When I become accomplished at any of these things, spaces in my heart will open up like popcorn.

The man in question was raised up in the South and says "hey" instead of "hi." He calls me "baby" and sometimes "my baby" but I like it best when he speaks the trinity. His name is Black Jesus — at least that's the name on the marquee and his CDs and cassettes. I refuse to discuss with Eva why my Ph.D. in Comparative Literature does not prevent my heart from freezing up and then thawing when I hear this man's foolish talk.

"I am interested," Eva says while I write my lyrics, "in this reluctance to identify what you want most out of life." She adjusts the pink turban that swaddles her head. The turban has nothing to do with religion. It's purely decorative, and modern as well. It fastens with tiny strips of Velcro.

What rhymes with "seen"?

"I'm pleased to see you taking notes, however," she adds.

Eva's not quite a real therapist. She's working on her doctorate in psychology, so I get a cut rate for being a university guinea pig. If I had the money to blow, I'd go to someone with a degree and a nice office full of caladiums. Instead, I'm stuck with Eva. I've been seeing Eva for four months. I'm trying to get my head straightened out in time for my wedding.

Lean? Fiend?

"Would you care to share your notes with me?"

I clear my throat. "Woman I got / Meanest woman I ever seen."

"What?" She pulls out a thick psychology text from the shelf behind her desk. Other books collapse into the empty space.

"Ask her for a drink of whiskey / She give me kerosene."

"What do you mean 'she give me'? Why are you using grammar like that? Is that what they call — wait — Black English Vernacular?" She's scanning the table of contents. "V," she flips to the index. "Maybe it's Vernacular Black English. Oh, I can't remember."

"Woman I got / She the meanest woman I know."

"Are you attempting to express anger at your mother?"

Know, Monroe.

"Yes or no?"

"Ask her to meet me downtown / I hear she over in East
Monroe."

"East Monroe? What on earth? Lacy, where are you
today?"

"University of Houston, Houston, Texas, your office."

"Thank you, dear. I already knew that. Are these original
lyrics?"

Eva's office window has a great view of the university
lawn. I see a girl who could be the mean woman in my
song — proud spine, electric hair. She inspires me to finish
the next verse.

"Woman I got," I read, "Meanest woman I ever done."

"Lacy," Eva says, "I think we should discuss some of
these sexist overtones. Words like 'done' imply —"

"Ask for the shade of her oak tree / She leave me in the
burnin sun."

The girl strides across the courtyard, her face lit with
purpose. The loose skirt can't keep up with her long, fast
steps.

"Perhaps," Eva attempts, "you are telling me that you
did not receive what you needed from your caregivers. That
they left you in a scorching desert of psychic need, rather
than providing you the nurturing shade of love and encouragement."

"Perhaps."

She waits for the next verse, pen poised over her notebook.

"The End," I say, though I know it's not.

Eva slams the book shut and claws at her turban, elbows
red as they press into the pasteboard desk. I'm spoiling her
dissertation research. Or maybe she just doesn't like the
blues.

"Why do you even come to therapy?"

"Maybe it's the answer?" I twist a curl of my hair, the
color of a blood orange, around one finger.

"One of many answers," she corrects. "And who are you today?" she begs softly, her New York accent stretching and twanging on the barbs of some private sorrow. To soothe her, I answer her question truthfully.

"I'm a white girl from Dallas," I say.

"Did you become intimate with this Black Jesus right away?" Eva asks.

"No, not intimate. I fucked him."

Eva scratches, birdlike, in her notebook. I wonder if she writes down "fucked."

"And have you remained intimate with Ellis?"

"Last night we blackened some catfish," I say. "Ellis fed me the tail piece of his. The tail piece is the most tender — did you know that, Eva?"

"No, I didn't."

"I felt intimate with him, then. When I opened my mouth and he laid his fork on my tongue and that sweet, spicy taste started sinking down through the prongs of the fork, then I thought, *Damn, Ellis, I can marry you. I can't wait to marry you.*"

"And Black Jesus? How do you feel about him now? What feeling, if any, has he left you with?"

It's a difficult question. I feel a flush along the skin of my throat, I feel a knotting and unknotting between my hipbones. I feel something like industrial-strength cleaning fluid in my stomach when I think of his hands cradling his harmonica. I feel my naturally red hair perspiring a secret shine.

CAN I HAVE YOUR AUTOGRAPH, MR. JESUS?

That first night at the club in North Houston, my voice feels frail when I ask him to play a song for me. Black Jesus says, "Damn, my grandmama used to play the hell outta that song." He remembers the music but not the words, and my hand quivers as I cram the words on a cocktail napkin for him. My memory is impeccable. He begins the next set solo, and I get to add the picture of the angle of his harmonica against his mouth, the notes he blew softly and the ones he blew hard, to those lyrics for the rest of my life. His acoustic guitar is varnished the sticky luster of caramel candy. His band is happily shooting pool. They pass the battered pool stick around the table as Black Jesus gradually signals one after another of them back, first Wells, the drummer, then Henry John Harrison, the rhythm guitarist who played with Black Jesus's famous grandmother, Vaughan Sharp, then Black Jesus's younger brother Marcy with his dark bass guitar, then finally Bill Wright passes the stick to a girl in cutoffs and a Harley shirt and goes on up to lay his hands on the keyboards.

When the set is over I start to gather my purse, my desires, and the leather jacket once worn by my dead daddy. Karl, Black Jesus's road manager, touches my elbow and says, "Come on back, girl, I know Jesus wants to visit with you." He guides me backstage, where Marcy holds a bottle of gin in one hand and a cellular phone in the other.

"We just got done," he says into the phone. "Yeah we did. You wanta ask Jesus? Jesus," Marcy says, "she says you as big a liar as I am."

"Marcy," Karl says, "tell that young lady you got to help me break down. Come on, now."

Black Jesus wipes his face and neck with a wet towel. He takes a long time doing it, as if there's soap and he's trying to raise a lather. He looks at me and says, "How'd you like the song?"

"I liked it," I say.

"I'm about to starve," he says. "I can't eat before my shows. You want to go somewhere with me?"

He gives Karl the keys to their van and we drive in my car to a restaurant where they never stop bringing warm tortilla chips and salsa so hot it drives confusion right out of your head. A three-piece band of elderly Mexican men wails out songs in Spanish. My Spanish is rudimentary, but I understand that people in the songs are being tortured by love. The musicians wander between the tables, their tasseled sombreros trembling. When they reach our table, Black Jesus hands a twenty-dollar bill to the oldest man.

"Say, man, lemme borrow your guitar for a minute."

The man smiles blandly and shrugs his shoulders. Jesus waves our waiter over to translate. When the old men settle in the corner with a pitcher of beer, Black Jesus strokes out a few chords, touching the guitar delicately. E? D minor? I have no idea, but each chord corresponds to a different space in my body. I'm a bigger fool than I previously thought.

"Let's you and me make up a song," Jesus says.

"I don't know how to do that," I say. What am I doing here? What if Ellis comes back early from his out-of-town conference? What if I say something inadvertently racist?

"You ever get the blues?" he asks, still working the guitar.

"About every day. I teach school." I twist my long hair up in my hands, as if to say, *See, I can wear my hair in a bun and make my handwriting pointy and clear and I'm getting over my chalk phobia, day by day.*

"Well, if you've had the blues, then you can make up a blues, cause you know how it feels, see?"

"You start it," I say.

"All right," he tells me. "This gonna be called 'Two Women Blues.'"

He leans closer to me and sings softly. "Got the two women blues, they gonna be the death of me." His skinny Jesus face expands in a smile. "There we go. Got the two women blues, they gonna be the death of me."

Something stirs in my heart, somewhere between the fiery salsa, the crisp scent of cilantro and warm tortillas, and the aching blue landscape I've walked through to get to where I am right now, leaning my elbows on a pink plastic tablecloth across from a man who caresses a borrowed guitar and seems to be singing to me. What if he could not sing, but could only call up the local radio station and dedicate a Sinatra tune to me, could merely take me in his arms and waltz me around the living room to the sound of another man's voice? Then I guess he'd be Ellis.

"How about this? 'One thinks I'm made of money, the other just won't let me be.'" I don't sing it, but I say it.

"Girl!" he says. "There you go." He sings the whole verse, then keeps stroking the melody while we think. "Got the two women blues," he sings, "one make her biscuits soft and fine."

"I like to make bread when I get mad," I say. "You know, the bread rises and then you punch it down to get all the air out."

Black Jesus laughs. "No one really makes biscuits. It's just for the song. Every blues song got to have some damn biscuits. Every blues song got to have a fuckin plantation, some corn, a mule, a woman stealin her man's moonshine. But I'll watch out if I see you comin with a big loaf of bread." He hums a little, then sings, "Got the two women blues, one make her biscuits soft and fine."

Is he handsome? Oh, yes. Yes, he is. Of all the made-for-TV Jesus movies I've seen, he is most like the Jesus who crashed barefoot into the temple, wrecking things blindly, rage blowing through him like a tornado's gathering whistle.

"I've got something," I say, then whisper in his ear, "I know she got another man, the other say she mine all mine."

"Hey my baby," he says. "That's the way."

I start revising my list of One Hundred Things I Want Out of Life to fit him in. Things I don't expect to say are twisting out of my throat disguised as a song. *Look at that white woman pressing her knees together under the table while a black man sings to her.* Sometimes I think of myself in third person, to get the picture clearer. "Got an uptown woman," I say, "her heart's made of ice and stone."

"This song can't be about you," he says, "cause I know you sweet as the day is long." Is he full of shit? Is he just a crazy and/or sleazy musician? Is he infected with a sexually transmitted disease? He plays the melody over and over, but it never sounds the same. I start promising myself I won't fuck him without a condom.

"Got an uptown woman," he sings, "her heart made of ice and stone. But my downtown woman, she got a smokin fire down below."

I laugh, but become conscious of my laughter and it bubbles and dies. "You know how some people say uptown and some people say downtown but they're talking about the same place? In some towns at least," I add. "Where are you from?"

"New Orleans," he says. "My daddy moved out to the country after my mama passed on, but most of my people still in New Orleans."

Our waiter sets a plate of enchiladas between us.

"Okay, my baby," Black Jesus says, "we better finish this damn song so we can eat."

"Excuse me," a young Hispanic girl says, lightly touching Jesus's shoulder. "Can I have your autograph, Mr. Jesus?" She shifts from one foot to the other, as if she's eaten something spicy and the heat of it just won't go away.

After Jesus lost his temper in the temple, did he go somewhere to be alone and laugh with the joy of it? Did he feel spaces opening up in him the way the sky opens after a rain?

Jesus signs a paper menu for the girl. She presses it against her pink T-shirt as she walks away.

"I love my two women," I sing, lullaby-soft, "but I swear they're gonna wear me out."

"I love my two women," he echoes, "but I swear they gonna wear me out." He tastes the enchilada, and the song tangles in its heat. "One make me weep and tremble, the other make me holler and shout." I watch the sharp angles of his jaw working under the Christ-like beard. The Hispanic girl winks from across the room. I wink back at her. She rapidly looks away.

"Isn't hollering and shouting the same thing?" I ask.

"Damn, you are a schoolteacher," he says. "Now, let's see. I think hollerin's more like like you got so much of somethin in you it just comes out in a holler, happy you know. Shoutin's more like you tellin somebody somethin."

He jumps up and takes the guitar back to the old man.

"You gonna have to help me remember our song," he says.

"Do you really have two women like that?"

"My baby, I've got the No Women Blues, I mean to tell you."

"Maybe you'll get one soon," I say.

"A woman or a blues?" Before I can answer he kisses me quickly, softly.

"Both," I say, and I'm thinking, this man is *black*. I am so white. I come from a lengthy tradition of Texas racism. I bite straight into the jalapeño that tops my enchilada. I don't flinch or quiver, I welcome the soft explosion in my head. I don't even glance at my glass of water, I refuse to acknowledge the tears rinsing my eyes. One deep breath, and I'm ready for another bite.

WHO THAT BITCH

Monday morning I become a teacher again. I wear a sweater dress the color of chalk. My eighth-graders think I'm an easy target and lobby relentlessly for games: Scrabble, hangman, videos. Instead, I mercilessly dictate a vocabulary quiz.

"No fair, Miz Springs, you can't give us a quiz," Tirzo says. "It's Monday. No quizzes on Monday."

Number 17 on my list: I write a hit blues song and Ray Charles sings it at the Grammys, Ray wearing not a tuxedo, but tails.

"Fragile," I say. "Definition, part of speech, and use it in a complete sentence."

"You didn't say we had to know parts of speech," Anna Dominguez whines from the back of the room.

"Second word: dubious," I say.

"You're goin too fast, Miz Springs," says Ronnie Stiles. "Start over."

They constantly make up rules, all to their benefit. It's a habit I'm trying to pick up. You can't hurt me today, it's

Monday. You mustn't forget me, it's September. You're not allowed to be cruel while I'm trying to live out my life in the form of a human being. No fair, slow down, start over.

Two weeks and three vocabulary quizzes later, Black Jesus and the Down Brothers have a gig in Dallas, at the Soul Hole. I figure it's a good time to visit my mother. My daddy has been dead as long as I can remember, although his money remains, a pale green residue of his life. Dinner with Mama features endless talk about Jesus (her Jesus, not mine), Junior League, money, and real estate. Escrow, let's go. I sever my slab of pot roast into a hundred tiny pieces.

"You're not still a vegetarian, are you?" Mama says. Her skin is plastic-smooth. Retin-A. She doesn't wait for my answer. "Yes," I spell out across my plate with the triangular bits of pot roast.

By dessert I'm caught up on every person in north Dallas who's had a face-lift or a divorce, including which dermatologist ran off with a woman from whom he'd removed more than twenty melanomas, leaving a profanity carved with a scalpel in the rotting oak of the deserted wife's front door. Two more drinks and Mama goes to bed with her Bible. Samson is her favorite character, big muscular motherfucker pulling the temple down over his own gorgeous body. Mama's learned a lot from the Bible. About leprosy, for instance.

"Your earlobes will fall off if you sin," Mama used to tell us. "You won't be able to have your ears pierced."

After Mama goes to sleep, I spend some time in front of the scalloped blue dresser in my old room, the dresser with a mirror so wide it reflects all of the brass bed, and beside the bed, the cluster of lonely dolls heaped on the chaise longue. Before I can step away, the mirror reaches out its silvery arms and pulls me back through years of looking at myself, back to the moment when I was startled by the new breasts pushing against my T-shirt. Mama walked by my door and said, "Lacy, quit staring at yourself in the mirror," but I was too fascinated with the power of my body to turn away. She rushed into my room, her hands twisted my nipples and gathered my breasts cruelly into their grip, but there was not enough flesh to fill her palms and she scraped at the bones beneath, shoving me back against the dresser — tiny china figurines leaped to the floor.

"Is this what you're looking at?" she hissed. "These little things? Pygmy!" She let go when my tears began to wet her hands.

I vowed to be tall like a skyscraper, my limbs dangling from me like scaffolding from a building.

"Your breasts will never grow," she said, smiling. "Men will never look at you. Your nipples will fall off from leprosy before you're fourteen, you little sinner!"

She ripped the mirror from the dresser, leaving two metal rods jutting weirdly from the dresser's base. For the two years I was not allowed to look in a mirror, my reflection was the dull blue flowered wallpaper. I learned to braid my hair and get dressed without it. Irene, my older sister, cleared the sleep from my eyes and parted my hair with the yellow comb, saying, "Hold still, Lacy. I can't get it straight when you're moving." Mrs. Watson helped me fix whatever was crooked when she picked me up for carpool. On my fifteenth birthday, Mama finally ordered Nacho, the kind black man who kept the yard, to hook the mirror back on my dresser. I still could not get enough of looking at myself. The glances in bathroom mirrors at school and at my girlfriends' houses had not been enough, and I drank in my reflection until I knew it well enough to lie down and dream of my own face.

Now I am grown up and can look in the mirror all I want. I take a good look — my legs please me most with their excessive length. I undress slowly and pull on my black leotard and naturally ripped jeans. I hear Mama snoring lightly in the next room. I want to bang on the wall, I want to wake her by screaming every catchphrase Eva and I toss between each other.

"Inappropriate behavior! Lack of boundaries! Sexual abuse, you fucking bitch!" I imagine she is dreaming her past away, replacing with elaborate fantasies the things she is most ashamed of: that she grew up poor, in a shotgun shack in Memphis, that when she got a full scholarship to SMU in Dallas she couldn't go out for sorority rush because she didn't have anything to wear. She met a rich man anyway, even without the sorority, and his mother worked that white trash upbringing right out of Mama. Speech lessons and dancing school. She's never been back to Tennessee. She's a Texan, now, weirder than ever. I don't feel sorry for her. Instead of banging and screaming, I put on too much makeup, drive to the Soul Hole, and walk straight to the backstage door. Karl leans against it, smoking a cigarette.

"Hey, Tex," Karl says, grinning.

"Forget my name already?"

"Nah," he says. "But ain't you a Texan?" he says with a fake drawl.

"I am," I say. "Is Jesus around?"

"Come on, I'll take you back."

Inside, Black Jesus is doing shots of gin with the rest of the band.

"Hey, y'all," I say.

"Hey my baby," Black Jesus says. He sets down his shot glass and gives me a kiss that clears all the loose things from my mind. "Listen, they got me workin like a dog signin these damn posters. Motherfuckin agent made me miss an interview today cause it wasn't on the damn list."

"What posters?" I say. He points to a stack of them on the table next to his guitar case.

"Don't let me stop you," I say. He turns back to scrawling his signature across the posters.

"Lacy, you like to rap?" Marcy says. Six inches of red boxers show over his low-hanging pants.

"I don't know." Marcy's gold teeth are so interesting it's hard to think. His initials are carved in the front two, "M.D." He sees me looking and grins big.

"Marcy Downs, the Doctor of Rap," he says, trying to shove his pants lower.

Black Jesus looks up from his stack of posters. "Your name ain't Downs, and you better be the Doctor of the fuckin blues tonight, you hear me, little brother? I don't want to hear none of your rap bullshit. The blues is our damn bread and butter right now, and don't you forget it."

Marcy doesn't even look at his brother. "Let's write a rap song, Lacy."

"Okay," I say. "What should it be about?"

"Gonna be about my girl, Dorinda," he says. "About how every time she be backstage like you are now, and some young lady come back want to tell us how much she like our music, Dorinda say who that bitch. Get this look in her eyes."

"You best be takin care of Miss Dorinda now," Karl says, "cause the good Lord has blessed her."

"That's the truth," Henry John says. Everyone except Marcy laughs.

"You motherfuckers shut up," Marcy says. "Me and Lacy writin a song."

"I think I got it," I say, digging in my purse for some paper. "Jealousy, right?"

"It don't have to be perfect, cause I'll just make most of it up while I'm rappin."

"I'd like to know when you goin to be doin all this rappin," Black Jesus says, "when we in the middle of a tour and got another album to cut!"

Marcy pulls me back to the corner, away from Jesus. "It's gonna start like this," he says, tapping out a rhythm with his combat boot. " 'I be walking down the street with my bitch by my side / When a girl come up to me' — damn, now what? What goes with 'side'?"

"Fried? How about 'when a girl, I mean bitch, come up to me / she be lookin kind of fried'?" We both giggle.

"Yeah," Marcy says. "Fried. That's the shit. Write that down, Lacy."

"Hey, why is the girlfriend a bitch and the other girl's a girl?" I say.

"Cause I ain't fucked the other girl yet. When I do, she be a bitch too."

Black Jesus is signing the posters faster and faster.

"I got it," I say. "Bitch start to freak / When that girl say I know you / You the Doctor of Rap / You don't sing no fuckin blues."

"Yeah," Marcy says. "I knew you'd have a feel for this shit. Jesus told me about the song y'all wrote. You got a good woman here, brother," he says to Jesus. "Knows how to appreciate a man who can rap."

"You can look but don't touch, little brother."

Alarms squeal in my head, but I drown them with imaginary rap music.

"Okay, I got it," Marcy says. "My woman gettin pissed / Her whole body start to twitch / Then she look me in the eye and say, 'Who that bitch?' "

"Hold on," I say, writing as fast as I can.

"Then I can say 'who that bitch' a bunch of times, like a chorus or whatever."

"Y'all got the worst rap I ever heard goin on over there," Bill says. Bill never takes off his sunglasses. Jesus says one of his eyes doesn't have any white to it, but he can see out of it just fine.

"Shut up, Bill," Marcy says. "You don't know shit about it."

"I know what I like and it definitely is not your so-called rap."

Number 46 on my list: I want to be reincarnated as a Stradivarius, but not one that sits in a museum — I want to be played every day. They lose their tone if they're not played.

"Lacy, what do you want to drink?" Black Jesus asks, crumpling a poster into a ball.

"Red wine, I guess."

"Karl, get Lacy some wine."

"Thanks, Karl," I say.

"Your turn, Lacy." Marcy's smile is a shield of gold.

"Okay," I say. "Goin to a party / With my woman so fine / We be drinkin Johnny Walker / We be smokin the kind."

Marcy laughs. "The kind. That's sweet. I like that, the kind."

"What next?"

"Lacy, I'm gonna be in New Orleans next weekend," Black Jesus says. "Got a break in the tour. Why don't you come on over and see me?"

"Hold on," I say as I finish scribbling the verse on the back of my electric bill.

"You sure you got a break?" Karl says.

"Shut up, man."

"I got it," Marcy says. "Young lady at the party / She be checkin me out / She say I seen how you be rappin / And I know what you about."

"Speakin of the kind, let's light one," Black Jesus says. He walks over, pulls a joint from a baggie in his guitar case, and puts it to my lips. "You flirtin with my little brother, Lacy?" he says, smiling.

"If I were it wouldn't be any of your damn business." I get a definite thrill from talking back to a man named Jesus. I draw a sweet, deep breath of smoke. "My turn, right? 'My woman drag me out the door / Then she push me in a ditch / While I'm brushin off my clothes / I hear "Who that bitch?" ' "

"I wouldn't let no damn woman push me in a ditch," Marcy says.

"Just for the song," I say. "And it rhymes with bitch."

"I like it, Tex," Karl says, handing me the wine. "Marcy, don't tell me Dorinda ain't never pushed your ass nowhere."

"She ain't."

The pale club manager opens the door and drones, "Fifteen minutes, y'all." Each of her eyebrows is pierced with four silver rings.

"Hey there," Bill says from behind the dark glasses. "Did you misplace an earring?"

"Fuck off," she says, closing the door.

"Damn, Karl, help me sign some of these posters," Black Jesus says. Karl takes a stack and starts writing.

"Okay, the ditch stuff is good," Marcy says. "Write that down."

"It's kind of dumb, don't you think?" I say.

I hand him the crumpled envelope with the lyrics written on it. We laugh together over the stupid song.

"Lacy, let's go out to the bar for a while before I go on," Black Jesus says. "Yo" is carved into one thigh of his jeans, "Dare" into the other. Fringe flares around the words.

"Hold on," I say. "So for the end, let's switch it around and instead of her asking 'who that bitch' have him say 'you that bitch' sort of like an answer to her question and also as a way of saying, you know, don't be jealous."

" 'You that bitch,' that's pretty good," Marcy says.

"Come on, Lacy," Black Jesus says, "why you wastin your time with this bullshit?"

He pulls me out to the bar and we drink wine and I tell him how good his show will be and how I can't wait to fuck him later on, but most of the time I'm thinking of Marcy and his dreams and how if Dorinda showed up she'd probably say who that bitch, talking about me. I think about the way jealousy makes women toss away their power like cheap Mardi Gras beads, how I already like Black Jesus less than I did, but somehow that makes me like him more, how it feels like an affirmation of something to have a Christ figure let me down again. I think of my desire to get a good, long look at Marcy's gold teeth and the letters etched into them.

OYSTER BLUES

The next Saturday, I drive three hours from Houston to New Orleans to meet Black Jesus at Antoine's for lunch. The Antoine's part was my idea. We sit at a linen-covered table like civilized people who fuck each other and aren't afraid who knows it. We order a bottle of red wine, a platter of raw oysters. People stare at us from every angle. I realize in a flash that I hate the men, white dicks like worms.

Black Jesus wears a pink silk tie. I touch the end of it.

"You are gorgeous," he says. I already know this, I think — I'm wearing pearls and a white linen suit that wrinkles everywhere he touches me.

"I'm gonna write a song about you for my next album," he says.

"Are you?" I start to imagine what it will be.

"And it ain't gonna be no damn rap song."

Our waiter brings the wine but does not wait for me to taste it, glamorous wine with intricate French words all over the label. As Black Jesus fills my glass I see a young black woman walking toward us. She's not dressed for

Antoine's, she wears a leopard skin shorts set, not real leopard skin but cotton printed with a leopard pattern. The
sharp-boned maître d' hurries after her, his mouth gaping
like a puppet's. I see that she is beautiful, even in the tacky
printed outfit that should make any woman look like a
majorette gone wrong. I try to remember that I'm beautiful, too.

She walks right up to our table and says, "Who this
bitch?" staring at Black Jesus and not even bothering to
look at how gorgeous or not gorgeous I am. Her voice is a
pitch too high.

Jesus turns about as pale as a black man can look. I take
pity on him.

I offer my hand to the woman and say, "Lacy Springs
from the *Houston Chronicle*. We're just getting started on
our interview, but you're welcome to join us if you won't
be too bored."

"I'm Jocelyn," she says.

Black Jesus jumps up and pulls out her chair. I hand
her my menu. I'm suffocating under yards of bright white
linen.

"You're just in time," I say. "We've only ordered appe-
tizers."

I sift through my huge purse and find a memo pad and
a pen. I take a slow sip of the sharp wine. Jocelyn finishes
Black Jesus's glass. I pour her another before he gets the
chance.

"Now," I begin, "after *Solitaire Blues* we're all anxious
to know what's coming up on your next album. Can you
tell me what you have in the works?"

I want Black Jesus to be stunned by my cool profession-
alism, my dazzling journalistic skills. I want him to be
shaken by his position at the table where he is flanked by
two lovely, venomous women, the black woman who hates
the other even if she is only a bothersome journalist and

not fucking Black Jesus, hates her for her obscene red hair and her luminous pearl necklace and because her chair was too close to Black Jesus's chair until she half rose to shake the woman's hand and moved the chair away as she sat down again, and because Black Jesus can say she's a journalist or an executive from Alligator Records or the editor of *Living Blues* magazine and Jocelyn will never have any way of proving that the woman is none of those things; and on the other side the white woman who hates the black woman but knows she was there first, knows that long before Black Jesus held her in his arms and whispered the words to "Steal Away" he whispered them to the woman in the coarse leopard skin print, he squeezed *her* hair at the nape of the neck and asked, "This gonna be my ass?" said it again and again until he was no longer asking but telling, and that woman said yes first, *yes, yes, yes.* He said *This is my sweet southern down-home country girl* and each woman thought *this* meant her, and afterwards loved being sweet and southern and down-home and girlish and loved being from the country, although neither woman really came from the country at all — one came from Dallas and one from New Orleans — but each started noticing all the things that gave her these supposedly country ways.

I want Black Jesus to know that I am full of lying, I have stuffed myself until I perspire lies, I have lied myself silly to come to New Orleans and sit at this table across from a woman he swore to me didn't exist. But he is not stunned, he answers smoothly in his interview voice, the voice that speaks slowly enough for him to consider how every word will look in print. I can't stand hearing it, as if it's a voice he keeps for another woman.

"I have a few things going," Jesus says. "We've got a couple more shows then I've got about a month before my next tour, so I'll have some time to write. My brother Marcy wrote a song we'll have on the new album, so we're excited about that. It's more funk-based than some of the traditional blues rhythms we've been working with."

"What's the name of it?" I say. I write *fuck you* over and over in shorthand as he talks.

"Oh, we haven't decided on a name yet. That's usually about the last thing we do, give all the songs names."

"Interesting," I say. The waiter drops the plate of oysters in front of Jocelyn so hard the flesh trembles in the rough shells. "Tell me about some of your influences. I know your grandmother was a fairly successful jazz vocalist."

The kitchen doors swing open as a waiter pushes through them with a stack of empty plates. Their rhythm is rough, nothing I can work with. Jocelyn pulls a tiny bottle of hot sauce from her purse.

"Yeah, I started giggin with my grandmama, Vaughan Sharp, when I was about fourteen. She knew what time it was. Most people called her Nana, but she wouldn't let no one she didn't take to call her that. 'Miz Sharp is my name,' she'd say, to white and black folks alike, in this voice that made you want to crawl in a damn hole and hide. She was an old motherfucker — don't write that down — but she could sing."

Jocelyn coats an oyster in red sauce and lifts the iridescent shell to Black Jesus's lips. She tilts the shell until the oyster slides into his mouth.

"Being raised by a great jazz vocalist, how did you end up working in the blues medium?" I ask.

"Nana, she'd sing the blues for us at home, just messin around, you know, but she was uppity — thought the blues was trashy, just work songs, not somethin to get up on a stage and sing, you know what I mean? But two of her boys made a livin playin the blues, and one of those was my daddy, so we just outnumbered ol Nana."

"But do you still consider her a significant influence on your style?"

"Oh yeah," he says. "She taught me the bones. Taught me that music is a language you can read and write. Taught me to listen to the bass instead of the drums when I'm singin. Taught me it's your ear, not your voice, that make you a good singer. Taught me how to sing from my gut and not my throat so my voice won't wear out. But I was always surrounded by the blues," he says, mouth full of oyster. "Our house was always full of musicians — matter of fact, Slim Harpo gave me my first harmonica. He was a friend of Nana's. He'd come over and sit on her front steps some days, play a song or two."

"So that was your first love?" I say. "The harmonica?"

I'm not listening; I know the answers to all my questions. I start writing lyrics in meticulous shorthand. *He slimy as an oyster/ Mean as a rattlesnake/ Don't know why I keep on givin/ When all he do is take.*

"Yeah, I didn't start up on the guitar until a couple of years later. Then I played bass for a while but I don't do that too much anymore now I got my brother Marcy playin bass for me."

Our waiter passes our table and drops the check at my elbow without missing a step.

"Let's go over to Sonny's and get some ribs or something," Jocelyn says. She's fussing over another oyster, forcing hot sauce into every crevice.

"How do you like the road?" I say.

Jocelyn stabs the oyster with a tiny fork, drips liquid into each small wound. *He lazy as a hound dog/ Lyin out in the shade/ Don't know why I keep on slavin/ He take everything I make.*

"I tell you, it get old fast. I get so tired, I don't even know what's goin on."

"I can imagine."

"But I got great fans everywhere I go, and that make up

for it. And the label's givin me a new touring bus — I can't wait to get goin in that bad boy."

He's so relaxed now he's talking his old way, the way he calls *down home,* the language my supervisor calls BEV, Black English Vernacular, and writes endless racist memos about. BEV is strictly off limits at our school. Jocelyn shuts him up by holding the sharp edge of an oyster shell to his lips.

"Thank you, my baby," he says.

My handwriting swerves raggedly across the memo pad. I shake my pen, pretending it's out of ink. *I must be crazy as a polecat/ To love him like I do/ Gonna go find me a new man/ Don't give me them oyster blues.* I stand up and shake Black Jesus's hand. I wonder what exactly a polecat is.

"Well, that's about all I need," I say. "Thank you so much for your time. I'll have a copy of the article faxed to your agent when it comes out."

I look at Jocelyn's breasts, cruelly bound up and offered in the leopard skin vise. "We're doing a series on Louisiana blues," I tell her. "Gatemouth Brown, Jelly Roll Morton, and so on. This will be the last article in the series." Everything I really want to say is in the word *last.* No one notices.

"Oh, one more thing," I say, tearing a clean sheet of paper from my memo pad. "Could I have your autograph for my husband? He's a big fan of yours."

"Sure," Black Jesus says. He doesn't know if I'm kidding or not. "What's his name?"

"Ellis."

He writes something on the paper and hands it to me. "Ellis, thanx 4 your support. Black Jesus."

"He'll be overjoyed," I say.

I leave enough cash on the table to cover the check and walk out of Antoine's to the rhythm of my blues. *Oyster*

*blues is when your man/ Slide right away from you/ He
eatin from someone else's plate/ While you sing them oyster
blues.*

I walk two blocks in the wrong direction before I'm calm
enough to turn around and find my car. I rip up the autograph and the interview notes and let them flutter out the
open window as I drive. The *give a hoot don't pollute* song
pounds in my head. I have to turn on my Elmore James
tape to drown it out.

I get to Interstate 10 without thinking. Speedometer,
odometer, temperature. I watch the needles quiver without
knowing what they say.

It's almost true that I have a husband. He accepted my
lie about wedding dress shopping, and he was thrilled to
get out of that Dallas trip a couple of weeks before, the
dinner with my mother, the society gossip.

"I owe you one," he said to me when I told him about
my shopping plans. "I can use the study time."

"It's okay," I told him. "You can make it up to me in
sexual favors. You can start right now," I had the nerve to
say. He closed his heavy textbook and kissed me hard,
pulling me across the couch while papers scattered and
crumpled between the cushions. While he unbuttoned my
shirt I thought of a sentence Tirzo Ponce used on his vocabulary quiz: *In the seventies, my mother used to listen to the
Dubious Brothers.* Then all the way to New Orleans I'd
thought about the gentle curve of Ellis's fingers brushing
my hair back from my face, the softness of his voice whispering *Te amo ahora y siempre.* Ellis loves to speak foreign
languages while we fuck. He's fluent in Spanish and
French, but he can whisper love talk in six or seven different languages. I can pretty much tell what he means. Driving away from New Orleans and Black Jesus, my head
swirls with Portuguese, French, and the many words for
love. The most I can decide is this: I will drive back to

Houston and will not look at the calendar, I will not count the number of squares between today and the day I will marry Ellis at Mama's church in Dallas. Instead I will drink some more wine, take a long bath, devise a quiz on the eight parts of speech so hard it will ruin my eighth-graders' day. When they complain I will tell them, It's a hard world, kids. You do what you can. You struggle through until you find someone to comfort you, someone who can take all your weight in their arms and still have the strength to whisper *My baby, my baby, my baby.*

LORD I'M A POOR
FOOL

"What did you expect?" Eva says at our emergency Sunday afternoon session. "That someone who is playing the role of the other man in your life would be exclusively faithful to you?" She taps a pen against the desk top, as if ticking off the seconds before I must answer.

I don't want to talk about the other man or the not-other man, oysters or leopard skin. I want to talk about the dinner table I sat at when I was nine years old. I want to tell how small I felt in the chair with the plastic slipcover meant particularly for me. I still don't know the feel of that dark green velvet upholstery, velvet textured with a pattern of roses. I know the coolness of the clear plastic, the look of the roses crushed beneath. I'd like to know the taste of the food I ate. I'd like to throw away the caution of lifting my fork slowly to my mouth, hoping the food balanced there will not fall. I'd like to forget the strain of my jaws as I try to open my mouth wide enough so my fork will not touch my teeth and make the clicking noise that unleashes the demon in my mother, the sound that makes her jerk me from my chair and say, "You can eat in the kitchen with the dog until you learn some better manners!" I never hear the click. I never know the exact moment when the sterling silver touches my new front teeth and starts the anger swirling in Mama's dark eyes. I know the feel of the kitchen floor, the time it takes to count nine crumbs, my age, in the grooves between the grainy oak planks. I know how quickly the sun tumbles into the dark pond outside the kitchen window while I arrange those crumbs in a delicate line, largest to smallest. The sun stays in the pond all night long, cooling in the mossy water. Nacho, the yardman, told me so. I know the hateful dog who crunches her sandy food with yellowed teeth while my dinner cools and congeals on the floor next to her dish. I never let her have it, even if I don't want it myself, the Maltese dog who was born before I was and given my grandmother's name, the elegant, glamorous name that should have been mine: Marcella. Mama loves to brag of the silence between her and my grandmother, loves to tell how she gave the dog my grandmother's name so she would never have to give it to a child. You don't give children and dogs the same names, you know, but you can make them eat right next to each other, you can come into the kitchen and pour out the dog's water and scrape the little girl's food into the red plastic water dish ringed with white dog hair and set it next to the dog food. You can make the child eat out of that dish with her fingers so she'll learn to appreciate the luxury of a fork, and you can fill the dog's dish over and over until the child's food is coated with a sprinkling of powder, the brown powder that sifts from the dog food bag and clouds up from the bowl as the star-shaped bits of dog food cascade into it. If you wait long enough, darkness will crush against the kitchen windows and the child will be afraid and will choke down the cold food while the gorged, stinking Marcella growls. The child will swallow every bite because sitting in the dark kitchen with the live oak contorting itself into a monster right outside the window is worse than going to bed and begging God to keep her from the curse of leprosy, praying that God will place His holy finger between her fork and her teeth so the two will never touch and the child will be spared the wages of sin and can stay on the plastic slipcover and dine almost like the adults do.

Eva is fascinated. She pulls a sturdy textbook from her desk drawer. She flips to the back, consulting the index, I assume. Dog: eating habits of, 82; precedence over child, 108. *See also* Animal. While I wait for her to find the chapter that pertains to me, the specific paragraphs that will identify my problems and instruct her on the method for dissolving them, I compose the song Black Jesus should write to win me back. I call it "Poor Fool."

> *Got a big house on the hill*
> *Eat prime rib every day*
> *But since my woman left me*
> *Ain't nothin gone my way*
> *(Chorus)*
> *Yesterday I was a rich man, thought I had it made*
> *But my good woman left me, I'm a poor fool today*

I imagine Black Jesus's new white Porsche; I picture its tires ripening like dark plums, its body erupting in a rash of rust.

> *Limo in my front yard*
> *Cadillac out the side*
> *Garage is full of cars*
> *But I ain't got my pride*

"What are you writing?" Eva inquires. She's slapping pink Post-it notes all over the book.

"Got rings of yellow gold," I say, "Diamonds in my ears / But since my woman left me / My eyes been full of tears."

"Lacy," Eva says. "It's interesting that your verses are always composed from a male point of view. Can you tell me anything about that?"

"Chorus repeat," I say. "Yesterday I was a rich man, thought I had it made / But my good woman left me, I'm a poor fool today."

"Have you ever experienced sexual desire for another woman?" She closes the book.

"Closet full of whiskey / Cupboard full of wine / Hundred-dollar champagne / Won't make that woman mine."

"Have you ever fantasized about making love with a woman?"

"Got alligator shoes / Guitars and caviar / I'd rather have my woman / Than all them fancy cars."

"Have you ever experienced these fantasies while making love with Ellis or Black Jesus?"

"I haven't ruled it out," I say, then softer, "Lord I'm a poor fool / I'm a poor fool today."

THE OYSTERS ARE
BETTER HERE
ANYWAY

I get up early Monday morning. The taste of oysters lingers, inexplicably, in my mouth. I play *Solitaire Blues* so loud it sounds fuzzy. I gaze at the cover photo that looks nothing like Black Jesus. I've got a picture of him in my head. It's something that's mine. Ellis doesn't like Black Jesus's CD, would rather listen to Eric Clapton or the Allman Brothers. White blues. He's already awake, typing frantically, his blond hair still shaped like sleep.

"What is it?" I ask.

"The bibliography," Ellis says. "I have to get a draft to my committee by noon. Can you turn that down?"

"No," I say. I love saying no. I say it as much as I want, and Ellis lets me. It's one of his best qualities. "No!" I shout, just for the hell of it, and it feels so good I turn the music down anyway.

Ellis laughs, his round glasses sliding down his nose. I rarely shout.

"Love me?" I say.

"Absolutely," he says, his long fingers stilled on the keyboard.

"How much?" I say.

"More than I did yesterday, and less than I will tomorrow."

This is our mantra. Sometimes I think if I say it enough, it will stop me from betraying Ellis again. Other times I think nothing can stop me.

Number 5 on my list: I become a nice southern married lady. I take my wedding ring off only to smear gardenia-scented hand lotion over my fingers a couple of times a day.

I take a long shower and trace lyrics in the fog on the glass shower door. The letters melt and drip into each other, then steam fills up the spaces again. I get out of the shower but leave the water running. I sneak out of the bathroom to get the cordless phone and slip back in. I hear the steady clicking of Ellis's keyboard. Black Jesus answers his phone on the first ring.

"She don't mean nothin to me," Jesus says right away. "Are you really married?"

"Yes, she does," I say, "but so what. It's silly to pretend like we're being faithful to each other when I'm married and you have other involvements, and I barely know you anyway."

I wish Eva could witness this burst of semihonesty. He's just a fuck, I'll tell her next time I see her. I wonder what she'll say to that.

"You're married?" he says. "You're married? Damn, I can't believe I been messin with a married woman."

The water's still running hot; I stick one hand under it until my fingers turn pink.

"I know I should have told you, and I'm sorry, but I'm telling you now. I'd still like to see you when I can." I cross my fingers, tight. Almost no water gets between them. "Jesus," I say, "I just want to see you sometimes. I don't want to be your girlfriend or make lots of future plans or keep you from seeing someone else. I just want to see you sometimes. I mean, what do you think?"

"Yeah," he says.

"Want to go to my father house?" he asks. I love the way Black Jesus talks. I give my eighth-grade English students demerits for speaking like this.

"Desperately," I say.

All week I tell myself it means nothing to go to his father's house in Louisiana, that he asked me there because it's easy, because it will make up for Jocelyn, because his father's house is out in the country, away from New Orleans, and no one will see us go there.

Wednesday in my school mailbox: a note from little Josh Jackson, my most pathetic eighth-grader, and something from Black Jesus. Josh writes: "Dear Miss Springs, I am sorry I brought my ninja turtle to school I will not do it again no matter what. P.S. Can I have it back." Mrs. Craven catches me before I can open Black Jesus's letter.

"Lacy, you're on lunch duty," she says. "Get in the cafeteria before someone gets hurt and we all get sued."

I go to the cafeteria to make sure no one chokes to death on the sloppy joes. I stand in the corner by the sticky Coke machine to read the letter. Josh Jackson pulls on my sleeve.

"Can I have it back?"

"Not now," I say. "Go eat your lunch."

"I already did." I can see by his stained shirt he is telling the truth.

"Which turtle was it?" I say. I have a drawer full of the nasty things.

"Michelangelo. Can I have it back?"

"Who was Michelangelo?"

"He's a Ninja Turtle, Miz Springs. Can I have him back?"

"You come tell me who Michelangelo really was and you can have it back."

"What do you mean really was?"

"Figure it out, my baby," I say. I retreat to the kitchen where I open my letter by the vat of seething sloppy joe meat.

It's a song written on the back of a paper placemat from a restaurant called Crazy's. *The oysters are better here anyway. I'll sing this for you next time I see you.*

My baby takes all day to let her stove get hot
She keeps on rollin that dough until it feels just right
Takes a sweet southern country girl to satisfy my head
You know my baby don't eat no storebought bread

"Miz Springs," Josh says from the kitchen door, "When God made people did he take black people and suck all the color out of em to make white people, or did he take white people and shoot color into em to make black people?"

"I'll have to get back to you on that one," I say. "Now get on outta here."

"Ms. Springs, I wasn't aware you'd joined the kitchen staff," Mrs. Craven says from the doorway, her fingers lightly tapping a cleaver on the counter. Her smile is a frozen slash as I pass her and sit down at a table full of writhing adolescents.

She got a Mississippi move make me holler and scream
I hear that soft Texas drawl, Lord it's got to be a dream

"What is that Miz Springs? Is that a love letter?" Anna's mouth is full with braces; they shove her plump upper lip defiantly outward. "Is that a letter from the guy you're sposed to marry? Is your name gonna be different after you get married?"

"Everything's going to be different. Life will be sweet like a rhapsody. Go eat your lunch, now."

"What's a rhapsody?"

"It's a musical composition that has an irregular form."

"That means the musician writes it however he wants?"

"However he or she wants, that's right. Now go on."

When my baby gets to bakin she make the sweetest bread around
I'll just stay out in the country, you won't see me around town

"Miz Springs has a love letter."
"Hush up."

I've had my share of city women from New York to New Orleans
If you've loved a country girl then you know just what I mean
Takes a sweet southern country girl to satisfy my head
You know my baby don't eat no storebought bread

Is it about me, or some generic blues whore? Or am *I* some generic blues whore?

I fold the placemat with the song on it small as a dime and tuck it in my shoe. All afternoon I make my eighth-graders write essays while my tongue imagines some combination of oyster, ocean, and Black Jesus's neck.

After school, when the last child is safely on the bus, I go to the copy room and wait in line behind the Spanish teacher.

He finishes his copies and leaves; I tap my code into the

buzzing machine and jiggle the paper trays, letter and legal. The screen reads "READY" in urgent, blinking letters. I unbutton the tiny pearl buttons of my white silk blouse and let it fall from my shoulders; I drape it over the fax machine. I unhook the contraption of my bra. I lean over until my breasts graze the warm glass of the copier. I press the green "Start" button, watch the dark copy slide out. I lift myself off the glass until only my nipples touch it, then only the tips as they stiffen. Start. I unzip my skirt, slip it down over my hipbones. An incoming fax ripples under my blouse on the other side of the room. I lift myself over the machine, press my right hip against it, then curve down until my navel expands against the glass like a small soft flower. Start. The hot bar of light sweeps beneath my stomach. I hear the metallic slam of a locker door, voices in the hallway. I snatch up my shirt, spill the fax, button the top four buttons. I have to reach back inside to hook my bra. I fold the copies of my naked breasts into my grade book and go out to the hall.

It's Tirzo, my favorite eighth-grader, a gun in his locker. Someone has betrayed him.

"You!" Mrs. Craven says. "We need the combination to his locker. The kids say he's got a gun in there."

"I don't know the combination," I tell Mrs. Craven, her mouth gathered into a bump. I was supposed to write it down. I was supposed to inspect Tirzo's locker weekly. I'm a goddamned teacher of English. I teach kids their mother tongue so they can tell about Tirzo's gun. Shut up, shut up. Motherfuckers are almost retarded, but smart enough to get our asses sued. One more sniff of spray paint and some of them will definitely be retarded. I don't know much more than the heights and depths of Black Jesus's voice, the many tones between. When officially retarded, they will still tell about the gun and everything else they know: Firebirds, freeways, fucking. Tirzo wrote a fabulous essay titled

"My Man Sam." My favorite line was: "My man Sam's face is dark and crumpled like a Milky Way wrapper."

"Oh man," Tirzo says, shifting from one unlaced Air Jordan to the other. He takes mercy on me, his homeroom teacher, and opens the locker himself. "It ain't loaded," he says, jerking open the dented metal door. "It's my brother's, man. It's unconstitutional."

Shut up, shut up. I'm busy wanting.

MY BABY DON'T EAT NO
STOREBOUGHT
BREAD

"Lacy," Eva says, staring out her office window, "let's try to find more substantial ground for this relationship than what kind of song Black Jesus writes for you."

"What could be more substantial than that?"

"Remember, girlfriend, songwriting is his business."

I shove the crumpled placemat across her desk, Black Jesus's atrocious handwriting squeezed between hot sauce drips. Jesus finished the ninth grade, went on tour playing bass for Buddy Guy, and never went back to school. His handwriting shows it.

Eva reads for a long time. I find an emery board in my purse and start filing my brittle nails. I hear a thump and look up. Eva's head is on her desk, twisting in her open hands.

"Eva?" She grinds her head into her wet palms, discolored hairline emerging from the slipping turban.

"Why doesn't anyone write me a song?" she whispers. Her eyes glisten under a sheen of tears.

"Eva, you're the one who just said songwriting is his

business. He probably wasn't even thinking about me when he wrote it, just about how much money he's going to make on his next album."

"You think you have problems? You have a fiancé *and* a rich lover with an enormous penis who writes songs for you!"

"I never said one thing about his penis!"

"You don't have to," she says. "I *know!* I'm almost a psychologist! Just tell me, it's enormous, isn't it?"

I finish filing the nail of my little finger. "Size is relative," I say.

"Isn't it!" she yells, tearing the turban from her head. The Velcro separates with a grieving sound. Her short, not-naturally red hair stays flat against her skull in the turban shape. "Isn't it!" she demands.

"Yes," I whisper. "It's quite large."

She balls up the placemat and throws it at me. It lands in the rubber plant.

"I hope you're not charging me for this," I say. I get up to retrieve the song.

"It's just not fair!" Eva sobs while I pick dirt from the crumpled placemat. "You have so much love in your life and I have nothing."

"I have so much *sex* in my life," I say. I walk behind the warped pasteboard desk and help reattach her turban. Its edges are stained with a beige line of sweat and makeup.

"I'm a terrible therapist, aren't I?" she sobs.

"No," I say. "We're both just learning." I pick a fleck of lint from the turban. "You're going to be great," I say. I wonder if I will be great, too.

A quick knock, and Dr. Troy, Eva's dissertation adviser, leans against the doorway.

"Everything okay in here?" His pen hovers over his memo pad.

"Great," I say. "We're just doing some anger work. We didn't disturb you, did we?"

"Not at all," he says. He slouches in the low doorway, stroking his tie.

"Eva's doing a wonderful job," I say. "She's showing me how to express all the anger I've never been able to get out because of my oppressive southern upbringing and all."

"Splendid," he says. His face and his tie are both the delicate color of salmon. "Good work, Eva. I'll let you ladies get back to it."

"I love you," Eva says when the door is closed.

"I love you, too. Feel better?"

"Yes, dear," she says.

I start to tell her that size isn't everything, but instead I grab a tissue from the industrial-size box on her desk and dab at the damp skin below her eyes. I'm a Texan, as you know, so naturally I've been trained to think bigger is better, and dicks are no exception.

"Don't go to Louisiana," she says. "I'm advising you as your crazy therapist."

SALAD

I ignore Eva's advice and devise a series of lies to go visit Black Jesus. I tell Ellis I have to go to a teachers' conference. I complain violently about the dull speeches to which I'll be subjected. The history teacher was supposed to go, but she's sick and I have to go in her place. There's a virus going around. I reel off a short list of people we know who supposedly have this same virus. Ellis gets the vitamin C from the kitchen, offers me the open jar.

"Here, take some," he says. "You don't want to be sick for your conference. Maybe you should eat some garlic, too — Eric just finished this big study showing that garlic stimulates the immune system. You should read it." He says he's looking forward to writing in a quiet house. He's composing a novel in addition to his folklore dissertation. I prefer the novel. I try to be extra loud the day before I leave.

Saturday morning, I get up early and drive the three hours to Black Jesus's place in New Orleans. I bring him a loaf of my homemade bread. Pumpernickel.

"I like the song," I say.

"Hey, married girl," he says.

"Don't call me that," I say. "Don't ever call me that."

We fuck on the floor of his living room, each of us trying hard to please the other. I make my mind a tunnel, a long, dark tunnel with an explosion of light at the end, a tunnel Black Jesus pulls me down and down, a tunnel warmed and dark and fragrant with our bodies, scented with the honeysuckle that clings to the windows and makes the light come in frayed patterns, a tunnel where Black Jesus's voice echoes off the smooth walls, *Just fuck me good, baby*. It's safe to melt in the tunnel, this space will let me fall apart and will piece me together again, will let me loose the coil of pain from my heart and spill it in a laugh, will let me float in that dusky space without thought or feeling. My senses return gradually: I taste the hard calluses that round his fingers, I feel his weight on my thighs, I see the yellow honeysuckle light that flecks the room, I hear a blues beating in my ears.

Late afternoon, we stand in the kitchen naked. We drink some wine, eat some of my bread obscenely smeared with butter and jelly.

"Damn, I can't believe I got me a woman knows how to make bread," he says.

"You think you got me?"

"I just had you."

"You're Jesus," I say. "Don't you have everything — all the sexiest angels, the streets paved with gold? What are you looking at?" Suddenly I realize he's staring at me.

"You," he says. "how white you are."

Everything in the kitchen changes from the usual background blur to real life. The white refrigerator with the blue dishtowel slung through the scratched metal door handle, the black gas stove with an empty cast-iron skillet sitting on the front left burner — none of these will hide my nakedness. I breathe, the moment passes, everything softens, and I am happy to have Jesus looking at my strong, young body.

We smile at each other until Black Jesus ducks his head down, won't look me in the eyes.

"Now what's the matter with you?" I say. I touch his chin, try to get him to look at me.

"You make me feel shy," he says. He's picking apart the wine cork with nervous fingers.

"Bullshit. How can you feel shy with me when you get up on a stage every damn night and sing? Tell me that."

"I can do that stuff," he says. "Singin and playin guitar and actin crazy, but when I get with you sometimes that's when my shyness come out."

"Is that so?" I say.

"Yeah, that's so," and he kisses me like someone who's never been shy in his life. He's probably full of shit, but I don't really care.

On the way to his father's house the Louisiana breeze, tasting like salt and smelling like soft shell crabs, rushes through Jesus's Porsche loudly enough so I can hum some of my original lyrics very softly.

"We get in the taxi / You give that driver a wink / Next thing I know / Girl I'm out on the street / (Chorus repeat) You got eyes in the back of your head / And they ain't lookin at me."

Black Jesus's father meets us in the driveway. He has slaughtered a pig in our honor.

"Killed a buck this mornin, too," he says. "It's back in the shed."

"Pops, she's vegetarian," Black Jesus laughs. "She don't eat no meat."

"Marcy and Karl sposed to be comin out for dinner, they'll eat it up."

I cannot ignore the pig. It seems there is no one more

important to impress than Black Jesus's father. I have not eaten meat in seven years, but I swallow twelve generous bites of the salty, pale pork. It takes forever to chew. My tongue puffs with thirst. Black Jesus kisses me while his father whittles second helpings from the pig. I bite his tongue gently in rhythm to my blues: *Girl I take you to church/ Oh you kneel down and pray/ You been through more hands/ Than that offering plate/ (Chorus repeat) You got eyes in the back of your head/ And they ain't lookin at me.*

Marcy and Karl show up in time for dessert. Marcy hangs outside the screen door for a moment, darker than a shadow, then kicks gently in.

"Don't be kickin my door," their daddy says. "Get you some meat, Karl."

"Don't be late for no more gigs, man," Black Jesus says to Marcy. "I'm tired of that shit."

"Wasn't so late."

"The hell you wasn't, and you wouldn't even be in this band if you wasn't my brother. I could get Lucky Boy or Robinson playin for me anytime."

"Then get em. I'm gonna get me a rap band."

"The fuck you are. We got thirty gigs in the next sixty days, then we goin in the studio. And I don't want to see your fuckin underwear anymore, man. Pull your damn pants up."

Marcy shoves his baggy jeans even lower. "Fuck you, Jesus," he says.

"Can you believe this boy?" Jesus says to me. "Eighteen years old and can't keep his damn pants up."

"Leave him be, Jesus," Karl says.

Dessert is Jell-O, red. Marcy gives his bowl a shake.

"Jell-O ain't dessert, man," Marcy says. "Jell-O's a damn salad. How you doin, Lacy? You sure look pretty."

"I'm just fine," I say.

Black Jesus and Marcy's daddy takes a glass of rose-colored whiskey out to the front porch. His rocker squeaks between words.

"Jell-O's a dessert, Marcy," Black Jesus says. He lifts a spoonful elegantly to his mouth.

"It's a salad, man," Marcy says. "Fuck that dessert bullshit."

"Motherfucker, it's a dessert."

"Man, then how come at school they always had it with all the fuckin salad stuff?"

"Cause they don't know shit at the school."

"Stupid motherfucker, *you* don't know shit." Marcy jumps up; his spoon bangs against the floor.

"I don't know shit?"

"That's right, man," Marcy says. "You don't believe me, man, me and my nine'll take care of that."

He pulls a gun from his jacket. Nuzzled in Black Jesus's ear, it's the shiniest thing in the room.

"Say it's a salad," he whispers.

Black Jesus takes another bite, twisting his head as if to wedge the gun further into his ear. I use my spoon to carve a rudimentary tulip in the surface of my Jell-O.

"Say it's a salad, man!" Marcy yells. A sheen of sweat lights his face.

"Marcy, put that damn thing away," their daddy says from the porch. "I don't need no guns in my kitchen." The rocker stops whining.

"Say it's a salad, motherfucker!" Marcy's voice sounds like something falling a long way, like an echo that can't quite duplicate the tone of the voice that made it. "Nigga, say it's a salad."

I have not heard Black Jesus raise his voice except in song. It's quiet now, and steady. He wraps one hand around the gun where it meets his ear, holds it like it's something he loves.

"Brother," he says, "I changed so many of your fuckin diapers I can't even count that high. I was the cream of the crop, man, and you was just the trash out our daddy nuts. You think your shit don't stink?"

Marcy holds up his free hand, squints up at it like he's trying to look at a too-bright sun, then he raises the gun and blows one bullet through his hand. It knocks his arm back like a violent wind, a wind of blood that coats the screen door and hangs translucent in the tiny squares of wire until their daddy slams open the door and the wire web of blood shakes and settles farther down the screen. Marcy reels against the counter and swipes the bowl of leftover greens to the floor. He makes a sound I've never heard before, somewhere between singing and screaming. He crumples in a circle of scattered iceberg lettuce and blood.

"Fuck you, Jesus, fuck you," he's saying, but the words are slurred and blood seeps from his mouth where he's bitten his tongue from the pain.

I'm the only one still sitting at the table. I horrify myself by taking a bite of Jell-O. I quietly spit it into my napkin, then ease it back onto my plate. I try, with my spoon, to graft it into its former place. No one is looking at me.

Black Jesus crouches over Marcy saying, "Calm down, man, we gotta get you into town." Jesus strokes the hair that Marcy tries to curl like his but it ends up more like dreadlocks, strokes Marcy's hair and says, "It's a salad, man. It's anything you fuckin want it to be."

GRACELAND

Eva is especially professional for our post-Louisiana session, her turban crisp and pressed.

"Sorry about the freakout," she says. "Very dysfunctional of me."

I can't remember what she's talking about. My head is swirling with the emergency room, my plate of carved-up Jell-O, and Marcy's bloody hand.

"It's okay," I say anyway.

"Thank you, dear Lacy. It is time," she says, "for you to do some ritual, some healing, some replacing of negative energy with positive energy."

"Okay," I say.

"It is time for you to journey to the home of your child-hood. It is time for you to show your precious inner child that she no longer needs to be frightened of the place which was once so unsafe for her."

"What do you mean 'journey'? You mean sort of medi-tate about that house, right?"

"No, I am speaking of a physical journey, on which I

will accompany you. Your recent honesty, or semihonesty, with Black Jesus signals to me that you now have the strength to make such a journey. Lacy, you must do some healing work on your sexual abuse before you marry Ellis."

"What do you mean, 'semihonesty'?"

"I mean you told him you are married when you are not yet actually married."

"Close enough," I say.

"Lacy, I'm hoping this trip to Dallas will help you begin to distinguish between truths and untruths, by way of facing some truths about yourself. And I'd like to do this soon, Lacy."

"Just tell me, Eva," I say, "is this an assignment? I mean, is this part of some paper you're writing or do you actually think it will do me some good? Because I'm not putting myself through torture just to help you get your degree."

"I like the strong voice I'm hearing today," Eva says. "And I say to you, dear Lacy, that you are safe with me. That the needs of your spirit will never be sacrificed to the demands of academia."

"Just checking," I say.

"Dallas?" Ellis says when I meet him at the university coffee shop after my session with Eva. "You're going to Dallas with your crackpot therapist?"

"She's not a crackpot, Ellis. She's unique."

"Use whatever euphemism you want, I think it's a terrible idea. How much is she charging you?"

I slowly sip the foam off my cappuccino, bubble by bubble. "She's not charging me anything."

"You're not charging me for this, are you?" I ask Eva when she picks me up Friday afternoon.

"Of course not," she says. "Don't be silly."

The four-hour drive to Dallas takes six hours because we have to stop at every barbecue place on I-45 so Eva can pass out gory animal rights literature. By the time we get to the Hawg Shack in Corsicana, I'm exhausted and my clothes smell like hickory smoke.

"Eva, I'm staying in the car on this one," I tell her. She's busy gathering her pictures of flayed monkeys, afflicted rabbits.

"Lacy," she scolds, "we must present a united front."

"Eva, it's embarrassing. It's not that I'm against animal rights, but I just don't like bugging people about it, you know? People who make their living selling meat don't want to hear about this shit."

"I don't always like doing this, Lacy."

"Yes you do. You love it. I'll go in," I bargain, "but this is the last restaurant for this trip. Okay?"

"Agreed."

The woman behind the cash register looks tired and hot. She's fiddling with a radio that alternates uncontrollably between country music and Rush Limbaugh.

"Sister," Eva addresses her, "I'd like to share something with you, if I may." She spreads her fliers on the sticky counter.

"My God!" the woman says, but she keeps looking at the photos. "Albert!" she yells.

"You are right to be alarmed," Eva croons. "The torture of our fellow creatures is an alarming phenomenon."

Number 72 on my list: I'd like to be reincarnated as one of those beautiful black ladies who stand behind Aretha Franklin and sing *sock it to me sock it to me sock it to me sock it to me.*

"Albert!" the woman yells again, looking back toward the kitchen. "Y'all go on, now," she says to us, "we ain't interested in whatever you're selling."

"We are selling the concept of peace, of healing," Eva says cheerfully. "We are asking you to consider the torture done to the very animals devoured here in this restaurant. The chickens you use in your chicken-fried steak are raised on factory farms where their beaks are cut off and their claws literally grow into the bottoms of their cages because they have so little freedom of movement."

"Come on, Eva," I whisper. "Chicken-fried steak doesn't even have chicken in it."

"What is it, then?"

"It's not chicken and it's not steak. It's like, beef that's dipped in a batter and deep-fried. Then you put white gravy all over it and have it with mashed potatoes or something like that."

The woman nods approvingly. "It ain't chicken and it ain't steak," she says. "Now listen here. I ain't done nothin. You fancy folks at County Health think y'all can come in my business and tell me how to run it, well I got somethin to tell you." She's angry now, doesn't need any help from Albert. "I'm sick of your kickbacks." She pulls a rifle from under the counter and levels it at our collarbones. *Get yer biscuits in the oven and yer buns in the bed,* someone sings on the frail radio. "I ain't never had cause to use this, but if y'all keep pesterin me, I might find a reason. I'm runnin a clean ship here and I paid all I'm gonna pay. So y'all just get on outta here and don't lemme see you on my place again." She raises the rifle to eye level, the butt pressing against her tired perm.

Before Eva can say anything I scoop the pamphlets from the counter and pull her out the door by her sleeve. The woman keeps the rifle aimed at us through the dirty window.

"That's a woman who is filled with anger," Eva says when we are safely in the car, "a woman in desperate need of therapy."

"Well, she's not going to get it from you, so let's get out of here," I say.

"I didn't even give her the best one," Eva says, examining the vivid image of a ruined monkey.

"Drive, Eva!" I yell.

"What's the matter with you?" I reach over and turn the key to start the car.

"I just don't like guns," I say. "Black Jesus's brother, Marcy. I saw him shoot himself in the hand. It was so gross." I start to cry. Eva pulls onto the highway, then parks on the shoulder and spends a few minutes sending healing vibes back to the raging barbecue woman and east to Marcy in Louisiana. A man in a Ford pickup pulls up behind us, taps on Eva's window, and says, "You ladies need some help?"

"Yes," Eva replies. "We all need help from each other."

"We're fine," I say.

"Car runnin okay?"

"Just wonderful," I say, and when he walks back to his truck we start driving again.

At our motel room in Dallas, we shower out the barbecue smell and paint each other's fingernails, waiting for midnight.

"Imagine," Eva says between blowing on her nails, "we are mere miles from the spot where John Kennedy departed this earth."

I think Eva has some kind of crush on JFK. She often works him into our sessions.

"Dallas is a city of much pain and much pride," she continues. "A good city in which to do healing."

When our fingernails are dry, we drive to my mother's house and park half a block away. We walk quietly up the long brick path, through the disfigured live oak trees that seem to hold more than shadows. I'm surprised when my key fits the lock, when I remember the code to the burglar alarm, when my feet know where to step so the oak planks don't make a sound.

"Step where I step," I whisper to Eva.

We walk first to the tiny bar bathroom, the bathroom where, if I reach back through layers of denial thick as a good pastry, the fat teenage boy baby-sitter drags seven-year-old me. He sits on the closed toilet lid and pulls me onto his lap, saying, "I'm going to spank you, Lace, you better turn over," tickling and tickling, but the laughter clings to my throat and spills as a gurgle. He doesn't really want to spank me, he wants only to do what he does next. "If you don't turn over, I'll spank you right here," and he touches my tight seven-year-old vagina, first through my dress, then my panties with the lace eyelet edging, then his fingers push inside me and his breath is jagged as he hauls the fat pink slug from his jeans and jams me down on it, and there is not enough room inside me. He tugs me down angrily until something breaks and deflates inside my body and his Dallas Cowboys T-shirt rides up on his fleshy stomach and I can hear the television in the next room where Irene is laughing at *Laverne and Shirley*. Afterward he scoops water from the toilet and stuffs toilet paper inside my raw wound and I lie in bed with my panties full of damp toilet paper and the elastic tight around my legs and Donny comes into my room and kneels by my bed. I turn away from him and wish he will catch leprosy so the big thing will fall off of him.

"Who's number 56, Lacy?" he whispers. He has taught me the numbers of all the Dallas Cowboys. This is a game we play often. I make my body as small as I can. I hide my voice deep in my throat.

"Who's number 83, Lacy? Come on, Lace. Didja forget already?" He touches the ends of my hair. I turn my head to pull my hair from his fingers. "Just tell me one, Lace. Who's number 56? I know you know it."

"Hollywood Henderson," I whisper.

"Atta girl," he says, satisfied, and I hear him walk out and after a long time I hear Mama come home from her party. I hear the tap of high heels against the hardwood floors, the happy jingling of her jewelry. Ice rattles in her final glass of the evening; owls fuss and coo in the backyard. I hear leaf brush against leaf hour after hour because I never sleep that night and when it is almost light I tiptoe into the bathroom and pull square after square of the stiff, darkened toilet paper from the hole in the middle of my body. When Irene wakes, she tells on me for making a mess in our bathroom and I am spanked and have to eat my breakfast on the floor next to perfumed Marcella, but I do not feel the spanking and I do not taste the food, I concentrate only on not telling, not telling, not telling, because I know if I tell he will do what he warned, he will do it to Irene, he will do it to my mother, and I know it is up to me to keep him from pulling them down on his huge, gushing slug.

Eva pulls a bundle of sage from her pocket, lights the tip of it with her Bic lighter, blows on the end of the bundle so it smokes gently.

"Eva, what if she smells it?"

"Shhh, don't think about her. Think about you."

She waves the burning sage stick in every corner of the bathroom, around the base of the toilet, under the brass faucets.

"In this room," she whispers, "a child was harmed. In this room a child was taught that she did not have the power to say no. In this room a child was taught that her body was not her own, that her only worth was as a sexual being. I acknowledge the soul-stealing that took place in this room, and I say to that child, no more. No more will you be unsafe. No more will your needs be ignored. No more will you be touched without your permission."

She offers the sage stick. I don't wave it, I kneel and hold it over the toilet where he held me. My voice is small in my throat. I remember the hand towel he jammed in my mouth, how it drew the moisture from my tongue, the cries from my throat.

We glide out to the kitchen, crouch by the pantry.

"Here?" Eva whispers.

"Yes," I say.

"Here," Eva says, "a child was not treated like a child, but like an animal. I say to that child that good parents support and encourage their children, they never degrade or humiliate them. I say to that child that her dinner table is now a safe place, a place of communion and laughter and nourishment. I ask that her table never again be a place of recrimination and fear."

I take the smoking stick and hold it over the worn place where Marcella's dog dish once sat, where the wood is splintered in a circular pattern. It is the one flaw in Mama's spectacular house.

"Upstairs," Eva whispers.

"It's too dangerous," I whisper back. "Her room is right next to mine. And she's probably got her fucking lapdog in there with her."

"Come on, girlfriend," she says. "Where there is fear let there be courage."

I know the stairs like my own body; each step has its silent spot.

I feel bravest in my old room; these walls know my stories, they believe me because they saw. Still, my voice is small.

Eva traces the sage around the edges of the dresser mirror.

"In this room," she whispers, "a young girl was taught that her body was not her own. In this room, she was taught to be ashamed of her body, ashamed of her beauty.

I say to that girl, you will grow to be a beautiful woman, an angel woman. Love yourself and your body, in its every stage, in its every season. There is no shame for this woman."

She hands the smoking stick to me. In the next room I hear the shallow, strained breathing of my mother and the rasping suck of the dog next to her.

"Eva," I whisper, then a squeak, a cascade of beeping, and after an instant of stupidity I realize the smoke alarm is wailing. I grab Eva's hand and we run down the stairs, hitting every noisy spot. I drop the sage stick, pick it up and crush it in my armpit to stop its burning. I hear my mother's steps as I grope for the doorknob. "Marcel?" Mama slurs, and the dog is shrieking as we run out the door into the fresh night air, down the walk and then the half block to Eva's car.

"Do you have the keys?" she gasps, and I can't answer because the sage has burned through my shirt where I clutched it under my arm and I drop the stick and stomp on it to put it out and Eva is patting all my pockets until she finds the keys, jerks them from my pants, and shoves me in the car. We drive like hell back to our motel room that smells like fingernail polish.

We collapse on the bed and I tear off my T-shirt to look at my burned skin.

"Aloe," Eva says, "we need aloe for that burn. I'll call the desk clerk and ask if they have any aloe up there."

"No," I say. "Don't call anyone."

"Don't be a victim," Eva says, gripping the phone.

"Eva," I say, "we just broke into a house and set off the smoke alarm. How's it going to look if we go asking for aloe to fix a burn?"

"You're right," she says, and wets a washcloth and holds it against the burn while we flip through the channels hoping to find a silly movie. We settle on a M*A*S*H rerun and I'm almost asleep when I hear Eva saying, "Lacy, good work tonight. Really good work."

"What's next?" I ask.

"Graceland," she says, and laughter is the last thing I remember before sleep.

WHITE IS VERY OUT
RIGHT NOW

"Robbed!" Mama says over the phone. "And with your wedding right around the corner!"

"We could put it off for a little while."

"Put what off?"

"The wedding."

"Oh, no, not with the invitations already sent. I wouldn't dream of it."

"What did they take, anyway?"

"Who?"

"The robbers, Mama."

I put the phone down for a minute and get a bottle of red wine from the cabinet.

"And I just know if I hadn't heard the smoke alarm," she's saying when I return, "well there's the sterling silver under your bed, and Lord knows what else they might have gotten their hands on. And I think they were smoking *marijuana*," she whispers. "The maid found some ashes, and there was a strange smell. Can you imagine the nerve?"

"So they didn't really take anything."

"Except my peace of mind! I bought a gun yesterday."

"Mama, get rid of that thing. You'll end up shooting yourself in the toe or something."

"Lacy, strangers came into my house. I haven't slept right since."

"Why don't you go have a nap?" I take a long sip of wine straight from the bottle.

"Because we need to talk about the wedding, Lacy. You simply must go down to Neiman's and choose your china pattern immediately. People don't know what to get you, and your aunt Eileen made a fool out of herself insisting to the sales girl that you're registered, when the fact is you're not. Of course, I realize the Houston Neiman's isn't quite what the Dallas store is, but that's no excuse, Lacy."

"I've been very busy," I say.

"Well, that's what I've been telling people, that you're just so busy with your teaching, but that's getting to be old hat."

"I'll be getting a new hat anytime now."

"Listen to me, Lacy. The first step is to decide if you want to be a blue person or a green person."

"What?"

"Do you want the theme color of your home to be blue or green? Because it can't be both."

"Why not?"

"Because blue and green don't go together. You can bring in other colors around your theme color, but you need to choose one color that will draw together your whole decorating scheme."

I look at our living room walls to see if we have a theme color. A huge Texas flag, topographical maps of the Guadalupe mountains, my black-and-white Miles Davis poster. I don't see marriage changing our decorating scheme, or lack of one. Suddenly I can't remember why I'm getting married. I'll ask Ellis when he gets home.

"Bye, Mama," I say, and hang up.

The phone rings almost immediately.

"Lacy," she says, "if you don't get yourself registered by the end of this week, I'm calling up Gayla Barris over at Neiman's and registering you for Wedgwood White. Then you won't be a blue person or a green person," she says spitefully. "You'll be a white person, and white is *very* out right now."

"Goodbye, Mama," I say again.

Number 22 on my list: I want something to accidentally interfere with my wedding. This something — I'm not sure what — needs to occur within the six weeks between now and my wedding date. Death? An academic tragedy? In the case of Ellis's death, I am prepared for a period of dignified widowhood, followed by a wild life on the road with Black Jesus and his band. In the case of my own, I'd enjoy being buried in my wedding gown, the innocent look and all. "They were so happy," I hope someone will whisper at the funeral. An academic tragedy isn't likely. Ellis has done very well in his doctoral work — American regional folklore is his thing. The university has paid to send us to Mardi Gras three years in a row. Folklore heaven, Mardi Gras is.

I unplug the phone, jam the cork back in the wine bottle, and drive straight to Neiman's. I race through the china displays until I find a pattern swirled with slate blue and bay leaf green. Why did I agree to marry? For a fateful moment I was seized with desire to be a bride, some sort of Barbie thing, and Ellis went along with it in his sweet, professorial way.

"Now I must caution you," the saleslady says through her tattooed smile, "Mikasa does have a nasty habit of discontinuing patterns, so if you want to be sure you can keep buying pieces throughout the years, you might want to choose something more stable, like a Wedgwood."

"This is perfect," I say.

When I'm done with the bridal registry, I walk around the mall to clear my mother's voice from my head. I'm looking in the Victoria's Secret window when I feel something hard brush against my arm. It's Marcy's cast, wrapped in black tape.

"Hey," I say. "What are you doing here?"

"I'm sittin in with a band called Fifth Ward," he says, then looks shyly at his cast. "I'm just rappin, I ain't playin nothin."

"You'll be better soon," I say.

"I'm gonna do our song," he says. "You know, 'Who That Bitch You That Bitch,'" and he does a little spin on the heel of his combat boot, ends up pointing at me. "Not you," he says, "I mean, you're never a bitch."

"Well, thanks," I say.

"You gonna buy that?" He points to the lace camisole strapped over the headless mannequin in the window.

"No," I say, "I'm just walking around."

"You'd look good in it."

"Well ... what are you doing now?"

"I was thinkin about checkin out the arcade, play a few video games. I got a couple hours till I gotta get ready for the gig." He tugs his pants down an inch or so with his good hand.

"Is Jesus coming?" I ask, looking hard at the camisole. "To the gig, I mean."

"Nah," Marcy says. "I think he's got somethin goin on in Austin."

We slowly walk to the arcade filled with twelve-year-olds. Marcy leads me to a glowing machine.

"I'll just watch," I say.

"No, it's for two people," he says. "See, you're the drug

dealer and I'm the narc," he says, "and you have to try to make your deals without me bustin you. Or you wanna be the narc?"

"I'll be the dealer," I say.

I get past the marijuana level and I'm turning a corner to pick up my load of crack. A bullet comes out of nowhere and my guy crumples at the bottom of the screen.

"Drive-by shooting," Marcy says.

"Damn!" I say. "Is that it? I lose?"

"Well, you're dead."

"I guess I consider that losing. Let's play again."

This time I'm more careful, and I maneuver through both the marijuana and PCP levels. I'm so busy watching for another drive-by that it seems almost accidental when Marcy brushes up against me from behind, then puts his arms around me and his hand over mine.

"Here it comes," he says, and makes my hand move the control lever as a bullet flies past my man.

"Thanks," I say, but he leaves his hand over mine even after my man is safe. I'm looking at the screen but I have no idea what's happening. I know only that numbers are flipping on my side of the scoreboard as Marcy racks up points for me by grinding his hand over mine, I know that he is pressing his body against my ass, that my jeans feel tissue thin as my stomach and thighs are shoved up against the warm machine. I know that my ear is almost inside Marcy's mouth as he whispers, "You beautiful, Lacy, you know that. You got it goin on."

I see cuffs slapped on my man, I see him shuffling away with his square head hanging down, I hear a wrenching car crash from the Indy 500 machine next to ours.

"Miz Springs!"

I push Marcy back, drop the control lever and there's little Anna Dominguez, mouth so full of chewing gum she can hardly talk.

"You play video games, Miz Springs?"

"Not really," I say, smoothing my shirt. "I'm just waiting for an appointment."

"A hair appointment?"

"Yes."

"Is this your boyfriend? Is this the guy who wrote the letter you were reading in the lunchroom? Is this him?" She points at Marcy.

"No. And don't point, please. It's rude. Good luck tonight," I say to Marcy, and I walk out of the arcade, trying to breathe, trying to get a breath of air that's not bubble gum or Marcy's neck or the sugary, sick smell of children.

I ride the escalator down to the bottom level by the ice skating rink and find a pay phone. Eva is thrilled to hear from me. I let her talk, because I can't seem to form any words. She thinks she has found the root of my problem.

"I want to talk to you," she says, "about your work on this plane, this plane which you have chosen to visit, and on which you will spend every moment of this lifetime."

Number 87 on my list: I move to Colorado where there are no blues, learn to snowboard on a Burton Freestyle, and work out my anger in the bumps. I don't tell anyone I'm from Texas.

"Yet in your striving to reach your God force," Eva continues, "or Goddess force, we should say, you constantly wish to enter other planes. And I say to you, dear Lacy, how can you learn to find the Goddess on your plane when you constantly wish to enter other planes?"

I think about Black Jesus's hands when he breaks and changes an E string. I think of a wonderful word Ellis used in our last Scrabble game: *quixotic.*

"You are not welcome in those planes," Eva says, "for you are not part of them."

A little girl in a red tutu spins and blurs in the middle of the rink. Her mother leans over the rail, clapping loudly.

"That's it, Brandi!" the mother calls.

"You want what you can't have," Eva says.

I agree enthusiastically. I want everything. I want Tirzo to earn straight A's while carrying two shining guns in a white holster slung low around his hips. Loaded. I want to be a blue person and a green person. I want Ellis, I want Black Jesus, I want to hear blues in the deep layers of my dreams, I want Jell-O to be both salad and dessert.

PARENTAL ADVISORY

Eva is fascinated by my encounter with Marcy. She wonders if she could interview him for an article she's writing on male sexuality.

"Absolutely not," I tell her. "Forget about that and listen to my side of it. The worst thing about it," I tell her, "was that I felt something."

"What do you mean?"

"I mean I felt a little bit, you know, aroused. I definitely could have fucked him. I could fuck anyone — it's really all the same to me." I'm ashamed to say it, and even worse, unlike so many things I say, this is not in any way a lie. The solemn drumbeat of truth throbs in my ears. *I don't want your dick/ Don't want your touch/ Don't want your mouth/ And I don't want much.* Parental Advisory.

"Lacy, you were taught by the adults in your life that your worth is as a sexual being. You were taught by your mother that your sexuality is a powerful thing, so frightening and powerful it made her behave like a crazy person."

"Well, she *is* a crazy person."

I think of my mother who, when asked where she comes from, names a different place every time, each more exotic than the last. "I come from a place," she once said, "where the most cherished delicacy is a woman's lubrication spread over a crème caramel."

"But you are not responsible for her craziness," Eva continues. "You did not, at the age of seven, seduce your baby-sitter. It is time for you to learn now that your sexuality is beautiful, and powerful, but that it does not by itself make up who you are."

There's a girl in Ellis's novel — Faith is her name — who's a lot like me. "Frail and reckless" is how Ellis describes her. Am I really? But who wants to read about someone who's strong and responsible, someone with a good credit rating, health insurance, and a 401(k) plan?

"There are many sides of you for you and others to discover," Eva says, "many ways in which you can be valuable to someone even if you do not take on that person's sexual needs."

I don't want your shit/ I don't want your talk/ Don't want your eyes/ Watchin how I walk.

"So what do I do?"

"I would suggest, my dear, and it is only a suggestion, a period of abstinence. A period in which you will let the sexual side of you rest, and heal, and give yourself time to appreciate some of your other qualities."

"You mean abstinence from sex, right?"

"I do indeed."

"Eva, that's my only fun. And it's not even that fun. Do you hear me? My job is hell, my relationships are a mess, and plus, my wedding's in two weeks, remember? I'm sort of obligated to fuck Ellis on our wedding night. I mean, my mother is expecting me to lose my virginity." I start laughing, and I cannot stop, and soon I'm choking on the tight, coiled laughter that fragments into tears because I realize I do not really remember being a virgin, because I'm jealous of the power of women who are able to choose when to ignite their sexuality, and I try to imagine some heated high school moment on the squeaking leather of a parent's Cadillac, the radio station changing as you accidentally kick the dial, but the static doesn't matter because an inner music is starting to swell, a song clear and familiar, a song only you can dance to, and if you dance lazily the music will slow to lull your every movement like the pair of enclosing arms that rocks you this way and that and that way and this, and if you dance frantically, wildly, your song will splinter until there is a note for every muscle, a chord for each joyful movement of the body.

Don't want your ass/ Don't want your kiss/ Don't want your tongue/ Don't want your dis.

I feel a touch and jerk away, then I realize it's Eva and I let her arms surround me.

"Tell me what you're feeling," she urges, and my head fills with the smell of her perfumed turban as I say, "Just now, when I jerked away, I think that might be the closest I've ever come to saying no to someone touching me. I really can't remember ever saying no. You know, if little Anna hadn't come up to us in the arcade, I think I would have let Marcy fuck me right there, back in that corner — I mean, I would have been screwing my boyfriend's brother in a filthy corner surrounded by beeping video games. That is gross, Eva!"

"You haven't had enough practice saying no, my dear. It's a learned skill, and you were not given permission as a child to learn it. How can you be expected to say no as a grown person when you were not permitted to practice that skill as a child?"

"I don't know."

"The answer is that you must begin practicing now. You must say it as much as possible, and perhaps a period of sexual abstinence will be an excellent way to begin."

"Okay," I say. "I'll give it a try."

I tell Ellis about the abstinence idea as soon as I get home. He stops typing.

"Three weeks," I say.

"What about our wedding?"

"Oh, the wedding ... the wedding's just a technicality. We'll have the rest of our lives to fuck."

"I can't believe I'm hearing this. A technicality? Who's the person who had to have the gold bands and a white lace wedding dress and the printed napkins and the goddamn lifetime supply of engraved stationery? Not that I don't want you to have any of that stuff," he adds.

"I know, I take it back. I just mean, we're gonna be married whether we fuck on our wedding night or not, so why can't you just let me do my abstinence thing and then we'll get right back to it. Eva thinks it's really important for me."

"Eva! I'm sorry, Lace, if she had any kind of credentials at all, maybe I'd buy it, but from what I can see she's just a grad student in a turban."

"She's in her last semester, Ellis. Plus, we can still make out."

Ellis starts laughing, and he kisses me and whispers, "Make out?"

"Yeah," I say, giggling. "Make out. You know, kiss and stuff."

"Like this?" and he kisses me softly.

"More like this," I say, edging my tongue into his mouth. "I thought you liked my wedding dress."

"I do," he says, pulling me back to his mouth.

I feel better knowing I won't be fucking anyone for three weeks. It's easier to face the fact that I'll be getting married in two weeks. It's easier to find something to wear in the morning, the freeway entrances seem longer, my students are more amusing.

"Don't be dissin me, bitch," is the first thing I hear when I walk into my classroom with my newly celibate body.

"Miz Springs, tell Darnell to quit callin me a fuckin bitch, I mean a bitch," Christine says.

"In your seats," I say, checking off my roll sheet as I talk. "This morning we're going to talk about synonyms. Who remembers what a synonym is?"

My question inspires a deadly quiet.

I raise my hand. "Oh, teacher," I say, "I know, I know. A synonym is a word that means the same thing as another word. So if two words mean the same thing, those two words are synonyms." I wait for applause. "Straight A's for me," I say. "Too bad I already graduated. Now, let's think of as many synonyms as we can for 'dis.' First of all, who knows what dis means?"

Every hand raises, but I call on Darnell since he started it.

"When you dis somebody, it's like you put em down."

"Okay, so if we're going to think of synonyms for dis, we need to think of other words that mean to put someone down."

Anna raises her hand. "How about to rag on someone?"

Darnell's already up at the board, wiping it off with his sleeve. I'm thankful I don't have to touch the chalk. "RAG," he writes in big swerving letters.

"Insult!" Josh, the Ritalin junkie, yells out.

"Good one," I say, "but let's wait until I call on you."

"Darnell," I say. He's waving his hand that's already coated in chalk dust.

"Slam," he says.

"Okay," I say, wondering if *slang* is a word I should discuss at some point, but my gut tells me no because words are words to my kids, and I'm hoping to teach them as many words as I can so they'll have some kind of choice when they're talking. I think choice is where it's at.

We get out the thesaurus and succeed in filling up the blackboard, and I even manage to get *degrade* in there. I ignore Mrs. Craven's disgusted stare when she comes by to pick up my roll sheet and sees DIS in foot-high letters at the top of my blackboard. As I watch her dried apple face shrink into a frown, I hope some day I'll feel the freedom to say Hey, bitch, don't be disrespectin me now.

I KNOW WE WILL
ENJOY IT IN THE YEARS
TO COME

Mama calls me late at night when Ellis is busy kissing my neck. He doesn't notice my tears spotting his thick hair as I begin to hate myself more with each kiss.

"We must discuss the dinner mints," Mama says over the phone, "we can't let another minute go by, Lacy."

Ellis shifts around to let me lean against his chest as I talk.

"What dinner mints?" I say. I wish I had not answered the phone. I wish I'd kept on with the kissing and useless crying.

"For the cake table," Mama says. "We'll have a silver bowl of dinner mints at each corner of the table. They come in all the pastel colors, so we could stay with our pink theme, but with salmon as the main course that might be too much pink. It might clash, actually, because salmon isn't a true pink, you know — it has those orange tinges."

"I thought everything had to be either blue or green," I say.

You probably never fucked a nigga, Black Jesus said to

me the first time I undressed in front of him, smaller with
each piece of clothing I removed.

No, but I've fucked a black man, I told him.

"I have no time for your sarcasm, Lacy," Mama says.

"Mama, you hired a wedding consultant. Why don't we
just let her choose?"

"Because we want your *personality* to come through
somewhere, darling."

"In the dinner mints?"

"You have a choice between atlantic, I think that's green,
petal pink, cornflower, sandstone — now what would sandstone be?"

"Probably beige," I say.

"Well, we don't want that," Mama says.

"That's the one," I say. "I want beige, I mean sandstone."

"Lacy, don't be ridiculous. Beige is so unflattering."

"I'm not *wearing* it, Mama. We're talking about candy.
Anyway, what kind of idiot is going to waste time eating
dinner mints when there's a big cake sitting right there on
the table?"

"They're decorative, darling. Now, I think cornflower
will do nicely. Don't be contrary, please."

"Then why did you call me?"

"Because you're the *bride*, darling."

"Yeah, I am."

"Irene's coming over Thursday and we'll just have her
try on your dress so you won't have to make an extra trip
up here — you two are still the same size, aren't you?"

"I think so."

"Well, if you're not, one of you needs to lose weight."

"Bye, Mama."

I get out the stack of papers I'm supposed to be grading
and look through them. I love looking at my students'
handwriting. It is not what it will be when they are older.

It is adorable in its effort to be neat, to be curvy, to stay within the lines. I try to forget my mother's voice and the terrible precision of the wedding plans — the color-coordinated bridesmaids' dresses and dyed-to-match shoes, the thee's and thou's and everyone with a particular place to stand and sit and now the mounds of cornflower dinner mints like tiny chips of shame. And my sister, Irene, whose personality was crystallized for me the time she came to Houston on business and stopped by to see me. We sat on the front porch with gin and tonics and saw a child trip on the sidewalk just past my house. I ran out to brush him off and touched my nose with my tongue to make him laugh, and sent him on his way. When I sat down again with my drink, Irene said, "At least he was past your property line so you're not liable. But you're just renting, aren't you?" Tort law, every square of earth a broiling patch of liability. Who is liable for the gun, Marcy's torn hand, the flecks of Thousand Island dressing and blood that splashed against the cabinets as he swiped the food off his daddy's kitchen counter, clenching his bloody fist as he fell?

I put away the stack of ungraded papers and get out my engraved stationery to work on my thank-you notes. *Thank you for the lovely gift,* I begin each one. *I know we will enjoy it in the years to come.* I studiously avoid writing anything I really feel, yet I try to feel the things I do write. I compose my most sincere note in thanks for a wooden salad bowl sent by Mama's accountant. According to the tag on the bowl, a man in the Ozark mountains carved the bowl solely with a chainsaw. I love the bowl and its rough elegance. When I'm freaking out, like I am right now, I enjoy imagining this bowl full of delicious, expensive ingredients that Marcy could swipe off his father's kitchen counter in a tantrum: wild capers, sun-dried tomatoes, grilled shiitake mushrooms. Sometimes I imagine more disgusting ingredients as well: processed cheese of a color not found in nature, for example. Sometimes I get furious thinking of the occasional wisdom that comes out of Marcy's slack, temperamental mouth. *Why don't you marry Dorinda?* I asked him one time. He answered: *Because we do so good not married.*

FUCK JESUS

"I urge you to postpone this wedding," Eva begins the next session. "I would like to suggest to you, dearest Lacy, that you are allowing the details of this wedding ceremony to keep you from feeling your feelings. I would like to suggest that your panic about dinner mints and dyed-to-match shoes points to a deeper, more serious panic about the covenant you are about to enter." She puts her fingers to her lips as I start to protest. "I am not saying you should not marry Ellis. Ellis is a fine man with an uncanny understanding of women's folklore, I might add, but for you to enter into the covenant of marriage at a time when your spirit is in such transition — my dear, you must not do it."

"I have to do it," I say. "I already have my dress, the invitations are out, and all the presents, and the thank-you notes. Plus, it was my idea to get married in the first place, Eva. I can't back out now."

"What was that idea, Lacy? Tell me about your desire to marry."

"I guess I'm hoping it will make me act better. It'll be

a fresh start, you know what I mean? I think I can be faithful if I'm married. I really think I can do it, Eva. I'm crazy, right?"

"Who says you must be committed to one man? Who says you must construct a life in which you are constantly struggling to be faithful?"

"Jesus. Christ, that is. He'll send me to hell if I can't be faithful."

"Fuck Jesus, Lacy."

"I do." I start laughing hysterically.

"You know what I mean. Lacy, you are allowed to postpone this wedding. You are allowed to defy the commands of a less-developed Lacy, a less-strong Lacy than the one I see sitting before me."

Number 43 on my list: I become a woman who speaks her truth.

"Will you speak to Ellis about postponing the wedding?" Eva says.

I wait for a song to swell in my ears to block out Eva's words, but no song comes and the silence grows oppressive. I stare at the carpet, imagining it covered with spilled salad ingredients: asparagus spears, a dusting of fresh oregano, crumbles of feta cheese.

"Lacy," she says. "If you cannot talk with Ellis about postponing the wedding, then I urge you to tell him about Black Jesus."

Water chestnuts, calamata olives, a touch of pimiento.

"Ellis must learn to recognize that many of your behaviors are typical of sexual-abuse victims. I believe that if he can do so, you will have a powerful ally to help you change some of those behaviors."

Flakes of crabmeat, morel mushrooms.

"... promiscuity, inability to say no ..."

Cherry tomatoes, hearts of palm.

"...dishonesty with self and others, codependency, a compelling desire to violate taboos..."

Eleventh grade, a St. Marks boy invites me to the Junior Symphony Ball. It's a big deal, this dance, for rich kids like me. I have a fabulous red velvet dress, silk-lined. *Did you tell your mother I'm black?* my date asks me in choir the day of the dance. It is a wonderful Friday — choir and the dance later. Choir is the only class we have with boys. They ride over to Hockaday in a shiny, blue van, especially for choir. They are arrogant but handsome in their uniforms, gray flannel pants and white oxford-cloth shirts. On choir days they are made to wear ties. *No,* I tell my date, who has a beautiful baritone voice. *Should I tell her?* I haven't even thought about it. We sing madrigals for an hour. I can pick out his voice two rows behind me.

Mama is having a massage when I get home from school, her exposed shoulders pink and rubbery under Monsieur Louchard's fingers. Neither of them glances at me. The white massage table is set up in the living room. I stand by the grand piano that no one knows how to play.

"Mama," I begin, my fingers separating the pleats in my green and white plaid skirt. "My date wanted me to tell you, I don't know why, but I guess he's a little nervous and wanted to make sure there aren't any problems you know, that he's like black?"

Monsieur Louchard's fingers still almost imperceptibly, then begin their probing once more.

"Call him immediately and tell him you can't go," Mama says.

"You've been exercising, haven't you darling?" Monsieur Louchard says to Mama. "I can feel the lactic acid."

"Yes, swimming," Mama says.

"Why?" I say. I think of the velvet dress, of the extravagant crimson bow spanning the back.

"Lacy, I am attempting to relax, and you are only creating tension. Please go make your phone call and either arrange for more suitable entertainment or stay home."

"Why isn't this suitable?"

"Etienne," Mama says.

"Oui?"

"Tell my daughter how quickly she will find herself off the Social Register if she pursues this Negro."

"Immédiatement," Monsieur Louchard says, pausing to coat his small hands in a honey-scented lotion. He and Mama laugh together.

"A black boy!" Mama laughs to her masseur, and her flesh shakes under his fingers. "Have you ever heard of such a thing?"

"Relax, chérie, or you will ruin my shoulder work."

"That will be all, Lacy," Mama says. "Please go make your call."

My date with the fine baritone voice is named William Bird. No one ever calls him Bill or Billy. William Bird knows why I am calling. He makes it easy for me.

"Hey, better than getting chased away at the door," he says.

William Bird probably deals with this stuff all the time.

"Well, thanks for asking me anyway," I say. My face burns with the embarrassment of racism.

"Listen," he says, "some people are getting a room at the Hilton, so we'll have a place to hang after the dance. Come by if you feel like it."

"Yeah, maybe I will," I say.

"You know where it is?"

"Yeah, I know where it is. What room?"

"I'm not sure yet. It'll be under Grayson's name. Or you'll see people going up. Everyone knows about it. So maybe I'll see you?"

I hang the velvet dress in the back of my closet and start

reading my history assignment for the weekend. Mama comes to my door after a while and sees me with the textbook open on my lap.

"Don't be a martyr, Lacy," she says, and closes the door.

I wait until she goes to bed, then listen patiently for the whining breath to deepen and slow. I am thankful for gin, which makes Mama a heavy sleeper.

Irene comes into my room to watch me put on makeup. No one has asked Irene to the Junior Symphony Ball. She hates me passionately.

"Where are you going?" she says.

"None of your business."

"Mama's right," she says, clicking the cap on and off my best lipstick. "Cathy Ewell hasn't been invited to any of the good parties since the mothers found out she's dating a black boy. Someone from *public school.* She probably won't even debut now. Her mom is like having a fit."

I snatch the lipstick from Irene and fill in the line I have already penciled around my lips.

"I'm not giving you the keys," Irene says.

"It's my car too, Irene."

"Yeah, but I have the keys."

"Get out of my room, bitch."

When I finish dressing I walk out back, past the pond and the rose garden to the groundskeeper's house. Nacho is more than a groundskeeper. He's my only ally against Mama. I hold my breath while I knock on his door.

"Look at you," he says when he opens the door. "Up to no good, I see."

"Nacho, please let me borrow your car, please, please, please. Irene won't give me the keys to ours."

He stands in the doorway looking at my miniskirt, my black clogs, my perfectly colored lips.

"Lacy girl," he says, "I ain't gonna tell you no. You my heart and that's a fact. But lemme drive you so at least I'll know you ain't gonna have a wreck. That's a good thing. I'll wait for you until you done doin whatever it is you gotta do."

I truly love Nacho and his way of always finding a reason to say, "That's a good thing."

Nacho drives me in his Cutlass down Central Expressway to the Hilton. I turn the radio up loud enough so I can't hear my sister's voice echoing *white trash white trash white trash.* I will be white trash if I want and no one is going to stop me.

"I'm glad you came," William Bird says. He is a little drunk, his cummerbund slightly crooked. The other girls at the party are flushed and sweating through their shiny taffeta dresses. Someone puts a beer into my hand. I grab William Bird's arm with my other hand, lead him to the bathroom, sit up on the counter, and wrap my legs around him. He looks surprised.

"Have you ever fucked in a bathroom?" I ask him.

"No. Have you?"

"No, but I'd like to. I'd like to right now." I feel his dick getting hard against me. High school is like that.

This is not the baby-sitter, I think, ecstatic, as William Bird unzips his tuxedo pants and works himself inside me.

"Hey, I gotta piss!" Someone is knocking on the door.

William Bird puts his hand behind my head to protect it from the hard mirror. My beer falls into the sink and fizzes and swirls down the drain. William's other hand hits the hot water faucet and warm drops fly up against my ass and we let the faucet run and run and run and I love William Bird for no other reason but that Mama has thrown a flaming circle of shame around him like a dare.

"Oh, sorry," he says when he comes.

"What about?" I say. I will live years more without having an orgasm. For now it's enough to fuck someone who isn't a child molester.

The knocking on the door continues. "What the fuck? Open up!" someone says.

"We better get outta here," William says.

"Yeah," I say, tugging my skirt back down. "We better."

"Lacy, where are you?" Eva says now, in the present day, in my session with her where I'm supposed to be listening and responding. "Why do you pay good money to come here if you're simply going to tune me out? Although I might add," she says, "that the psych department is doing an experiment on concentration, and I think you'd be an excellent candidate."

Minced garlic, curls of prosciutto.

"I'm here," I say. "I'm all ears."

AS IS

"Mama, I can't hear you." I hold the phone away from my ear. Mama's rat dog yelps in the background.

Mama starts shouting over the dog's frantic soprano. "Windswept blonde, Lacy. Roberto will do a fabulous job, I assure you."

"Mama, put the dog out," I say. "I can't hear anything."

"There, whuz Mama's baby cryin about? Quiet down now, we're talking to Lacy on the telephone."

"Mama, back to earth, please."

"We were lucky to get an appointment, darling."

"Appointment for what?" I drag the phone across the room and turn on the radio.

"To get your hair colored. What's that noise?"

"Radio."

"Well, turn it off, darling, I'm trying to talk about your hair. I practically had to kill to get this appointment. But I *am* one of Roberto's best clients, and God only knows how many good contacts I've sent him, practically my whole tennis ladder, although I'm glad to do it because he is simply the best —"

"Mama," I say. "I was kind of planning on my own color. You know, the one I was born with? Red?"

"Darling, surely you don't mean, as is?"

"As is, Mama. That's me. I'm a redhead."

"I know, dear, but for a wedding red is just so, well, *whorish.* I'm going to keep the appointment on the books because I know you'll come to your senses once you realize how nice everyone else is going to look."

I hang up the phone and focus completely on the voice coming over the radio, the voice that says, "We have so much crabgrass we just don't know what to do." I breathe deeply while I listen to the gardening advice, the praise for composting, red wiggler worms, and ladybugs. "Compost is better than money," the host of the show says.

After a while I turn down the volume and call Dallas information to get the number for Roberto's salon.

"Your mother just called and said don't let you cancel," the voice on the other end says in a pseudo-British accent.

"I won't be there," I tell her.

"Are you sure? Don't you want to reconsider?"

"What, are we breaking up?" I say. "I'm just trying to cancel an appointment."

"Okay, okay," she says. "I hear you."

IT'S NOT TRUE

=======

"Lacy," Ellis asks me a week before our wedding, "are you sure you want to be my wife?"

I'm standing in front of the bathroom mirror, trying to twist my hair up into a French roll. I feel dizzy from holding my arms up so long.

"Are you sure you want to be my husband?" I say.

"I don't ever want to not be your husband," Ellis says, sliding his hands around my waist. My hair refuses to be captured.

I remember my hands speckled with flour once when Ellis reached from behind me and cinched me up in his arms while I was making biscuits, flour sifting over his jeans, mist of falling stars. What was it I liked about Ellis back then? He said romantic things to me, he said: "You have a tall soul capped in fire." He said: "Your eyes are like the map of a planet I want to live on." He said: "If I were a woman, I'd want your body, exactly."

"Love me?" I say, my elbows poking at his face as I struggle with my hair.

"Oh yeah," he says. His face is hot against my neck.

"How much?" I say.

"More than I did yesterday," he whispers in one ear, "and less than I will tomorrow," into the other. I'm not really listening to him, not because this is something he tells me every day, and not because of the French roll, but because I am busy thinking of Nacho, the old yardman who loved me so well a long time ago. I am thinking of how he tried to protect me, of how pretty he made our yard with the Mercedes rosebushes, the double-flowering peach trees, how he smoothed over patches of my life with the touch of an instinctive gardener. I cannot pay sufficient attention to Ellis, who circles his arms around me in our small bathroom, but I can devote endless hours to thinking of Nacho and the things he told me during the happy hours I spent out in the groundskeeper's house, listening to baseball on the radio and looking through Nacho's collection of books on John F. Kennedy. Nacho's room was a small shrine to JFK, with tattered posters and buttons pinned all over the walls. I can't remember what any of them said. Every once in a while Nacho would let me look at a disgusting picture he had of JFK's punctured head with its blood-soaked hair and rolled-back eyes. "Ain't that a shame, Lacy girl?" he would say. "It's a shame," I would answer, shivering with happiness over the gory photo. He once made a point of driving me past the spot where one of Jack Ruby's clubs, the Carousel, had stood. The day we drove by the old Carousel we were supposed to be picking up a load of calla lilies for a pool party Mama was having.

"That's it, Lacy girl," Nacho told me, letting the Cutlass idle in front of the blackened strip of ground. "Mr. Ruby owned that damn club, had strippers you wouldn't believe. Don't you ever be goin to none of them places, you hear?" he added.

"But you went," I said.

"Only to drive your mama out here when she wanted to come. I never set foot inside, and that's a good thing."

"How do you know they had strippers I wouldn't believe?" I said.

"Someone told me."

"Mama?"

"Nah. Someone you don't know."

"Did Mama come to see the strippers I wouldn't believe?"

"It was a complicated situation, Lacy girl, but she came out here to see someone, I don't know what for."

Nacho's car smelled of tobacco and calla lilies, and he talked to me like I was a grownup, although I was only eight. *Strippers strippers strippers,* I said in my head.

"Do strippers take off their clothes?" I said.

"That's what they do, Lacy girl. Take em right off. Damn, I shouldn't be tellin this to a child, but Lord knows you a messed-up little thing already."

"Was I a baby when the strippers took off their clothes?"

"You was indeed, the prettiest little baby that ever lived, and one night your mama couldn't get no one to keep you and she wanted to come out here like nobody's business, so you know what she done?"

"Took off her clothes?"

"Naw. Get that outta your head, girl. We brung you on out here little as you was, not off the tit even, and I held you in the car all night long with the baseball goin over the radio. When the crowd got to yellin over the radio you'd start up to cryin, and when they was quiet, you'd quiet on down, too."

"What did you do when I'd start up to cryin?"

"I can't remember, Lacy girl. But after a while your mama and another woman and Mr. Jack Ruby himself come on out to the car so your mama can show you off a bit, and your mama was in a happy mood from the drink and she said, 'Nacho, I'd like you to meet my friend, Mr. Ruby,' and the window was rolled down and Mr. Ruby asks if he can hold the baby for a minute, that's you, see? So he reached in that window before I have a chance to say yes you can hold this baby or no you can't and he pulls you out and holds you for a minute, real gentle, like he's afraid of you."

"Did Mr. Ruby think I was the prettiest baby that ever lived, Nacho?"

"I'm sure he did, Lacy girl, unless he'd already gone back on his reason. But you know what you did?"

"I made him go back on his reason?"

"Nah, you spit up on his shoulder, right on his coat, most likely ruined it, you sweet thing. Your mama and her friend laughed to beat the band, and Mr. Ruby, he passed you right back through the window. Then you and me listened to our game some more and they went on back in the club to do some more drinkin. You know who Jack Ruby is, don't you?"

"He killed the president?"

"He killed the man that killed the president, he did indeed."

"Did he hold Irene, too?" I asked. I squished Nacho's pouch of tobacco between my fingers.

"No, he didn't. Irene was in the hospital with one of her baby sicknesses, and your daddy had just passed on, which was what made your mama get so wild."

"Why did she get so wild, Nacho? Did she go back on her reason?"

"You might say she did. She got filled up with sadness. She married your daddy for his money, see, so she wouldn't have to be white trash no more, but then she started lovin him and it took her by surprise. She knew she'd love his money, but she didn't reckon she'd love *him*. So when she did start in to lovin him it hit her like a freight train. And when he passed on like he did, that was a whole nother freight train runnin right over her. Them two trains made her wild, you understand?"

I plugged my nose with my fingers and breathed all the tobacco smell out of my skin. "Nacho, are you white trash?" I said. Nacho started laughing.

"Naw," he said. "That's one thing I ain't. You gotta be white to be white trash, you understand that?"

"You're black," I said.

"I am."

"Am I white trash?"

"No, you ain't."

"What happened then?" I did not want him to stop talking. I did not want him to drive us home.

"Thas all. Don't mean much to you now, but when you get raised up some and learn some history, you remember that Mr. Jack Ruby held you in his arms for a minute when you was just a little ol thing. He didn't have long to live, then. You probably the last baby he ever held. What you think about that?" And he started the car and drove us on home, the calla lilies swaying in the back seat.

"What are you thinking about?" Ellis says as I slide the last bobby pin into my French roll.

"Nacho."

"You think about him a lot, don't you?"

"Ellis, Nacho said Jack Ruby once held me in his arms," I tell him, as if I am confessing an infidelity.

Ellis kisses a line from my ear to my collarbone and says, "It's not possible, Lace. You were born in 1966. He must have been thinking of something else."

"I'm sure he was thinking of me," I say, and I don't care if I am too young to have been held in Jack Ruby's arms. I like it that Nacho worked me into his story. I think about what it means to be enclosed in someone's arms, about how we pass children around like sacks of potatoes without re-membering that a baby feels love or the absence of it from those who hold her, the way she will later feel in the space between her body and her lover's a field of love, or lust, or a perfect combination of both, or nothing, the way she will sometimes feel the power of human touch.

YOU DON'T HAVE TO THINK
ABOUT A THING

The day of my wedding is a cold day in Dallas; there's talk of a freeze. I wear red long johns underneath my ankle-length wedding gown. In the church dressing room before the ceremony, I pull up my dress to show Irene the bright red underwear.

"How completely tacky," she says. "Take those off right this minute and put this on." She dangles the blue-and-white garter that's supposed to be my something blue. I take it from her and run my fingers around the puckered silk. "Lacy," my sister says. "I hope you'll be happy."

I lunge toward Irene and hug her. I want to hold on long after she begins to stiffen in my arms.

"I'm freezing," I say. "And I just don't want to feel, you know, naked in front of all those people."

She reaches around my neck to adjust my pearl necklace. "Clasp was in front," she says. "You look beautiful."

"You do, too," I say.

The wedding consultant cracks the dressing room door and pokes her head in. "Five minutes, ladies," she sings.

"He did it to me, too," Irene says when the consultant has left us alone again.

"What?" I whisper, fingering my pearl necklace like a rosary.

"Donny did it to me, too." I cannot get a breath; the tight wedding gown presses the air from my lungs. "After you were in bed," she says. She twists the blue garter in her hands, not looking at me.

"In the little bathroom?" I say.

"In my bed," she says. She looks at me accusingly. "He said if I told anyone, he'd do it to you, too. And I didn't want him doing that to my little sister, but I hated you because you didn't have to fuck him." Her dark eyes ignite slightly when she says *fuck*. I can tell she doesn't say it often. She stands with her arms crossed next to a painting of Jesus on the cross. Jesus archs up against the wooden cross like it's a lover, like He can't get close enough to the splintered wood.

"Every time," I say. "He fucked me every time he baby-sat." I sink down onto the plush velvet couch.

"Me, too," Irene says, pulling me up. "You'll wrinkle. And you know what?" she says, checking her hair in the mirror. "It was a long time ago. I've gotten over it, Lacy, without the help of therapy or any of that crap you're into. I think you should get over it, too." She says, louder, "If I can forget about it, you can, too. I got through law school and I bill my time out at one hundred and seventy-five dollars per hour and I never think about him." She spins around to face me. Her hair is frozen in a perfect French roll. Mine hangs loose under my veil. "I'm telling you these things, Lacy, because you're about to get married and you're going to have promises to keep and you're supposed to be a good wife to Ellis and maybe have babies even, or maybe do something with your degree besides waste your life teaching high school, and you can't just keep being as self-absorbed as you are and as, as fucking selfish!"

"Why didn't you tell me before?" I say.

"Because I'm over it."

"Have you been over it your whole life?"

She doesn't answer me. We are both crying. Irene catches her tears with a tissue before they leave her eyelids, but I let mine roll down my cheeks and into the sweetheart neckline of my lace wedding dress. I quickly change Number 41 on my list from a wish for friendship with my sister to a wish that my father will return from the dead and right all that is wrong with my life. I feel sure that he would beat to a pulp any baby-sitter who so much as looked at his daughters funny, that he would teach us to be kind to each other, he would compliment me on my obscene red hair, validate my fears and sorrows, and he would walk me down the aisle I am about to walk down alone. He would not stop at the end of the aisle to hand me over to Ellis, the preacher, the four groomsmen in their tuxedos, and the four bridesmaids in their petal-colored dresses and dyed-to-match shoes. He would keep walking, I'm sure of it. He would guide me out the back door of this church where people marry in a pathetic effort to recycle the flawed families of their childhoods, this church where people receive the blessing of Jesus Christ on their desperate fucking. He would walk me through the parking lot and across Northwest Highway, past Northpark Mall where all the sinners go to shop on Sundays, past Turtle Creek where I rode my purple bike with the purple banana seat the day Mama said we were old enough to stay by ourselves, the day I knew I would never have to fuck Donny again and could use all my strength to fight my two remaining enemies, Irene and Mama. I sat by the creek that day and looked at my elongated reflection in the dark water and knew that my body would soon be my own.

"It's time, ladies," the wedding consultant says. Irene

and I stare at each other. "Everyone's already seated," the consultant says. "Irene, you know where to go, right? Lacy, you come with me and I'll tell you when to walk. You don't have to think about a thing."

We leave the dressing room, Irene hesitating as we pass through the door single file so we won't have to touch each other.

"Look, she's so happy," I hear someone whisper when I finally start down the aisle.

When I am halfway down the long, carpeted aisle, Ellis flagrantly violates the wedding consultant's blueprint and walks forward to meet me. He offers his tuxedoed arm. I gratefully slide my hand through the bend of his elbow, and we walk the rest of the way together. The people are twisting in their pews to watch us. I notice several women in the audience crying. I wonder what about.

NOTHING TO SEE HERE,
MOVE ALONG

The completion of the wedding ceremony has opened up a few spaces on my list of One Hundred Things I Want Out of Life. The first Monday after our celibate honeymoon, I scribble in the changes during my free period, between eighth-grade English and eleventh-grade special needs. Number 22 becomes a wish for Elvis's reincarnation, thinner, drug-free, minus the white panties fetish. I figure a lot of people, my mother included, will be pretty happy if that one comes true.

"Ms. Springs." Mrs. Craven stands in the doorway of my classroom, a small black boy in her clutches. Mrs. Craven's fingernails could give you nightmares. I shove my list in my pocket. "You're free this period?"

"Yes. I'm grading papers."

"This child needs to miss his lunch period. He needs some time to think about how one pronounces the word 'ask.' If you don't mind, I'll seat him in here until your next class. Sit!" she commands. The child chooses a desk in the far corner of the room. Mrs. Craven slams my door as she leaves. I run down the hall to catch her.

"Problem?" the old lady says. A hundred lines gutter her face.

"I've noticed," I say, "that the kids have a hard time concentrating on their afternoon classes when they don't eat. I think it's a blood sugar thing, something about the brain.... I'll be glad to work with him, but —"

"If he's hungry, he can learn to speak the English language. I won't have this nigger trash talk in my school."

"I guess not," I say, and walk back to my classroom. The boy runs one finger over the graffiti carved into the desk. I sit down at the desk beside him.

"You ever been to another country?"

He looks at me suspiciously. "Nah. I mean, no ma'am. Have you?"

"Yeah, I've been to a few. Been down to Mexico a bunch of times. You know what the weirdest thing about Mexico is?"

"What?"

"You have to talk differently, or the people there won't understand what you're saying."

I get up to look through my desk for a snack. I come up with a small pack of M&Ms.

"You like these things?" I say, tossing him the pack. I sit down beside him again. He eats the candy politely, piece by piece. "You going to Mexico anytime soon?" I say.

He giggles. "No, ma'am."

"Well, when you do go, you can't talk like you talk here in the United States. If you eat a bunch of jalapeños and you get really thirsty, you can't ask for water — you won't get a thing — you need to ask for *agua*. Then you'll get something."

"Agua," he repeats.

"You got it," I say. He runs his finger over the letters in the desktop that spell *dope*. "When you come to school," I say, "it's kind of the same thing. You need to talk the school talk, and that means saying 'ask' instead of 'axe.' When you're somewhere else and you know everyone's gonna understand you, then maybe you'll want to say 'axe.' But what you need to remember is that wherever you are, you gotta talk so the people there understand what you're saying. That's your best chance of getting what you want, sometimes." He offers me the last piece of candy. "Thank you, my baby," I say. "Now if you and I go on down to Mexico, what are we gonna ask for when we get good and thirsty?"

"Agua," he says.

"Sí. And when we're at school?"

"Ask."

"That's the way."

Mrs. Craven opens the classroom door, sees the boy with the empty candy wrapper clutched in his hand, and sucks in her breath. She slams the door and stomps down the hall, her high heels pounding an angry shower of footsteps. She returns clutching a wooden paddle.

"Up against the wall!" she commands the boy. He drops the wrapper on the scarred desk. We both stand up, but I don't let go of his shoulders.

"Children need to eat lunch!" I say. "He can talk perfectly fine, if you'd just give him a chance!"

The old woman circles us with the paddle held forward like a divining rod.

"Ms. Springs," she hisses, "you and your namby-pamby teaching methods will not stop me from whipping this child. His parents signed the release. Let go of him before you get yourself into real trouble."

"What are you going to do?" I say. "Spank me?" The

bright map of Texas on the far wall of my classroom starts to melt into the shape of some less interesting state. Mrs. Craven is quivering. "I quit," I say.

My hands are shaking on the boy's shoulders. I drag him to my desk, grab my purse, and pull him out of the classroom and down the hall. Mrs. Craven runs behind us yelling, "Stop right now! Right now!" and some other stuff I don't even hear. She can't keep up with us in her high heels. We both get in the driver's side of the car somehow, and I lock the doors. Mrs. Craven bangs on the hood with the paddle as I back up and drive out of the parking lot.

"Where do you live?" I ask the boy at the first stoplight.

"I don't know." He clicks the glove compartment open and closed, open and closed.

"Do you know the name of your neighborhood? Your street?"

"I forget," he says.

I know I have done a terrible, unprofessional thing. I know I will not be able to teach again in the Houston Independent School District. I know the feeling of wood against flesh, of missed meals and a stomach too small to hold my rage. I know the bewilderment of standing in the knee-high monkey grass trying to choose a switch from the red-tip photinia bush, I see the shower of soft, red leaves as Mama strips them from the stick and squeezes me against her bronzed legs and white terry tennis skirt so there is nowhere to pull away from the burning slashes except into Mama's stomach that smells of suntan lotion. I know the arm that possesses the best serve on the Brookhollow Country Club women's tennis ladder will not tire easily, but after a while will shove me away and Mama will say, "Damn, my skirt," but my tears never stain the white terry cloth, they only dampen it.

I hear the siren but don't realize it's meant for me until the boy closes the glove compartment, touches my arm, and says, "Miz Springs?"

I look up and see the rearview mirror churning with red. I pull over in the parking lot of a convenience store.

The officer's moist face fills my window. "Please step out of the car, ma'am."

Another cop car pulls up behind us. People start to come out of the store and they wander toward me instead of going to their own cars.

"Nothing to see here, folks," the officer calls, "move along."

I get out of the car as gracefully as I can, thankful for my high-necked schoolteacher blouse, my rich cherry hair, and the blank spot on my list. I feel certain the officer will see that I am someone who has the best of intentions, someone whose kindness can be seen in every curve of my face, if he will only look closely enough.

SO,
SHE'S A TATTOOED BITCH

Mrs. Craven didn't really want to press charges since I could easily tell about how she altered our school's overall PSAT scores by not sticking to the time limits on the test and making all the teachers tell answers to the students she wanted to do well. And how Lyle Cobb was failing my English class with an average grade of 43 until his parents gave Mrs. Craven an all-expense-paid luxury cruise to Cancún, and she took the pencil right out of my hand and changed his grade to an 82, making a mess of my grade book. I'm sure the Texas State Commission on Education would love to get an earful of that. You can't change a grade in Texas for anything that doesn't have to do with football. So the D.A. dropped my kidnapping charge down to a misdemeanor harassment. I have to do two days in the county jail and sixty hours of community service, which shouldn't be too hard seeing as I'm now unemployed.

When Ellis drops me off at the Harris County jail to do my two days he holds me tight and says, "I'm gonna start working really hard on my book and maybe I'll sell it

and you can stay home and eat bonbons all day or whatever."

"Yeah?" I say. "What kind of bonbons?"

"Those chocolate-covered cherries with the chocolate
cream in the middle."

"How do they get that chocolate cream into the middle
of those cherries?" I ask, kissing him between words.

"It's one of the secrets of the universe. We'll find out in
the afterlife."

"It's the first thing I'm going to ask God when I die. I
can't wait to hear what she says."

Then he hugs me again and he's gone and a young guard
leads me in and they make me change into a horrible orange jumpsuit. Orange is not my color, let me tell you. It
makes my red hair look like ketchup, tacky as can be.

My cell is a little gloomy but there's a radio and another
woman who's sleeping on the cot across from mine. I refuse
to reflect on my crime for even a moment, for I will not
let my government get the best of me. Ha! I dig a draft of
Ellis's novel in progress from my overnight bag, the lovely
tapestry bag Mama gave me to carry on my honeymoon.
I've hardly had time to read Ellis's book between my teaching job and my secret weekend travels. I plan to look on
these two days as a vacation. Catch up on some letters, some
sleep, some sexual fantasies. I used to do the same thing
when Mama would send me to my room for days at a time.
It wasn't bad, really. I made a heaven out of my blue flowered wallpaper and my bookcase full of Shakespeare which
I read until my eyes popped out, and the little mirror I hid
under my mattress that I could look into for hours without
finding a trace of the evil Mama swore she saw in my face.
Shakespeare, that's the stuff. Adventure and true love. By
the end, everyone's either ecstatically happy or dead.

"What're ya readin?" my cellmate says, waking slowly.
Her hair is a kinked mass of electric moss.

"Oh, it's something my husband's writing."

"Oh yeah? Got a brainy husband, do ya? Mine ain't worth a shit."

"Sorry to hear it."

"Tell me the story, will ya? I'm tryin to make the time go."

"Okay. Um, my name's Lacy."

"Mine's Laverna."

"That's pretty," I say.

"Is it now?" Her face is puffed with too much sleep. "Hold on, I gotta go," and she stands and yells "Hey," through the bars until the guard comes and takes her to the bathroom. I'm glad to know how to do it. I flip through the pages of Ellis's book looking for parts about Faith, my favorite character. Ellis tries to disguise her, but I recognize her like I would a sister. She doesn't look like me; she's a blond, although she's bald-headed for much of the book. Self-inflicted. At her core, although it's wrapped in the most fragile of textures, the flimsiest of scarves following the wind's every gesture, is a band of steel — I recognize the glint. Faith is heavily influenced by her aunt who raised her, one of those women, plentiful in the Deep South, who consider every happening in life (and perhaps in death, as well) the result of either the presence or absence of good breeding. Only whores and children wear red shoes. Only prostitutes and gypsies have pierced ears. Serving dark meat in a chicken salad is a sure sign of lunacy. I could go on for the length of a gossip column. Ellis implies that the aunt's complicated belief system is some sort of harness on Faith's soul, that if she could burst the leather stitching and leave the brass bit dangling, if she could prance and scuff the softest red leather, toss her head until the slender earrings whirl like uncooperative hair, all would be righted, the earth would sweat with joy, the universe would become riddled with moist patches of happiness. None of this prevents the aunt from acting foolish in chapter 4. Although she is not a Catholic, she angrily flings a rosary against the wall, an heirloom rosary carved of ivory and onyx, a rosary as vain and beautiful as sin, and it hits the china cabinet that holds none of the Wedgwood china, for Faith's aunt keeps that in a secret place with the sterling, but instead of china, the cabinet houses the violin Faith's uncle successfully bid on at a Sotheby's auction in London, a violin crafted by the German violin-maker Leopold Widholm in the distant year 1718. The door to the china cabinet is slightly ajar, because Faith, who is musically talented, has just finished playing one part of Bach's Concerto for Two Violins in D Minor, which she does as a service to her uncle because, as any cultivated young lady should know, an instrument loses its tone if not played. The violin in question is very fine indeed. The uncle kneels on the floor with the maimed instrument in his hands, looking through the dented, gaping F-hole at the German maker's intricate label. I enjoy that moment when the two exquisite objects clash and sink together, the rosary and the violin shined and proud and freshly played. I'm a big fan of Ellis's. I can't wait for the next chapter.

The cell door slams and Laverna collapses on the bunk again. "So what's happening in the book?" she says.

"Lots of fucking," I say.

"Like who's fucking what? Tell me." She lights up a cigarette.

"Want one?"

"Yeah, I do." She tosses me the pack and the lighter.

"You don't really smoke, do you?" Laverna says, watching me light up.

"I do now." We grin at each other. "So Faith, she's the main character, she's married to this guy but she's fucking a musician, a Mexican guy. He plays in a flamenco band."

"This Faith, she a white girl?"

"Yeah, well, pretty much."

"I had me a Mexican boyfriend once, he couldn't get it up. So I don't fuck spics no more. I think that was God tellin me, Laverna, don't you be fuckin no more spics."

"Yeah? Well, the Lord works in mysterious ways, right?"

"Pretty damn mysterious. Ain't nothin worse than a dick with no starch in it."

"That's the truth, sister," I say.

"My husband . . ." Her face begins to tense and change. Her small chin shows a tiny band of muscle. I turn a page of the manuscript, and that moment passes when she could have let the tears start, could have told me what a motherfucker he is, could have told me more about the time he stayed out drinking all night and broke through the living room window after losing his keys somewhere along the way, and instead of knocking on the door he broke the glass with one hard slap of the garden hose nozzle and Laverna was picking splinters of glass out of the couch for weeks and the kids had to sit on the floor to watch their cartoons while the couch stood empty, a shimmering upholstered dagger, and when she whined "Why? Why didn't you just knock?" he looked straight into her dark eyes and said, "I didn't want to wake you." Then all the time she spent thinking about what that meant, whether he believed it as he said it or whether he saw the broken window as she did, one more misjudgment in a long series of mistakes: the furniture bought on credit, the DUIs, the four hundred dollars spent getting a patent for the gadget that scoops paint from the rim of the can and puts it back in, the hours spent calculating the difference that amount of paint would make to someone, the alcohol always seeping out of his body in his sweat, the split-second decision to shoot the next time she saw someone outside the living room window, someone who could be her husband and was, in fact, him. But the crackle of page 82 of Ellis's book quiets Laverna and when she says, "Oh, it's all a bunch of garbage anyway," I'm relieved that I won't find out what happened with her husband, if anything happened at all. Something usually does.

"So what about Faith's spic?" Laverna says. "He gets it up all right?"

"Seems like it. See, Faith isn't really white, I mean, she started out white but her whole body's covered in tattoos, because every time something really important happens to her, she gets a tattoo having to do with that thing, so her whole body's like a map of her life."

"No shit. You got any?"

"No," I say.

"I got one," Laverna says, blowing two tendrils of smoke out her nose. "But it's in a place I can't show you."

"But you're black."

Laverna laughs. "And I thought you wouldn't notice."

"I mean, it still shows up?"

"Of course."

The cigarette is making me dizzy. I'm seized with desire to see Laverna's tattoo.

"So this Faith, she's a tattooed bitch," Laverna says. "Well, go on."

"Yeah, well it gets her in good with the Mexican guy, because she's not really white, see, she's all these different colors. She can relate to any color person because she's got that color on her somewhere. And it's not just on her skin, it's sort of in her soul, because every tattoo represents something painful that's happened to her, or something that's changed her somehow."

"Damn. Your husband's got some imagination. He really know someone like that or did he make it up?" She stubs her cigarette out on the concrete floor.

"I'm assuming he made it up," I say. "I think Faith is supposed to represent some kind of multicultural synthesis kind of thing, you know, everybody getting together and acting nice no matter what color anyone is."

"Ha! Your man's got some crazy-ass ideas," Laverna says.

"Yeah, he's got a few. But the cool thing about Faith is that her tattoos act as a shield, so once she gets a certain tattoo and she's clear about what it represents, it's like a shield that deflects that particular kind of evil away from her. But she's not all closed off, like most people are who have to shield themselves from something, she's a very warm and loving person."

"But you don't want to mess with her, or you'll end up in one of her tattoos, cause this Faith don't take no shit, do she?" Laverna mumbles, almost asleep again.

"No, I guess not," and I lean over the bunk and stub my own cigarette out on the metal leg of the bed, then lie back with Ellis's book to see what happens next.

The next day at noon Laverna flips on the radio.

"Prison show," she says. "My no-good husband better remember to call."

Ellis and I have listened to the show on the public radio station a few times, and we've always gotten a kick out of it. It's run by a prisoner's advocate, an ex-con who is always vague about her particular crime. Inmates who have radios can listen to their families and friends ramble about this and that. Today, Ellis himself is the second caller, right after a woman who says, "I'd just like to say to my husband J.C. up in Huntsville Unit B, J.C., I'm just mowin the lawn and we went to church and Evelyn Baird inquired about you and sends her love and here's little James, oh I guess he don't want to get on the phone but he says daddy I love you, sounds like that's what he's sayin." Ellis says: "Am I on now? Okay. Hey, Lace, did you know that Elvis wore diapers for most of the last five years of his life? Seriously, I just found out."

"We have a lot of callers waiting, honey," the prisoner's advocate cuts in.

"Is that you he's talkin to?" Laverna says. Her face shines with cheap makeup. "Damn, you're only in here for two days and you already get a call. That boy's talkin up his ass about Elvis, though."

The next caller says, "Henry, I written you three letters in a week and I ain't heard a word from you. I sure would like to know how you are. Everybody's wonderin but I guess I'm wonderin the most."

"I hear you, sister," Laverna says.

"Our next caller is phoning from Amarillo."

"Yeah, uh, I'd just like to say that Elvis never wore no damn diapers."

"I'm with you, sir," Dee, the prisoner's advocate, says. "We all got a right to express our opinion, but this ain't an opinion — it's a fact that the King did not wear diapers, and I thank you for calling to set the record straight. Hello, you're on the air."

"Worse than diapers." Ellis is back. "His guys just pinned bath towels around him. Luxury-size bath towels. See the Goldman biography and testimony of Elvis's head housekeeper."

Something shifts in my cell structure and I love Ellis fully, then my heart constricts, afraid and unfamiliar with so much love, and it stills for a beat until Dee's voice breaks in again and love flows out, a slow, relieved exhale.

Laverna doesn't like me as much now that she knows I'm married to an Elvis doubter. It's cause for suspicion, and being a Southerner myself, I completely understand. I think about why I love Elvis in spite of the diaper thing, which I assume to be true because it was spoken in Ellis's voice. I think it's that Elvis is the only thing I know of that my mother wanted and couldn't have. I think I like the idea of Mama languishing in her tiny shotgun shack during the very hours Elvis was performing at Russwood Park in Memphis, that while the other eighth-grade girls were squealing their small voices away, Mama was left to the tender clutches of Jesus and my grandparents, who thought rock and roll music would lead her dancing down the path to hell. Mama was left to wait who knows how many more years for the sight of a man's pelvis grinding back and forth, and I think if she could have unsealed that moment later and remembered the wanting, she might have been less cruel.

I pretend to sleep until the guard comes to get me at five o'clock.

"Well, bye," I say to Laverna. "Maybe I'll see you some-time."

"I doubt it," she says. "I think we probably run in different circles. But if you ever go drinkin at the Tall Texan, up on Studemont, well, that's where I do my partyin."

Number 52 on my list: I walk into the Smithsonian and find it empty, alarms off, cases unlocked, glass doors invitingly ajar. I go to the Americana wing, find the mannequin who wears the pink suit Jacqueline Kennedy wore when someone sprayed her husband's blood and brains all over her. The suit is still flecked with the president's dried blood. I wriggle it off the mannequin. Where the mannequin should have a vagina is a plane of smooth, sealed plastic. I try the dress on. It fits perfectly.

Ellis's car is right in front of the jail, a box of chocolate-covered cherries waiting for me on the front seat.

"Thanks for making everyone in jail hate me, you damn Yankee," I say to Ellis, putting two cherries in my mouth at once.

"Hello, you beautiful, unemployed jailbird. Are you horny?"

I pretend to be horny because no girl in her right mind should not be horny for a man as sweet as Ellis, but I'm not

in my right mind and I'm not sure I've ever been there — I
don't think it's part of my legacy. Was my mother in her
right mind when she asked Nacho to drive her out to Russwood Park the day after the Elvis concert so she could scour
the grounds for souvenirs? Nacho was a young man then,
living next door to my grandparents. At the paint company
downtown, my grandfather put lids on the paint cans and
Nacho slapped the labels on. I imagine that slapping motion was still lively in his hands when my mother climbed
into his truck and he drove her out to the empty baseball
park to search for dirty fliers. Nacho stayed in his truck, he
didn't tell Mama what he had heard about the concert from
the blissful secretaries at United Paint, he didn't tell what
they said about how so many women climbed up the
chicken wire behind home plate that the people sitting in
that section couldn't see a thing through the wall of ecstatic
bodies. Was Mama in her right mind when she ran out to
the infield and dropped to her knees in the dirt where the
members of the Memphis Chicks infield had let so many
ground balls rollick past them? And as she gave in to her
girlish grief and lay down along the third base line, were
the groans that came from her throat genuine, because the
noises I make during my just-out-of-jail-fuck with Ellis are
fake and shallow, and I can't for the life of me figure out
what makes me so dissatisfied, or why I have to think so
much about Black Jesus when he doesn't give a damn about
me and Ellis loves me fully and truly, but I'm going to find
out, I swear I am.

STRAIGHT EDGE
BLUES

Monday morning when Ellis goes to the university, I call Black Jesus at his hotel in New York City. He's recording his new album, probably fucking all kinds of Yankee women. I don't really give a damn. I can't wait to hear the album, though — it's called *Straight Edge Blues.* Jesus's agent thinks it's going to be a big hit, and perhaps he's right. I figure I need to hurry up and fuck him a few more times before he gets too famous and catches AIDS. Then I'll start living right, I swear I will.

"Why don't you come with me on the southern part of my tour?" he says. "We're doin Houston, Dallas, New Orleans, Nashville, and Memphis, all in one week. Can you get away from the man?"

"That's my problem," I say. "You shut up about it."

"Well, you got an invitation, baby. You can hook up with us in Houston and catch a flight back from Memphis, or however you want to do it. But I got a reporter comin over right now so I gotta get goin. We'll be in Houston

Friday night, so come on by Rockefeller's with your stuff if you want to come along."

"I'll think about it," I tell him, and hang up. I want to go so bad I can't stand it. Now that I'm not a teacher and will never be a teacher again, I want to be as bad as I can be. I spend all day thinking of an excuse that will satisfy Ellis. In between my possible excuses, I consider being a faithful wife. I think of Nacho, the only person I've never lied to. I remember what Nacho used to tell me when we'd go riding around Dallas in his Cutlass, sent by my Mama to look for some fantasy plant: "You special as a flower, Lacy girl, special as this flower we ain't gonna find, I'm tellin the truth."

"Go find me the Flower Which Opened at Queen Elizabeth's First Menses and Never Dies," Mama would command Nacho. "It's an annual."

"Yes, ma'am," Nacho would say, and we'd drive up and down the LBJ Freeway until he felt brave enough to go home and tell Mama they were just all sold out.

"Then bring me a dozen bulbs of the Flower Whose Essence Makes Horses' Hooves Strong. Elvis Presley gave one to Priscilla on their first date. It's of German origin. Now hurry, Nacho, we've got to get those bulbs in the ground before dark."

"Yes ma'am," Nacho would nod, and we'd go out to drive the freeways some more.

Number 96 on my list: I bring my mother a bouquet of all the flowers she's ever imagined — Thelonious Monk lilies, the star-covered Rebel Rose, the Iris Which Opens When a Billie Holiday Record Is Played. She begins to love me.

Number 61 on my list: I move to a galaxy where I can simultaneously be married and not married. In this new band of stars I enjoy the comfort of having someone to come home to, someone who gives me a diamond the size of Texas, who fucks me like he might never have the chance again, but whose scent and voice are as familiar to me as my own. Perhaps I will be married and not married to the same person. I'll find out when my wish comes true.

"Ellis," I say when he comes home to make pasta for us, "I really want to go to Graceland."

"Investigate the diaper thing?"

"No, I just want to see it. I mean, I just want to go somewhere while I'm not working my ass off for once, and I think it would be really cool to see Graceland. You think it's stupid?"

"I think it's the great tourist trap of the South. No telling how much money his estate makes off all the tours and souvenirs."

I slip my arms around Ellis's waist as he stands at the stove. I lean my cheek against his shoulder blade. "You're such a Yankee boy," I say. "I know it's goofy, but I really want to go."

"Is this Eva's idea?" His back muscles move under my cheek as he stirs the sauce.

"No. I haven't even told her I'm going."

"She'll probably want to go with you. It's just the kind of campy thing she could turn into something profound."

"Well, she probably could," I say. "That's what I like about her."

"Lace," Ellis says, stirring fast so flecks of red sauce fly up against the side of the pot, "when you're ready, I want to be more a part of your life. I want to know what makes you so sad, whatever you and Eva talk about. I want to know what you want, who you want to fuck, cause I get the feeling it isn't me. I understand that you need some time and that you've been through some bad shit, but I just want you to know, I'm here when you're ready."

"Ready for what?" I whisper.

"For whatever. For dinner," and he moves out of my arms to drain the pasta and we put the heavy fiesta plates mounded with fettuccini on the table and eat like we're starving. We do not look in each other's eyes because I'm not ready to be that much of a person yet. I just want to eat enough food to crush the fear in my stomach, and then move on to dessert.

I COULD BE
A MILLIONAIRE
BY NOW

"I knew you'd come," Black Jesus says when I walk through the backstage door at Rockefeller's.

"No you didn't." I make my voice hard because my body starts to soften all over as I look at him, and I don't give a fuck about the blues or my marriage or Black Jesus himself, I just want his dick to be mine for an hour or so. Karl puts a glass of wine in my hand and I sit backstage by Jesus while Karl brings girl after girl back to get his autograph. As each girl passes through the door with a flush on her face and her makeup fresh and exact because the evening's only begun and no one's had time to sweat or get messed up yet, I see the disappointed look on her face as she sees me in my blue velvet dress and my black seamed stockings and my left hand that's bare because I left my wedding ring in my safety deposit box, and I wonder what her story is, if she came here with someone and what excuse she'd use to get away from him if Black Jesus wanted to fuck her, and most of the women are white but the black ladies are different, shimmering in sequined gowns even though

Rockefeller's is a dump, and they look at me with a sneer or don't look at all. It makes me feel powerful to sit there, all beautiful and high and no question in anyone's mind about whether Black Jesus is fucking me, because I'm the most gorgeous woman in the club so of course I'm his. And I'm thinking if I have to be a man in one of my next lives oh please let me be a famous musician, because they get the best women — maybe women who are a little crazy, who have to press their legs together and think of something else from the first note on or they'll be even crazier from the wanting, a woman who can take a song that's been sung over and over for fifty years and think he's singing it about her, a woman who dances gently and slowly, because her real dance will come later on, when he says, "Don't take that dress off, baby, cause I been makin love to you in it all night long," and she slides it up over her garter belt, then her hipbones, and fucks him until the seams of her stockings are all twisted around and he unhooks her garters and slides the stockings off her legs, kissing her calves all the way down. A woman like that, a woman like me.

"Lacy, this here is K-San," Black Jesus says when a tall thin black man walks in the back door. "He takin Marcy place."

"What about when Marcy's hand heals up?" I say quietly. Already I don't like K-San and the way he's letting Karl carry his equipment in and the way he's not Marcy.

"Marcy crazy as a motherfucker," Jesus says, "but he kin and if he still wants to play with me I guess I'll take care of him."

"Only cause he's your brother? Don't you think he's good?"

"Good and crazy. I was raised up with him, Lacy. All you seen is him shootin his own hand apart and lemme tell you, that wasn't so bad."

"Where we goin tomorrow?" K-San asks.

"Tonight, brother," Black Jesus says. "Goin to my daddy house cause we playin Baton Rouge tomorrow night."

"We ain't spendin the night here?" K-San says, tuning his bass to nothing in particular. "Damn, I got me some good pussy goin here."

"You can start fresh in Louisiana, then," Jesus says.

"You the only one gets it tonight?" K-San looks at me.

"Excuse me," I say. I go out to sit in the audience where the waiters bring me whatever I want because they know I'm with Jesus. Karl comes out and sits by me and says, "K-San ain't that bad, Tex, he just a boy, and he don't like white women much unless they his."

Black Jesus and the band come out and a few people start dancing and Karl says, "You and me, Tex?" We dance, and I like watching Black Jesus watch us, and it makes me lean a little closer to Karl because, as I think I've demonstrated, I don't like to be told what to do.

"Where I come from," I once heard Mama say, "women eat their children's placenta and their birthing wounds are immediately healed."

After the show I sleep in the back of the van while the band plays five card draw and Karl drives us to Louisiana.

"What the hell?" I hear Henry John say after a long time and then Jesus's voice says, "It's the fuckin man."

We climb out of the bus onto the soft warm grass of his daddy's front yard and see four sheriffs sitting on the porch, two creaking gently on the swing, one leaning back in the rocker, and one sitting on the steps with his long legs stretched across their expanse like a dare.

"Mr. Robert Sharp, alias Black Jesus?" the one on the steps says quietly.

"What can I do for you?"

"You can come with us, sir," the sheriff says, standing

now and stretching his arms up until his back cracks. "Damn, that feels good," he says and the other sheriffs laugh a little. "You got the summons, Bill?" and the sheriff in the rocking chair hands him a piece of paper. He walks down the steps and holds the paper out to Black Jesus and says, "Sir, I have a warrant here wantin me to bring you in to answer charges of third-degree assault against a Miss Jocelyn Jacobs. If you're willin we won't need no cuffs."

"I ain't willin," Black Jesus says, and they press him against the side of the van and lock his hands behind his back and as they lead him away his fingers move like they're playing a song, like they're Bill's fingers pounding his keyboards. I think of how Bill calls his keyboards his "bones." I think of Jesus's hands hurting a woman, playing the bones of her body just to hear the sounds she makes.

When they drive away, Black Jesus's daddy comes out of the house, slamming the screen door.

"I tried to call y'all in Houston," he says. "They been sittin here all night. Sittin here in my goddamn rockin chair. Come on in."

I don't go in, but I sit on the porch steps for a long time until even the crickets quiet to a soothing hum and I try to empty my mind out into that humming. I let every thought loose into that low wave of sound and let my worries be carried off into the moist southern night. Karl comes and wraps a blanket around my shoulders.

"Oh, Karl, it's warm out."

"You gonna catch a cold sure, Tex, sittin out here in the dew."

I let the blanket fall off my shoulders a little.

"We'll get Jesus out tomorrow, and then he can clear everything up," I say.

Karl pulls a lotto ticket from his back pocket. "I buy one in every state," he says. "This my New York one."

"Yeah?" I take the shiny ticket from him and feel its slick surface.

"I gotta check on it," Karl says. "I could be a millionaire in New York by now. New Jersey, too."

"There's probably a number you can call. We'll work on it tomorrow."

"Sounds good, Tex."

I bring the ticket to my lips and kiss it. "For luck," I say.

Karl looks off toward the magnolia, just holds his hand out and lets me lay the ticket across his palm.

"I can always use more luck," he says.

"He did it, right?" I say. "That's what you came out here to tell me?"

"Don't need to tell you, Tex."

"Did you see it?"

"I saw Jocelyn after. She done right to go to the police."

I pull the blanket tight around me. A fogged light starts to glow between the Spanish moss that drapes the trees all around us, a light that could be the end of one day or the beginning of another one, it's hard to tell which.

"The Florida lottery gets really big," I say. "Sometimes it's up to twenty million."

"That right?"

"Buy a ticket for me when you get there, will you?"

"Sure thing, Tex."

"If I win, I'll split it with you."

"Think you can make it on ten million?"

"Yeah, I think I can manage."

The first light glides across the lawn, and the dew holds the light so the grass is not green, but white.

"Why did he do it, Karl?"

"Don't know. Could be Jocelyn was ridin her bicycle backwards."

"What does that mean?"

"You a sight, girl, you know that? Means maybe she was cheatin on him."

"But he cheats on her."

"Tex, I don't even know if that was it. Could be she just buttered his toast wrong, you know? Jesus got a hell of a temper boilin up in him. It don't take much."

"You want part of this?" I hold open the blanket to invite Karl in, but he knows he is a big man and instead of taking the blanket he wraps it tighter around me and holds me in his arms. "What are you gonna do with your ten million?" I ask.

"I don't know, Tex. I'd get me a place out in the country, get me a good woman, have a bunch of babies and dogs and a couple horses. Never set foot in no damn night-club again. Grow tomatoes."

"I'd get a boat and some good-lookin man to sail it around for me, but I wouldn't sleep with him, you know, it'd be strictly business."

"I hear you."

"And I'd fill it up with books and just sail around and read in the sun all day. And I wouldn't ever let any men on my boat, you know, it'd just be my space."

"Now what about that fine sailor man?"

"He'll be a eunuch, so that doesn't count."

"A what?"

"A guy that doesn't have any balls."

"Tex, there ain't no guys like that. You got some crazy ideas, girl."

"Okay, if I can't find a eunuch, I'll get a gay man, I'll be a fag hag. We can trade clothes and paint each other's toenails."

"Girl, you wanna go use the phone to call your head-shrinker? What those men be doin is ... I don't know, it's disgusting."

"It's disgusting to you. To them the idea of fucking a

woman is probably disgusting. Know what I mean?"

"No, I do not, but I like listenin to you talk, cause you a sweetheart. You got it goin on in that department."

"The sweet department?"

"Couple others, too."

"I'm gonna have to go home, you know." Birds are starting up all over the yard.

"Today?"

"No, not today. Cause I want to see him again. I want to see him long enough to believe he could hit a woman, then I'll leave."

"Tex, you ain't known Jesus very long. And he been good to you cause he thinks you a spoiled white woman and he know he gotta act a little better. But I was raised up with him, girl, and I know him like I know my ownself. He ain't right for you, baby, and the road ain't right for you. Ain't nothin but smoke and booze and eatin in your lap, never a decent night sleep and women who'll cut you for an hour with your man."

"Well, don't sugarcoat it, Karl."

"Just tryin to tell you straight, baby."

"You think I'm a spoiled white woman, Karl?"

"I think you a strange woman, Tex, but I like you."

"You ever hit a woman?"

"Nah. Let a couple hit me." The vibrations of his laughter run through my spine. "But I wasn't raised up watchin my daddy hit my mama. He treated her right and learned me to treat women right."

"What was Jesus's mother like?"

"She stayed upstairs."

"What do you mean?"

"That's what people used to say to mean someone was crazy. Stayed upstairs. Jesus's grandmama did all the raisin with them children. Played her music and did the cookin and cleanin too."

"I'm surprised she got any singing in."

"You got that right."

"What was she like?"

"She didn't take no shit. She'd traveled all over the South when she was just a young thing, playin the blues, and then when she got a name she started singin jazz in the good New Orleans clubs. She could drink men under the table, or she could go on a sober streak a year long, stay clean as the board of health. When she didn't like somethin, she'd say, 'That's tacky as Florida.' Every girl Jesus bring around, Nana she'd tell him what she thought of his women — tacky as Florida.' "

"What does that mean?" I picture too-bright colors and synthetic seashells.

"Don't know," Karl says. "All I know is I had me a woman from Florida once, Jackie was her name, and she was tacky as can be. Couldn't get along with other women for nothin, always comin up with somethin nasty to say — *her hair's ugly, she don't know nothin*, that kinda thing."

"It's a common problem with women," I say, "although I like to think we're each other's natural allies."

"Ain't never seen that," Karl says.

"I saw Vaughan Sharp sing once," I say. It's something I've never told Black Jesus.

"No kiddin? You saw Miz Nana?"

"Nacho — he was our yardman, and my mama was always sending him out to look for some crazy flower that didn't really exist. Nacho would get sick to death of it, but I loved it cause she'd let me go ride all over Dallas with him, and that was about my favorite thing in the world."

"What do you mean about the crazy flowers?" Karl says.

"Oh, she'd say something like, 'Go bring me a flat of the tulip whose inner petal bears the image of the transfiguration of Christ.' "

"Damn," Karl says. "That's some kinda strange."

"Yeah. So we'd go out and drive around for a couple of hours, listen to baseball on the radio and then after a while we'd go back and tell Mama the florist was sold out."

"Why didn't you just say there was no such flower?" Karl says.

"Mama couldn't take it. She couldn't stand wanting something and being told it didn't even exist. Probably reminded her too much of wanting my daddy after he was dead."

"I know just what you mean, girl."

"So one time when she sent us out like that, it was nighttime, and Mama woke me up and sent me out in my pajamas. We were drivin around downtown, and Nacho saw that Vaughan Sharp was playing at some club. He talked the doorman into letting me come in with him, even though I couldn't have been more than ten and in pajamas, too. My pajamas had ballerinas all over them. I remember her singing 'Surrey with the Fringe on Top.' I didn't know what in the world a surrey was."

Karl sings the first couple of lines for me, looking down at his hands.

"Karl!" I say. "You have a wonderful voice! Why don't you ever sing with Jesus?"

"I do my singin in church, young lady."

"Well, you sweet thing."

"So you saw Nana sing. That's somethin."

"The other thing I remember about that night," I say, "is that she did a gospel song at the very end of her set. The crowd got so quiet you would have thought it was a church."

"You know what Nana's sister used to say?"

"What?"

"That there ain't no difference between the gospel and the blues — but in gospel we say Jesus and in the blues we say baby."

"That sounds right," I say. "The other thing I liked was she was wearing a wonderful hat," I say. "It was sort of a beret, but very big, and she had all her hair stuffed up in it."

"I know that hat. She'd put it on and say, 'Now ain't this tacky as Florida?' "

"Think she'd say that about me?"

"Oh no, Tex. Nothin tacky about you, girl. Now tell me some more about your people. You never say a word about em."

It's easy to lean back in Karl's arms and talk to him, not having to look in his eyes.

"My people," I say more to the cypress trees across the way than to Karl. "My daddy's been dead longer than I can remember, and my mama ... she grew up poor and she's spent the rest of her life trying to forget it. Maybe that's why she likes exotic flowers so much."

"Not havin money ain't nothin to be ashamed of, you gotta know that."

"I know it, Karl, but I don't think she does. My daddy had money, west Texas ranch money, cattle and oil. Mama says he'd just die if he knew I don't eat meat, but I tell her he's dead already. My mama came from nothing and didn't know much about how to act, manners and such."

"Your daddy money teach her how?"

"I don't know. I just mean, like when she got engaged to my daddy and she went to register for her silver pattern, they asked her what letter she wanted engraved on the pieces, you know what I mean?"

"I'm with you, girl."

"Well, my mama was so country she didn't realize it was supposed to be the letter of her last name, so she just blurted out her favorite letter: L. Then when the silver arrived my daddy's mama said, 'What on earth does L stand for?' and my mama was so embarrassed she just said, 'I guess it stands for love.' "

"Sounds fine to me," Karl says.

"I think so, too, Karl. I think it sounds just fine. But I think it shamed her, somewhere deep inside, that she didn't know how to act exactly like all the rich people around her. She said she named me Lacy so I could use that silver, and so I could have fun making big curvy L's when I write my name."

"Girl, I seen how you write. Your L's straight as anything."

"I know," I say. "I've never made them curvy."

"Now why not?"

"Just to spite my mama, I guess."

"Whatever helps, girl."

A red Firebird pulls up in the driveway, and Dorinda, Marcy's girlfriend, steps out. Her high heels sink in the soft ground as she walks toward us.

"Damn, how'd y'all let the man get holda Jesus? Marcy sent me over here to see what's goin on. I got some money. Is it the same amount as last time?"

"Don't know," Karl says. "I'd guess about seventy-five hundred."

"I got it."

"What Marcy doin to get that kinda money?"

"What do you think?" Dorinda's at the bottom step, squinting up at us. "Lacy, what you doin with Karl's arms around you? Black Jesus gonna have your ass. I won't tell, though."

"Nothing to tell," I say.

"That's good. Where y'all going today?"

"Baton Rouge."

"I'm gonna go with y'all. Maybe Jesus'll let me sing. I got an outfit you won't believe, Karl."

"I believe it, Dorry."

"Well, let's go on over to the jail before this money burn a hole in my pocket."

Number 25 on my list is a wish for a white house with an upstairs porch. I'll grow so much ivy all over my house it will surround my porch and make a soothing green light. When I hear someone coming up my walk, I'll look out between the vines of ivy and see who it is. If it's a man like Ellis, who sometimes comes into the bedroom when I'm hot and tired and presses a cool, wet cloth against the curves of my face, I might open the door. If it's a man like Black Jesus, who hits a woman and forgets about it as soon as the sting leaves his hand, I'll let the streamers of ivy fall back together, I'll stay in the moist green light of my porch and never think of going downstairs.

HE'S NOT THE REAL JESUS

"You couldn't get the money last night?" is the first thing Jesus says when the guard brings him out. His silk shirt is wrinkled; flecks of lint cling to his beard. "We gotta call the office today, cause I gotta be back here for court the day we sposed to be in Miami."

"There goes the twenty million," I say to Karl.

"It's okay," he says. "I could still be a millionaire in New York."

"I could still be poor in Texas," I say.

Black Jesus takes my hand but doesn't look me in the eyes. "We all gonna be poor if we don't get on the road. We gotta get our butts to Baton Rouge and get set up for tonight."

We go back to the house and wake up K-San and Black Jesus's daddy makes us pancakes and no one talks about the arrest, no one asks him if he did it. No one even seems to wonder.

As soon as I climb in the van the next morning, K-San hands me a beer.

"I don't drink beer in the morning," I say, "I'm a god-damned former schoolteacher."

Karl knows better, hands me a wine cooler. Raspberry.

"Lacy, we playin at a black club tonight, so you just get ready," Jesus says.

"What do you mean, a black club?"

"This white girl don't know nothin," K-San starts. "Don't drink beer in the mornin and say what's a black club."

"Shut up, man, she knows plenty," Karl says.

"How do you know?" Black Jesus says from the back. "It don't mean nothin, Lacy, just probably won't be no white people there, that's all. Don't worry your head about it."

Karl is driving; I can see him watching me in the rear-view mirror. K-San can't shut up; the only way to make that mouth stop flapping is to put his hands around his bass.

"Don't be dancin like you do," K-San says, "like you on some kinda downer or some shit. Get your white ass laughed right out the door."

"Leave me alone," I say. I make Henry John trade places with me so I'm sitting up front with Karl, but it's not far enough away from K-San. Now he's waking up Dorinda, saying, "Dorry, show Lacy how to dance."

"You motherfucker," she says, but she's already awake so she might as well fuck with me some. She's barely too tall to stand up in the van, but she leans over and braces herself against the side window with her arms outstretched.

"Okay, Lace," she says, and moves her hips forward and back in a hummingbird blur, faster than music. "You do like this, like you're gettin some, but faster."

"Like you gettin some," K-San repeats, laughing. "I like that. You gonna gimme some, Dorry?"

"Take a good look, motherfucker, cause that's as close as you're gettin, you hear?" Dorinda says.

"Lacy, get Dorinda to teach you how to dance," K-San says.

Black Jesus, Wells, and Bill are sleeping, Karl is driving, Dorinda's laying down again, Henry John's got his head-phones strapped over his ears, and K-San's getting drunk. Me? I'm consumed with shame, I want to move my hips like Dorinda, I want to wear clothes they won't make fun of, I want Marcy's hand to heal and become strong enough to punch that silly leer off K-San's face, I just want to be cool. How can I feel music so deep in my soul it's like water seeping up out of the earth, but when I go to dance that music, my body is never like water, but stubborn and stiff?

After a while Dorinda says, "Karl, if you pass a catfish place, I'm gonna knock you silly. I didn't get none of them pancakes."

"All right, baby," Karl says, but Dorinda can't see from the back he's passing all kinds of places. We speed by a hitchhiker, a young Asian woman with a sign that says, "Anywhere Please."

"Y'all wouldn't mess with no Japanese, would you?" K-San says.

Henry John lifts one earphone off his ear. "They women, ain't they?"

"They vaginas go sideways," K-San says, then can't stop laughing.

Karl is tired of K-San's talk and pulls over at a restaurant with an unappetizing statue of a catfish out front, a catfish miraculously standing upright with whiskers big as my arm.

I go straight to the pay phone by the bathroom and call Ellis.

"How's Graceland?" he asks.

"Amazing," I say. "It's a spiritual experience."

He tells me how he's been reading Shakespeare, how he's got a theory about Juliet and why she married Romeo.

"See, her family unit was completely fucked up. The nurse had the power over her that her mother should have had, but the mother was too caught up in the bureaucracy of ruling Verona —"

"Ellis," I interrupt, "do you think I'm a good dancer?"

"What?"

"I mean, do you like the way I dance?"

"Lacy," he says, "you have a woman's shape. You hear me? You have a woman's shape. You are everything the word woman should mean. Any way you move your body, God ... it's beautiful when you move."

"You think so?"

"Come on home, girlfriend, and I'll show you what I think."

I hang up after a few minutes and squeeze into a booth next to Black Jesus and Karl.

"Did you order something for me?" I say.

"Bitch ain't brought menus yet," Jesus says. "Let's get outta here, Karl."

"Give her a chance, man," Karl says. "Maybe she's just busy." But we're the only people in the restaurant.

The fat white man behind the cash register stares at us. He's got a burning cigarette in one hand and a forkful of food in the other. He takes a drag off his cigarette while he still has food in his mouth. He wears a faded cap that says "Happiness Is A Tight Pussy." It's hard not to stare at the amazing cap.

A waitress with a dirty apron and an out-of-control perm hands me a menu and says, "Can I get you some coffee, Miss?"

"Yes, I think we'd all like some, please."

"Let's go, Lacy," Black Jesus says. He's poking me in the ribs but I'm on the edge of the booth and he can't get out unless I move.

"I'm sorry, ma'am," she says, twisting the pencil behind

her ear, "y'all should probably go on and eat somewhere else." She looks at the man behind the cash register, about a hundred wrinkles popping out in her face when she does.

"Are you saying you won't serve us?" I ask. She's pleading at me with her blue-shadowed eyes to understand her secret code, the code that says, Sister, I see your man and he's gorgeous and there's nothin wrong with your friends except they're black and if my boss wasn't here I might fry y'all some catfish and take your money and send you on your way but if I don't get y'all out of here now it's my j-o-b and I got children at home.

"I'm just sayin there's plenty of places on down the road," she whispers.

"What do you mean? Are we in a time warp or something? You *have* to serve us. It's the law."

"Shut up, Lacy," Black Jesus says. He pulls me to my feet as he stands up and almost shoves me out of the booth.

I walk straight up to the man behind the register and say, "Are you the owner of this restaurant?"

"Who wants to know?" He stabs his cigarette out in the grease on his plate.

"Are you aware that we can file suit against you for refusing to serve us based on our skin color? Are you aware that what you're doing is illegal?" Even while I'm saying this, I'm not sure if it's illegal or not. It's nothing I've ever had to think about. Everyone else is already outside. Black Jesus is standing by the door of the van, urgently waving to me.

"White woman," he says, "you wanna associate with trash, that's your business. I got the right to refuse service to anyone." He pulls his apron aside and in the gap between the bottom of his T-shirt and the top of his pants so much pale, dimpled flesh converges that for a second I don't even notice the handgun that's shoved in there, for a moment I forget that he's not one of my students I can give a bad grade to or get suspended for bringing a gun to school, he's a real live motherfucker who can act as bad as he wants and I can't do a damn thing about it.

"You're tacky as Florida," I say, and walk out.

"Lacy, what the fuck you doin?" Black Jesus says when I get to the van. "You want to fuckin get us killed? I already spent one fuckin night in jail, that's enough for this tour."

"I was just trying to stick up for you," I say. "Don't yell at me," I add, remembering what Eva has tried to teach me.

"The fuck I won't," he yells. "Your white ass ain't the one gonna get messed with, so stay the fuck out of it. Damn!"

"Leave her be, man," Karl says. "She don't mean no harm."

"She don't mean no harm, like a motherfucker she don't! People like that, Lacy, you just walk away, you hear me, you just keep your goddamn white mouth shut and you walk away."

"God! I'm sick of being told what color I am! Just shut the fuck up!"

"*You* sick of it!" Black Jesus starts to laugh. "That's a good one. Hey, K-San, this goddamn white woman's sick of being told what color she is. Damn!" K-San's going through the cooler looking for a beer, watching us through the open door of the van like we're a movie he's seen before. "Lemme tell you somethin," Jesus says. "You want to be gettin on some big black nigger dick, but you want the rest of me to be white. Don't want me actin black for a minute."

Karl squats by the catfish statue, shaking his head.

"Is it acting black to hit a woman?" I say. "Is it?"

"Toss me a beer, man," I hear Wells say to K-San. "This gonna take a while."

"You're no fuckin angel, Lacy," Jesus says, "runnin around on your man like you do. Don't you be tellin me what time it is."

"I'll tell you whatever the fuck I want to tell you."

From behind Jesus's back, Karl puts his fingers to his lips in warning.

"Your man ever hit you, Lace?" Jesus's face shines with angry sweat.

"No."

"Then he ain't never caught you doin the bullshit you do. If you was my wife I'd fuck you up good."

"Yeah? I don't have to be your wife. Here I am, Jesus, go ahead. You like to hit women? There's one standin right in front of you. You beat the fuck out of Jocelyn, why not me?"

He pushes me up against the sliding door of the van and whispers in my face, "Don't you be feelin sorry for Jocelyn. You wish you had her black pussy."

"No I don't."

"The fuck you don't. I'll hit you better than your man and I already fuck you better, too."

"What makes you think that?" I whisper back.

"The way I make you come."

The metal door of the van burns through my shirt. He leans so close to me I can't get his face in focus, but I don't let my eyes leave his.

"Who says Ellis doesn't make me come?" I whisper. His grip tightens on my shoulder.

"Damn, you a cold bitch. I can't believe some motherfucker ain't knocked your pretty head a country mile." He stretches the fingers of his other hand around my neck so tight I can hardly talk.

"Maybe you could be the first. Motherfucker."

"Jesus, don't you hit that bitch," Dorinda whines out the window of the van. "I'm flat outta bail money, you hear?"

but Karl is pulling Jesus away from me because he knows
what's about to happen and he just wants to get us all to
Baton Rouge without having a race riot right there in front
of the van, so he says, "Jesus, forget it man, we got to get
to the gig, all right?" and we get in the van and drive until
we find a Popeye's with a drive-through and get a bunch
of chicken and biscuits. The biscuits taste like cardboard
but I lift them to my mouth over and over because I have
to move my hands to stop them from shaking. *He's not the
real Jesus,* I keep telling myself, *he's not the real Jesus,*
because the real Jesus is someone who'll dip you in a lake
of fire like it's chocolate fondue if you so much as sneeze
wrong. I've known Him all my life. The first thing I
learned about Jesus was that I should be glad for the pun-
ishments Mama dreamed up, that they were a treat compared to what I'd get if left to the mercy of the Almighty
Motherfucker. I learned that if she whipped all the evil out
of me while I'm right here on earth, maybe Jesus would
pass me by in His lazy search for something to feed the
lake of fire. Maybe if I ate nothing but dog food my body
would be too frail and small to make a satisfying *plop* when
He tossed me in. *He's not the real Jesus,* I tell myself, because I am not going to be afraid of this black man, and
sometimes I'm still scared of Mama's God. I try hard to
think of Jesus as a nice, sandal-wearing guy, as someone
who won't judge all the fun and anguish I've had on this
earth as sinful or good, but will see it for what it's been:
life as a human being.

When we get to the hotel in Baton Rouge, Black Jesus
goes right to sleep. He hasn't said a word to me since the
restaurant. I grab my bags, walk two doors down to Karl's
room, and knock on his door. A plump white girl opens the
door, stunning fake fingernails. How'd he get a girl in here
so fast? Karl comes up behind her, sort of guides her away
from the door.

"What can I do for you, Tex?"

"I'm sorry, Karl."

"It ain't nothin, now what's up?"

"Can you take me to the airport?"

"You goin?"

"I'm just gonna get a rental car and go on home." I pretend I'm not crying. I pretend it's not starting to rain.

"Hold on." I hear him say something to the woman, then he comes out with the keys to the van.

"Jesus ain't gonna be happy with me, I will tell you that," he says when we're almost to the airport.

"I know, Karl. I'm real sorry. But I would have taken a cab if you hadn't driven me."

"I know, girl. When you make up your mind to do something, you do it, ain't that right?"

"Yeah, I guess that's right. Who's the girl?" I ask.

"Aw, she ain't nobody," he says.

"Don't tell her that."

"I ain't gonna." A skinny arm of lightning stretches over the horizon, then retracts.

When we get to the airport he pulls up by the "Departures" sign and sits with the motor running. "You got a husband, don't you Tex?"

"Yeah, I got one."

"He treat you right?"

"Yeah," I say, "more than right."

"Then what you messin with us for?"

"I don't know." Karl has a way of talking that makes everything seem clear.

"You take care now," he says, and he sets his hand on my shoulder for a moment.

"I will." The windows are starting to fog, the rain beats a pattern of *go, go, go.*

"Lemme see your hand a minute," Karl says.

"Why?"

"Come on, girl."

I offer my hand and he takes it and guides it up to the fogged windshield.

"Stick out your first finger, now. That's right," and he guides my hand in the shape of a big, curvy L. Tiny drops of water hang in the curves. "Too much spite in the world already," Karl says, and I leave him, hoping he won't wipe it off just right away.

I rent a Ford Taurus and start driving back to Houston. Forty miles out of Baton Rouge, the damn car starts whining and won't drive more than forty miles an hour.

"Stop that," I say.

I pass town after town, but I'm not about to pull over. As long as the car will move, I'm driving, I don't care how slow. I think back to the restaurant, I remember the hard look in that man's eyes, the obscene jut of his stomach over his gun. He made me want to hold Black Jesus and never let him go, made me want to stay by his side always just to annoy all the racist motherfuckers in the world. It's a stupid reason to be with someone. It's nothing I can call love. And Black Jesus just makes me want to go to Jocelyn and hold her close like a sister and put tea bags on her eyes till the swelling goes down and rub aloe into her cuts and tell her there's some men out there who don't hit women or call us bitch/slut/ho, there's men around who'll call you by your name and make it sound like the name of a goddess, who'll breathe your name out with so much happiness it sounds like the first word ever spoken. I'd tell her I've got a man like that, that I'm trying to get my head straight so I can treat him right, so I can let him treat me right, so I can listen when he calls my name, and maybe even answer.

The orange "Service Soon" light on the dashboard blinks an urgent rhythm: "Stupid, stupid, stupid." To shut it up, I start to make up a blues. I roll down all the windows so

I can't tell if I'm singing in tune or not. I don't want to know. *Car won't drive, kids won't mind/ Boss won't pay my check on time (Chorus) Every morning I wake up/ Things start goin wrong/ If tomorrow ain't no better/ Ain't gonna get up at all.*

Black Jesus is probably at the club in Baton Rouge by now, touching one guitar after another, saying who's gonna be my baby tonight? I have to sing loud so his voice can't squeeze in my ears. *Garden won't grow, tractor won't plow/ My woman doin things that I don't allow (Chorus repeat) Every morning I wake up/ Things start goin wrong/ If tomorrow ain't no better/ Ain't gonna get up at all.*

I imagine myself onstage at the club, hundreds of black faces waiting for me to dance. My body is frozen like an ice sculpture, pale and white and still, and I wait for Black Jesus to play the one note so sweet it will release me, will melt the fear from my bones and fling me into dance. Somewhere in my bones I remember how to dance. Some woman before me must have danced, some woman whose blood is now my blood, she must have danced free and wild, I must possess a fragment of that ancestral movement in my bones, because women do not keep living and giving birth to new women for thousands of years without ever dancing once. *Woman won't love me, dog half dead/ False teeth about to fall outta my head (Chorus repeat) Every morning I wake up/ Things start goin wrong/ If tomorrow ain't no better/ Ain't gonna get up at all.*

I think I could dance to my own song. If the music comes out of me, I must have the movement to that music somewhere in me, too. It's just a matter of finding it, and maybe I haven't ever looked. *Holes in my shoes, guitar won't play/ Had them brokedown blues when I woke up today (Chorus repeat) Every morning I wake up/ Things start goin wrong/ If tomorrow ain't no better/ Ain't gonna get up at all.*

The "Service Soon" light darkens, and next to it the

"Service Now" light suddenly ignites, glowing a steady red.
I refuse to acknowledge it, just keep humming my blues. I
plan to tell Ellis his voice made me miss him so much I
just had to come on home. By the time I hit the Texas
state line, maybe this will be the truth.

I'm outside Lafayette, Louisiana when I remember that
Ellis asked me to bring him a souvenir. I stop at a gas
station to see what they've got.

"Do you have any Elvis stuff?" I ask the woman behind
the counter.

"Sure don't, sugar," she says. "You want some gas?"

"Yeah, I'll get some. But I really need an Elvis souvenir,
like a mug, or a key chain, or one of those little domes
where you turn it upside down and then back and little
musical notes fall all over Elvis, like the snowflake things
except they're notes? You know what I mean?"

"I don't know what you're talkin about, sugar. My mama's got a scarf Elvis threw to her at a big concert in At-
lanta, but she wouldn't part with that for all the tea in
China. Got some Kennedy stuff. You want to see it?"

"Sure."

She shows me a card with a penny stuck to it, a real
penny that someone's etched John Kennedy's tiny profile
onto so he's looking into Lincoln's face. The card lists several ASTONISHING COINCIDENCES between the two
men, such as: Both men were slain on Friday. Oswald shot
Kennedy from a warehouse and hid in a theater, while
Booth shot Lincoln in a theater and hid in a warehouse.
Kennedy's secretary named Lincoln warned him not to go
to Dallas, while Lincoln's secretary named Kennedy warned
him not to go to the theater. I'm convinced.

"I'll take one," I say, "but I don't think it's going to pass
for an Elvis souvenir."

"I didn't say it would, sugar."

"No, you didn't."

I buy a map of the southern states from her, then turn around and drive back to the Baton Rouge airport to trade in my rental car. I have to fill out several forms. My handwriting gets sloppier on each one. The boy at the rental counter is . . . oh, who cares. I'm not going to look at anyone until I get to Graceland. I'm tired of looking at people, their awful faces and the pain hidden away in some fold of their bodies. Instead I think about my friend Callie, about sitting across the kitchen table from her with a bowl of bananas between us, solemnly practicing blow jobs. Callie starts with the smallest banana, easing it past her tiny lips and back into her throat, a strangling noise and little bits of spit lighting the corners of her mouth.

"Are you supposed to put it all the way in?" she says, looking doubtfully at the long fruit.

"I don't know," I whisper.

"Why are you whispering?" and we giggle. "Your turn," she says, and I put my lips over a medium-sized banana and let it fill my mouth without ever gagging once, and Callie claps and says, "Excellent!" and I do not tell her that I already know the feel of a penis in my mouth, that it is so familiar to me I don't even know if it is strange or wrong, that I am participating in this bizarre practice session because I want to be a little girl, even if only for an afternoon.

After a while we start cheating by peeling the bananas because it's easier to put something in your mouth if it tastes good, and when Callie finally gets a whole banana all the way inside her mouth, lovingly, lips over her teeth so as not to scrape it, throat open and relaxed, her eyes popping out with pride at the accomplishment, Irene swings open the kitchen door, sees the intricate cut crystal bowl mounded with naked bananas, some glimmering with saliva, some bent and broken and covered with teeth marks from our more savage efforts, and she says, "I know what you're doing."

After Callie leaves, Irene tells Mama, who slaps me until my gums bleed and then searches deep inside herself for a glimmer of innocence so she can lecture me properly on the whole fiasco, so she can sit me down at that same kitchen table and tell me that oral sex is a perversion of a natural function. It took me years to figure out what the natural function is. I still love bananas, the educational fruit. But I don't want to ever participate in oral sex again, or sexual intercourse, or even conversation. I want to be quiet, chaste, alone, free to commune with Elvis, the white trash king of rock 'n' roll. I want to immerse myself in his intense tackiness, in his innocent country ways, in the affluence of grease that coats his abundant hair, in the violent swing of his pelvis, in the whole amazing aura of a white man trying to be black and driving women crazy with the strange combination of cultures.

I hum "Love Me Tender" for five hours until I get to Memphis and have to break my vow of silence by asking a policeman directions to the holy place.

"Probably closed up right now, ma'am," he tells me.

"That's okay," I say. "I still want to go."

He draws a crude map on the back of a McDonald's sack and says, "Be careful in that neighborhood, ma'am."

So many things I like about the Deep South, despite the racism, homophobia, and such: being called ma'am by policemen and having doors opened for me are two of them. It takes the edge off. And not having to open doors saves my energy for other things. Eva gets offended when men try to open doors for her, shoves past them with a snooty toss of her turban, but me? I save my feminist instincts for the big things. Like clutching the warm wrought-iron bars of the gate to Elvis's mansion, pressing

my cheek against a musical note and sobbing because
Graceland is closed, because I am locked away from Elvis
forever, because no amount of wanting will let me see the
red velour entranceway, the smoked-glass mirrors threaded
with fake gold, the bogus Louis XV furniture, although I've
seen it all in my dreams of this fabulous southern
whorehouse, dreams in which I loll across the bed with its
headboard of black quilted Naugahyde, dreams in which I
am comforted by the padded walls, the jungle room with
its soothing green shag carpeted ceiling, dreams in which
the black suede tassels dangling from the walls of Elvis's
bedroom swish all fear and sadness from my heart with
their sadistic twirling. Elvis doesn't bother me in these
dreams — he's on tour. Neither does my mother bother
me — she's chained to her bed, dreaming of exotic flowers.
And Ellis? Never met him in these particular dreams, no
hurt there. Black Jesus? Hates Elvis. The King don't have
a thing to do with the blues, according to Jesus. Has to
do with white teenagers, breathless with squeals, with the
National Enquirer, with fifty-year-old women who saw
Elvis years ago and still cherish the outline of his dick in
his polyester jumpsuit. Did he really wear diapers? I must
know. I start to bang on the gates.

"Let me in! Let me in!" I scream.

"They won't let you in," says a man who slumps against
the brick wall next to the gates, his shiny black hair framed
by loving graffiti.

"Elvis?" I say.

"Just a humble impersonator, ma'am." His belt buckle
is the size of a salad plate.

"Let me in!" I scream again.

"Hold up there, young lady," the security guard says
from the other side of the gate, fumbling with his hat as
he walks toward me from a small guardhouse.

"Please!" I sob. "Please let me in!"

"Now I can't do that, miss. Or is it Mrs.? Ya just look too young to be married."

"It's Ms." The guard is an older black man, dignified, with a kind face like Nacho's. In my highway-induced delirium, I start to think of him as Nacho, and as he opens the gate and offers me his arm, then leads me through as if we're entering some grand ball together, I accept him as our old yardman, and when I stumble suddenly and he rights me I whisper, "Thank you, Nacho," and he nods as if that's his name, as if people have been calling him that all his life.

"Fuck you!" the Elvis impersonator yells, standing now and clinging to the gates. "You always let the women in! She ain't gonna fuck you, man!"

"Don't worry bout him, missy. He one of our regulars," the guard says.

"She's Elvis's girl," the man yells. "If Elvis catches her bobbin on your knob in his yard, man, you're fired! Fuckin fired! You old nubby-dick motherfucker!"

"Ya ain't a reporter, are ya, miss?" the guard stops suddenly and we stand together in the electric aura of Graceland. Tiny blue lights follow the curve of the driveway up to the house. "Nah," he says before I can answer. "Ya too quiet."

His arm offers the tired, true comfort of an old man. No sex, ever again.

"I can't take ya inside, miss, but we'll have us a nice walk round the grounds here, if that'll make ya feel better."

"That sounds lovely."

"Ya a Southerner, ain't ya? Ya wouldn't know how many damn Yankees we get down here, want a bit a the King's ass. I can't count that high."

As we circle the mansion, the little blue lights fade in and out of focus. I try to concentrate on the huge white columns of the house, but I don't really see them. Instead

I see the gray house, my mama's house, as Nacho walks me around the yard, saying, "Now one more circle, we gonna be cryin a little less. Then the next time round we ain't gonna be crying a'tall. Then one more circle these here live oak trees gonna give you the courage to go on in there and face your mama, devil that she is." Leaves fragmenting under our feet. "Yes ma'am, she a devil, but you got a stronger devil in you somewhere, and your devil gonna beat the tar outta her devil one a these days." Wind snaring in the full branches of the live oak. "Wind, come on and feed the mouth o this devil child. She got a helluva mama, she need your strength." Moonlight making me and Nacho the same color. "Moon, you gots to do with women. We got a powerful little woman here need help findin her power." Grass bending with dew. "Touch this, Lacy girl." I bend down and press my palm into the cool wet grass while Nacho kneels beside me. "This here's the goddamn earth, Lacy girl. Feel how wet it is. That's a good thing. Gonna soothe all them dried-up rickety parts of you. I know you got em, young as you is. I can hear em rattlin around inside you there. Hittin against each other, makin everything hurt more. You gots to find the things that soothe em. Puttin your hands on the earth is one. You leave them little hands there, no, another minute, then we gonna go on in. Then I think we be able to go on in." I look up and into the deep folds of Nacho's face and realize he is frightened of Mama, too, that his rituals are not designed only for me, but for him as well. We press our hands against the wet grass until we start to shiver, then walk slowly up the long brick walk.

"What're ya cryin fer, Lord!" the Graceland guard says. "I wouldn't tell ya how many ladies I seen cryin over the King. If I had a penny fer every tear I seen, Lord! I'd be standin in tall cotton!"

I don't have the heart to tell him I'm not crying over

the King, that I don't spend much time longing for the sight of his rhinestone-studded American Eagle jumpsuit, his thousands of teddy bears crammed up in the attic, his diamond-crusted sheriff's badge belt, that I haven't tasted a peanut butter and bacon sandwich since Mama made us eat one, so we would know what the King ate. I've been choosing my own food for years now. I don't tell the guard that Elvis does not ignite anything sexual or womanly in me, that to me he is a sad symbol of my family: bloated, sick, innocence and privacy lost. No, it's not Elvis who interests me — it's Priscilla, the goddess of white panties and big hair, the woman who left the most desired man in the world for a poor karate instructor. Did she still wear white panties in the steam of her affair? Did she ever think of Elvis when she was in her lover's arms, did a snatch of song run through her head — "That's All Right, Mama," or "Don't Be Cruel"? I'd like to know, Priscilla, did you ever eat peanut butter and bacon? Is it true that Elvis despised the sight of a naked woman? How you must love to be naked, how you must have searched for the one who would rejoice over your body, and when you heard of Elvis's death, drugged and slumped over the king-sized toilet, how glad you must have felt to be in your own small beautiful body, far away.

"Look here!" the guard says, and we watch a swarm of fireflies pricking the darkness with small bursts of light. "This here's my favorite part of the grounds," he says. "Called the Meditation Garden." We walk around a small fountain and stand in front of the Presley graves: Minnie, Gladys, Vernon, Elvis, and little Jesse. The grass around the largest gravestone is covered with wreaths. One is made from black and white flowers in the shape of a record. "For the Record," tiny flowers spell out, "We Love You."

"We get flowers every day," the guard says proudly.

We circle around the garden, past a marble statue of

Jesus with the name Presley inexplicably carved in its base. It is too far from the graves to be considered a tombstone, and the effect of the Presley name so close to Jesus's foot is of a combination deity.

"I love that," I say.

"My wife don't like that one bit," the guard says. "Says it ain't right havin the Presley name on a statue of Jesus Christ. Me? I don't pay it much mind. It all ends up in the same place."

We walk back past the blue lights and down to the front gates.

"You been here a long time?" I ask.

"Longer'n you been alive, missy."

"You ever hear anything about Elvis wearing diapers?"

He laughs. "Missy, I ain't sposed to talk about the King, but you a Southerner and a lady, and I don't take you for a gossip."

"I'll never tell," I say.

"Well, I believe I did hear a little somethin about that, back a ways. But lemme tell you somethin else. The way Elvis was at the end of his life, that wasn't him. He was a decent boy, a fine boy, and don't you forget it."

"I won't," I say, shaking his hand. "Thank you for everything."

"Enjoyed passin the time with you, missy," he says, and unlocks the gate to let me out.

"Fuckin women," the impersonator mutters.

I shake hands again with the guard through the bars, and as he turns and walks back to his guard station, I remember Nacho walking away the last time I saw him alive, the day I started to eat the dog food when I was seventeen and boiling over with sorrow. I stood at the kitchen counter with Marcella yipping at my feet and stuffed handfuls of her food into my mouth. Nacho saw me through the window, dropped his hose in the backyard without bothering to turn off the water, and ran into the kitchen to swipe the red bowl off the counter. I can see the hose twisting and jumping in the backyard, I hear sprays of water slapping the windows, I watch the soggy crumbles of dog food scatter across the kitchen floor. I hear Nacho's voice yelling at Mama, "You been treatin this child like a dog all her life, and now she actin like one! You want a dog for a daughter or you want a girl?" I feel him hooking his arms under mine and dragging me outside to the acacia bushes, saying, "You spit that out, girl, I ain't havin you eatin no dog food," and he holds me and strokes my head while I throw up the tiny triangular pieces. Mama stands by with her photogenic smile. I throw up as long and as hard as I can, because I know that when my stomach is emptied Nacho will stop smoothing my hair back from my face, he will have to undo that safe circle of his arms and Mama will fire him and hire Donny to keep the yard because he is out of college now and has his own summer landscaping business. He's saving up for law school. The next time I see Nacho he will be floating face up in the pond he tended so carefully, a bullet in his head and the revolver already sunk deep in the mud, down among the catfish and dark weeds that mingle there. I will stand at the edge of the pond and watch him for a long time, watch the water flowing in and out of his slack mouth, watch his shirttail gradually work its way loose from the pants, watch his shoelaces swell and loosen. Before I phone Mama at the country club to say that Nacho has shot himself in our pond, not one week after she fired him and threw his things from the grounds-keeper's house out into the yard, ruining a Mercedes rosebush with Nacho's heavy radio so that the branches swayed out at crazy angles and the thick faces of the roses looked to the ground, before I do that I kneel and dip my hands into the pond. I wash my palms with Nacho's blood and the muddy water that is blood colored anyway. I send a

series of ripples from my hands out to his body and I remember, one by one, the things he told me: Plant garlic
next to roses to keep bugs away. Put your hands on the
earth and don't be afraid to ask her for strength. Human
hair spread around a garden keeps rabbits away. Don't let
things rattle around inside you too long, don't eat dog food
even if your mother tries to make you. I remember the
way he taught me to yank on the stem of a plant after
transplanting it, to make sure there's no hollow space
around the roots where air can collect. "You get the dirt
firm around the stem and loose around the roots, Lacy girl,
that's like havin your feet be cold and puttin on a pair a
garters to warm em." I'm working on it, Nacho, the rattling
things, the cold space around my roots. You, you've already
been at peace in the warm Texas ground for so many years,
and here I am, still working. What would you think of
me now, sitting here in my rented Ford outside Graceland,
unfaithful to my husband and myself, still trying like a fool
to please my mother, so much that I dressed up in a Barbie
doll wedding dress and covered my red hair with a white
lace veil to hide it? Would you understand the things that
turn me on — e. e. cummings, blues, Shakespeare, and men
named after gods? I think you'd be proud of how I stood up
for that young student, you'd like the taste of the tomatoes I
grew last summer, picked at night to keep their sweetness.
I think you'd tell me to work on standing up for myself,
too, to keep some of that sweetness for my own mouth. I
think you'd like the forty-ninth wish on my list: that so
many sweet things will pass through my mouth that I will
forget the taste of dog food, that I will not be able to recall
its dust in the back of my throat, that my tongue will forget
even its shape — triangles that break in half first, and then
crumble.

I JUST HAD TO
BREAK SOMETHING

"This is it?" Ellis says when I toss him the Elvis key ring I picked up at the gas station on my way out of Memphis. The tiny plastic Elvis looked a lot more interesting in the middle of the night. In the bright light of our living room, I see its flaws: the lashless eyes, the expanse of white where individual teeth should be.

"I was running out of money," I say.

"I thought at least a velvet wall hanging."

"Sorry. I'm just not cutting it as an Elvis fan." I close my eyes and wish for courage. "Or as a wife."

"What are you saying, Lace?" Ellis takes off his glasses and starts to clean them with his shirttail, as if clearer lenses will help him understand me better. I've spent so little time speaking the truth that this feels like a weird experiment.

"I've been fucking someone," I say. It comes out a little too loud, like it's something I'm proud of, but I didn't think

it would come out at all so I made my voice louder than
usual, hoping to get *something*.

"You're kidding," Ellis says. He walks to the kitchen and
gets a big plastic pitcher, fills it with water, and starts cir-
cling the living room, watering all the plants. "I forgot to
do them while you were gone. I'm really sorry," he says.
"I think they'll all be okay. I just got really busy rewriting
the last section of my thesis — the La Malinche stuff." I
follow him into the bathroom and watch him overwater
the aloe.

"Did you hear me, Ellis? I said I've been fucking someone. I've done a horrible thing and now you should probably divorce me or at least leave me. Don't let water touch
the leaves," I add as he starts on my African violets. "You
pour it in the dish and they suck it up from the bottom.
Here," and I take the pitcher from him and fill each small
plastic dish as he lifts the plants up. "That tastes good,
doesn't it," I whisper to my plants.

"I don't *want* to divorce you or leave you," Ellis says. He
still hasn't looked at me. He takes the pitcher from me and
I follow him into the bedroom where tiny cacti line the
windowsill.

"They don't need any, El." I can see that he badly wants
to water them. "Do the geraniums. They're probably dying
of thirst." We walk out to the back porch and I sit on the
steps while he soaks the plants, filling the pitcher again
and again with the hose.

"So," he says, when he has watered everything in sight
and has nothing left to do but sit down beside me, "who'd
you fuck?"

"A musician. I broke it off with him."

"Because you'd rather be with me?"

"Mostly because I'd rather be with me."

His face is wet, but now that I have tasted the truth

passing over my lips, I cannot stop. "I don't know if I can be faithful, El. I want to, but I'm telling you, I don't know if it's in me. And I don't think it's a matter of not loving you enough, because I love you about as much as I can love a man, but there's something in me that just doesn't want to follow the rules, you know?"

"Yeah, I know. I sort of like that about you. Except right now."

"Eva says that when I was sexually abused, it taught me that my only worth was as a sexual being, and that's why I have a hard time not fucking everyone. I know you probably don't care what Eva thinks, but there might be something to it."

"I care, Lace. I care if you care." The geraniums start to renew all around us.

"You're mad, right?" I say. "I mean, you should be."

"I'm scared," he says, and takes my hand and presses it between both of his. "I'm scared of how much I love you. I'm scared that I've just been sitting at my computer and going to teach my classes and going to the grocery store and just basically going through the bullshit motions of my life thinking everything was fine, when all this time you've been out screwing some musician behind my back. God, Lacy! How the fuck did this happen?" He starts to kiss my hand, finger by finger, then suddenly he's biting the flesh below my thumb, hard.

"Ouch! Stop it, Ellis!"

"You don't like the way I fuck you? Is that it?"

"El, you're freaking. It's not you — it's me. It's me and my fucked-up childhood — oh, I know that sounds like an excuse — but it's me never learning how to say what I wanted, never speaking my truth, ever, because I grew up keeping Donny's secrets and my mother's secrets and now all of a sudden every fucking thing in my life is a secret and I can't seem to get out of it. You know?"

Ellis pulls me to his mouth and kisses me hard, not a kiss of his I know. "Do you want to fuck me?" he says.

I push him away. "No! Goddammit, I don't want to fuck anyone! I'm trying to talk to you, Ellis."

"You wanted to fuck the musician. He's probably black, right? I know you like black guys. Why is that, Lace? You got some fucking psychological analysis for that, too?"

"No."

Ellis swipes a geranium pot off the porch. It breaks on the bottom step.

"Sorry, Lace," he says after a long time. "I just had to break something."

"No worries."

"So now you're gonna leave me and I'll never find anyone I like as much as you and I'll be bitter toward women for the rest of my life and I'll just end up some creepy old professor probably trying to fuck all my students out of desperation because I lost the one woman I really want." He's twisting his shirttail in his hands, lost in his morbid fantasy.

"Who says I'm leaving you?" I say. "You know what I want?"

"What?"

"You're probably not gonna like it."

"Did you even go to Graceland? Did you even fucking go there, Lacy?"

"Yeah, I went," I say. "I was there."

"Describe it! Describe one thing from that fucking whorehouse, cause I don't even think you went there."

I hear Mama's voice in my head saying, "Nacho, I've been reading about a flower I want you to find for me. When the wind blows through the petals an Elvis song comes out, a different one each season. Get me twenty flats. Lacy will help you carry them."

"I was there," I say.

"What is it you want, Lace?" He stretches his foot out to torture the broken geranium some more.

"I want to get divorced, and start over. I want us to make up our own promises. Maybe monogamy will be one of those, you know, I just don't know. But I was wrong to marry you. I did it because I thought it would be some kind of break with my mother, because I always felt like God was about to strike me down for living in sin with you. I did it for a million stupid reasons. Because by the time I started to figure it out everything was already arranged — the caterer and the dresses and the fucking dinner mints. About a million things stood between me and the truth."

"Don't forget the engraved napkins."

"And the thank-you notes. I still have at least fifty to write."

"You didn't finish them in jail?"

"I was only in there two days, El! And I was busy reading your novel."

"So what you're saying is I didn't really have to wear that fucking tuxedo or spend two days thinking up a toast to your mother that wouldn't make her sound like the evil bitch that she is?"

"Well, yeah."

"You're a lot of work, girlfriend."

"I know."

He reaches down for a clod of dirt and squeezes it between his fingers, catching the falling crumbles with his other hand and then molding the dirt into a ball again.

"Lace, I can't promise you I'm not gonna be mad about the fucking part — I mean, why the fuck did you have to go and do that? But I'm gonna try to understand why you did it and I'm gonna try to let it go. And I think your plan sounds pretty good. I'd love to be your husband, but if you want me to be your ... something else, well, let's try it. I guess."

I wrap my arms around him and he starts to cry again. I hold my husband without saying anything. I watch the slender, exposed roots of the geranium twisting up from the hectic clumps of dirt. Neither of us moves to pick it up.

WHERE ARE ALL THE PAINTINGS?

When I tell Eva what I've done, she runs from behind her desk to hug me. "You told Ellis the truth! Did you really?"

"I swear."

She grabs my shoulders and looks at me like something's different but she can't quite tell what, a subtle change of hair color or some minor dental work.

"We have to celebrate," she says. "What can we do?" She paces around the office, clutching her turban. "Of course we have a lot of work to do before you recovenant with Ellis. You need to grieve your marriage, brief though it's been, and you should probably do some cleansing work, and oh, I've been meaning to tell you for a while, I think we need to go back to Dallas for you to do closure on Nacho's death. I don't think you've ever let that one go, and the fact that he died on your mother's property makes it all the more difficult to accept that loss, because you experienced so many losses there. And we probably need to look into your choice of Black Jesus as a lover. We need to examine why you chose a batterer when you come from a childhood of physical abuse."

"Eva, don't forget, I'm unemployed. I got my retirement money out of them, but I don't know how long that's going to last. I don't think I can afford all that grieving and cleansing and closure."

"We'll work it out, Lacy. This is exciting work for me, too, you know. And I want to tell you, dear, that although your affair with Mr. Jesus was unfortunate from Ellis's point of view, I think it's possible that you knew he was a batterer all along, that you chose him specifically so you would finally have the chance to say no to someone who might physically harm you."

"That's sort of scary."

"No, not scary, my dear, wonderful. You're becoming so wonderful. Look at you. You can look me in the eyes. You can speak without having to communicate only through your lyrics."

"Well, what about our celebration?"

"What's something you've always wanted to do?"

"Oh, I don't know. You know me. I've always wanted to give myself an orgasm in the Rothko Chapel, but that's not possible."

"Why not?"

"There's always people there."

"Anything is possible, dear. Do you believe me?"

"It's a great theory, Eva, but it doesn't always work that way. We could settle for ice cream."

"Spoken like a true victim. We're not *settling* for anything, dear."

We close up Eva's office, walk through the university grounds where the Spanish moss hangs low from the live oaks, and find our cars in the vast parking lot. I follow her to her house and we rummage through her closet for special celebration outfits. She wraps a silk turban around her head while I change into an ankle-length kimono-type thing.

"Welcome to the seventies," I say.

"You look lovely," Eva answers.

"Eva, why do you always wear a turban?"

"That's where I store my wisdom, dear."

"Oh. Maybe I should get one."

"And cover up this gorgeous red hair? Absolutely not! You carry your sexuality in your hair, in its unavoidable color, and the way you toss it back from your face makes people open their eyes a little wider, my friend."

"Where do you carry your sexuality?" I ask her.

"In my teeth," she says.

"Your teeth!" I start laughing. "Damn, Eva. Let me see these teeth."

She smiles a big smile and I reach over and gently pull her lips back to look at her bright, even teeth.

"See what I mean?" she says.

"Whatever works, girlfriend."

In the Rothko Chapel six people are meditating on cushions throughout the beautiful room. Some close their eyes, some stare at the twelve dark, introspective canvases that hang at peaceful intervals. Eva and I each take a cushion from the center of the room, settle in the back and wait for them to finish. One leaves, then another. A woman in noisy shoes walks in. She looks around and whispers to her friend in dismay, "Where are all the paintings?"

"Shhh," he quiets her, and they turn and walk out of the smooth, calm, light-filled space. Perhaps the Houston Chamber of Commerce should not list the chapel with the art museums in its marketing pamphlets, because it takes more time than most tourists have to sit and empty one's mind of thought and become accustomed to the idea of being *inside* a work of art for an hour or so. Two more people leave, then the young man who I imagine is a medi-

cal student. When the last meditator walks out and we are
alone in that prayerful space, Eva whispers, "Celebrate,
my dear, for you have much to be proud of," and she walks
out and stands outside the door of the chapel. I see the
flash of her silk turban in the sunlight. I hear her telling someone, "I'm sorry, but we're closed for an hour to do
our weekly cleaning. It's not healthy to meditate in a
dusty space, you know," then the door closes and I am
alone.

I remember that I came here to masturbate, but I feel
dry and quiet, I feel that the room in me that houses the
sexual is a long walk away. I walk to the center of the
chapel and kneel on a soft cushion. I like the way my ass
feels against my heels. I spread my fingers and let them
enter my hair at the scalp, moving all the way through
that long red silkiness, and where my hair stops, my breasts
begin. I untie the three closures of my dress and let my
hands remember the shape of my breasts, let my palms
recall the weight of them, the weight of a perfectly ripe
plum. My nipples harden and rise in the small curve of my
cupped palms, and it is safe to grow stiff and proud in that
dark, gentle space. I feel the sturdy plane of my collarbones
and at their ends are my soft, round shoulders to be ca-
ressed. I've forgotten how my forearms love to be massaged,
how the blood gathers in my arms and turns my skin a
shy, morning color. I let the dress fall from my arms and
pool around my waist, and I look down in pleasure at my
torso rising from the soft ring of purple silk. I watch the
womanly curve of my waist disappearing into my dress the
way the stem of a summer flower curves gracefully into
the ground. I shake my head and enjoy the brush of my
hair against my bare back. I breathe deeply and watch my
belly expand and contract. I love the angles of my hipbones and the soft flesh that stretches between them. I open
my dress to reveal the triangle of wild red hair that joins

my thighs, and as I lightly move my hands over the triangle the hair tangles and swirls and I can see its many colors, brass and gold and the generous reds of an apple. As I part the deep auburn hair in the middle of the triangle, the flesh of my labia is a startled pink, slippery and delicate. I raise my fingers to smell them, and I fill myself with my own scent until my sex begs to be touched again, and I take my outer lips between my index fingers and thumbs, giving one hand to each side, and rub them prayerfully, and I love the double texture of hair on one side, and the softest flesh on the other. When I move to my inner lips they are swollen and wet, and I feel their lovely scalloped shape and how they curve up to the little sponge that is porous with my own fluid, that seems at this moment to be the center of my body, and a million strings run outward from this center, and when I press gently and then faster these million channels open to accept the steady flicker of pleasure that comes to me like a gift. When I am almost ready to let the web of channels merge and melt into one, I slide my hand down and let my middle finger enter the open, moist passageway. When my finger is all the way inside so that the heel of my hand now presses against my clit, I find the small, fleshy berry that lolls deep in the entrance to my body, and I touch it delicately. It is moist with its own secrets, and the heel of my hand and my finger work together to touch the two pulsing sponges. When my muscles begin to spasm around my finger and my breath snags and laughter collects in my throat and my palm is joyful with fragrance and fluid and small spry red hairs, I am so thankful to be a woman that it is almost a prayer.

Three people are waiting in line when I walk out of the chapel.

"Chinese men advise against wasting ginseng on your youth," Eva is saying to a young man with a large backpack strapped on his back. The weight of the pack causes him to bend forward slightly, but he watches Eva attentively. "Wait until you're older," she says, "and then see what it can do for you. Cleaning all done?" she says when she sees me.

"Yep," I say. "Ready for business."

"Thank you all for waiting," she says, "and please enjoy the Rothko Chapel."

"Thanks for the advice," the young man says. The back of his pack is covered in patches: Greenpeace, PETA, Grateful Dead.

"What was that all about?" I ask Eva as we walk away.

"Sexual energy, dear," she says. "How was yours?"

"Great," I say. "If you want something done right, do it yourself."

AFTERNOON TEA

"Lacy," Mama says over the phone. "I'm at the Ritz Carlton having tea. Come meet me here. I'd like to talk to you."

"You mean here? In Houston?"

"Of course, dear."

"What do you mean, 'of course'? You live in Dallas."

"Well, I have a car, Lacy, for heaven's sakes."

"Has anyone died or been maimed? Just tell me."

"No, dear. It's nothing like that."

"All right," I say. "I'll be there in about twenty minutes."

"Who was it, your black lover?" Ellis says when I hang up the phone.

"Ellis, please. It's my mother. She's in town for some reason, and she wants to talk to me."

"You don't have to go, you know."

"I know. But if I don't I'll just wonder all day what she wants to tell me. She'll drive me crazy whether I see her or not."

I recall Number 68 on my list: a wish that I will learn

to say no to my mother. Once I can say it to her, everyone else will be easy.

"Come here," Ellis says, and pulls me onto his lap. The first line on his computer screen reads: "All day in Mexico City she thought of getting back to the States, where every restroom had toilet paper and Jesus did not bleed."

"Don't read it," Ellis says. Then he puts his mouth to my ear and says, "Do you know how much I love you?"

"How much?" I whisper.

"More than I did yesterday, and less than I will tomorrow."

I put on a sundress and drive to the Ritz Carlton, Ellis's whisper soft in my ears. Mama wears a white sun hat with a white gauze veil that obscures her face from her forehead to the tip of her nose. Her dress is of the same white gauze, layer after layer. Something bulges near the stomach of the flimsy cocoon. She runs her hand over the bulge and it stills.

"Mama, what's in your dress?" I say as I sit down.

"Shhh," she whispers. "Don't alert them. It's Presley."

"Oh, Mama, why do you have to bring that damn dog everywhere you go?"

She pulls the bosom of her dress out a few inches and whispers down it, "She doesn't mean it, Presley."

"I do mean it," I say in the direction of her stomach. "Presley, I can't stand you. You're a rodent. Now what did you want to talk to me about?"

"I'm very upset, Lacy. I had a long talk with your sister, and she tells me you think you were sexually violated by that sweet Donny Greer. What on earth gave you that idea?" One hand strokes the obscene bulge in her stomach, the other grips a delicate teacup.

"It's the truth, Mama. It's not an idea I got. Donny fucked both of us, Irene and me, all those years he babysat."

16o

"Please don't say 'fucked,' darling. It's unbecoming."

"What would you like me to call it, Mama? Making love?"

"Lacy, you're getting everything so mixed up. Irene didn't say a word about herself."

"Because she's in denial, Mama. You know about denial, right? It's on Oprah all the time."

"Presley and I don't watch Oprah, dear. It's trashy."

"Would you care for something?" the slim waiter asks. His wrists are sharp and quick.

"No, thank you," I say.

"She'll have a cup of your black English," Mama says. "And a bowl of hot oatmeal, please. It's delicious, darling. Just what you need to clear your head."

"I don't want any tea or oatmeal, Mama."

"The oatmeal is for Presley," she whispers. "And the tea will do you good, dear. Aren't these cups wonderful? My favorite Wedgwood. Do you know that where I come from, the elderly get false teeth made from Wedgwood china?"

"Why don't you believe me, Mama?"

"Donny always did such a wonderful job on the yard," Mama says. "Didn't he, Presley?" she whispers down her dress. "He saved my tea roses that awfully hot summer when all those old people were dying in their apartments, remember? And that lovely Flower Whose Stamen Is a Sundial," she adds.

I stare across the room at a painting of a girl with a white parasol.

"Now, darling," Mama continues, "I spoke with Dr. Monk, who did my eyes, remember? And he said there are thousands — literally thousands, Lacy — of lawsuits against therapists for dredging up these false memories of sexual abuse. He said it's really getting to be quite a problem in the business — the insurance people are starting to get in on it, you know." She holds a thin slice of lemon over her tea and wrings the juice from it.

"Dr. Monk is a plastic surgeon, Mama, not a psychiatrist."

"But he's a doctor, dear, it doesn't matter what type. Doctors don't learn anything in med school, you know, they get it all on the golf course and at cocktail parties. I'm sure he knows what he's talking about." She touches the corners of her eyes with her index fingers, to demonstrate Dr. Monk's artistry.

If I don't blink for several seconds, the parasol in the painting seems to twirl slightly.

"Mama, Donny molested me." I say. "He molested Irene. I'm recovering from it, and it would help my recovery if you admitted that it happened. But I'm going to be healthy and strong no matter what your attitude is. I just want you to know that."

She takes a long sip of tea then leans back in her chair, her face calm as flan. "Don't you love this pattern?" she says, stroking the dark needlepoint chair arm. "I think it would go wonderfully in my living room." She rubs the chair harder. Her hands are a gleaming blur of diamonds and fingernail polish. "Did I tell you I had the library redone in a dark green Berber carpet, almost exactly like what they have here? Berber cleans so beautifully, you know."

"No, you didn't tell me that."

The waiter brings my tea and the steaming bowl of oatmeal. I hold the hot cup without drinking any. Mama pulls a gold compact from her purse and starts retouching her lipstick. She blows on the oatmeal, waving the tube of lipstick over it like a wand.

"We'll just let it cool, sweetness," she whispers down her dress.

"Mama," I say. "Can you hear me?"

"I just think you're confused, dear. If anyone molested

you, it must have been Nacho. That kind of thing happens a lot with blacks, you know."

The tea cup is shaking between my palms, and the hot tea splashes up and over my fingers. I watch my wet hands reach down the front of my mother's antique dress, snatch her rat dog up by its pencil neck, and shove its tiny snout into the bowl of scalding oatmeal. I hold its head in the hot mush. "Can you hear me?" I scream over the dog's shrieking. I let go of Presley's neck and he falls off the edge of the table and quivers on the Berber carpet. A waiter with a tray of scones steps carefully over him. I see the manager starting toward us from across the room.

"Bad Lacy," Mama whispers, her hand pressing the open lipstick against her stomach where the dog had been. The lipstick makes a long, tribal mark across her white dress. She starts screaming.

I wipe my hands on a white linen napkin and walk past the sharp-wristed waiter and the gilded statue of an unidentifiable Greek goddess. I go down to the cool, dark underground parking lot and sit in my car until I'm calm enough to drive.

"You watch your mouth about Nacho," I whisper, and start the motor.

BUCKLE UP — IT'S
THE LAW

"Water," Ellis says. "One gallon per person per day." He's writing a list at the kitchen table. Ellis is a dedicated list maker. "Tent and tent poles," he says. "The summer-weight bag and the midweight. Coffee, definitely coffee. The stove. We can pick up some propane on the way. The Thermarest? I don't think so, with all the water we have to pack in. A maybe on the Thermarest. A bunch of that dried black bean soup mix they have in the big bins at Whole Foods, you know? And some dried fruit for trail food. Chocolate. Fuck, yes."

"And a good book," I add. "We can fit a book, right?"

"Sure," Ellis says. "Just one, though. I'll read to you. Pick something you like."

Book, I add to the list. We have two weeks before Ellis starts teaching summer school, and who knows how long before I start doing something productive. We're planning to spend three nights and four days in the Guadalupe Mountains out in West Texas. Work those muscles. Get dirty, get soulful. Reinvent the marriage. I filed for divorce a week ago.

We tear the house apart finding all our backpacking gear, and I spend a day walking around the house in my hiking boots.

"Your legs are gorgeous," Ellis says. "Someday when you really like me can I play connect the dots with your freckles?"

"Absolutely not," I say.

Ellis and I have been joking a lot, talking about books, going to all the movies we can stand. No tears, no guilt. Just a deep hope that the West Texas sun will sweat our problems out of us, will send them scattering up to circle and dissipate around the rock formations that rise like jagged, interlocking steeples. Just a prayer that we'll stand under the biggest sky we've ever seen and its blue curves will be generous enough to absorb our fears and questions, that each point where rock punctures sky will be an answer, that the limestone cliffs will be porous and willing, that the prairie falcons will circle in patterns that form a blessing, that the deer prints in the soft mud along the West Dog Canyon riverbed will spell out a message, a message that begins, *You will love each other and here's how to do it.*

"Lacy," Ellis calls from the kitchen, "Eva's on the phone."

"Are you ready for this?" she asks.

"I guess."

"Have you and Ellis set the parameters for this new covenant?"

"Well, we're going to talk about that between here and there."

"Lacy! All those things you've been working on ... I don't know if an automobile is an appropriate place to discuss them. Cars draw negative energy, Lacy. I'm doubtful that any deep truth can be reached in a car."

"I know how you feel, Eva. But my car's different."

"We're not taking your car," Ellis calls from the other room.

"Yes we are, Ellis, or I'm not going."

"Call me from the road," Eva says, "And blessings on you, dear."

"Oh, Eva," I say. "I attacked my mother's dog." I'm glad she can't see that I'm smiling.

"Lacy, what on earth? You assaulted an animal?"

"Not an animal. A nasty little rat dog. I shoved its face into a bowl of hot oatmeal at the Ritz Carlton tea room."

It sounds like Eva puts her hand over the phone, then she's coughing.

"Eva, you're laughing," I say. "I can hear you."

"Lacy," she says. "We'll need to discuss this violent — oh, what the hell, your mother deserved it," and we both laugh until we hang up.

Ellis is measuring spices into film containers. "We're taking my car, El."

"Lacy, my car is reliable. Your car is not reliable. There's really no question as to which car we should take."

"I just had it tuned and I want to go in it. It's important to me, Ellis. You know I'm attached to my car, and this is an important trip for us, and I just want my car to be part of it. For good luck."

"God, I'm a pushover. All right. Fine." He lets the salt pour too long and it spills over the top of the film canister and onto the counter. "Fuck," he says. "The fucking Cutlass."

My car makes Ellis nervous, I think, because it is too much a part of my childhood, because the little girl who rode around in that car with Nacho was already broken in some crucial places, and those breaks are what have made me behave foolishly with Ellis. And the car, like me, is needy, sucking up gas and oil and fluids and then begging for more. It's big, American, difficult. But Ellis loads our backpacks into the trunk anyway and we take off for West Texas.

"Friendship," he says as we drive through the urban sprawl of outer Houston. "That should probably be first on the list. Honesty."

I write "honesty" in tiny letters.

"That's a hard one for me, El."

"I know. But are you willing to try?"

"Yep. But I just want you to know, it's not like I haven't *been* trying. But I grew up keeping secrets, so many secrets, and big ones, too. I get sort of a perverse thrill out of having a secret, you know?"

"I hear you."

"Could you pass that truck? I hate their sticker."

God, Guns, and Guts.

"No problem. So, let's say that we'll both make our best effort to be honest. In fact, everything in the ceremony or whatever we're calling it should be worded that way. I mean, the traditional marriage ceremony sucks that way, because you're saying I promise this and I promise that, and who the fuck can keep all those promises all at once for the rest of their lives, so you're just setting yourself up to fail."

"Amen, brother."

Ellis laughs. "So, we'll agree to make our best effort to be honest with each other, and when one of us screws up and lies to the other one, we need to sit down and ask ourselves if we were really trying, or if we lied out of some kind of laziness or boredom or fear, which is what it usually is."

"Agreed," I say. "Best effort," and as we speed past alternating catfish, barbecue, and chicken-fried steak restaurants, I wonder if I have ever made my best effort to tell the truth. I wonder what it will feel like when I do, because my best efforts so far have been spent in concealing, not telling, in making my voice smooth when Mama made me call Donny to tell him what time to come baby-sit, in pushing away my dinner and saying I felt sick when I was so hungry even the dog food interested me, because it was not worth the risk of touching my fork to my teeth and making Mama crazy, because I could not add one ounce to my body when I knew a baby would be growing inside me soon, and Callie had told me that's what happened when people *did the nasty*, because I did not know how I would fit a whole baby into my ten-year-old body. Was it my best effort when Nacho caught me shoving the garden hose nozzle inside myself, and shook me and said, "I oughta whip you, girl, but I don't believe in hittin children. Now who learned you to do that?" I lied, I said I saw it on TV and said it between gushes of tears because the idea of Nacho, my guardian and protector, whipping me was too much to stand. When he said "Lord, the things they put on television," I could not tell him that television was a sanitized dream compared to my life, that if only I could have had a TV family, a father and mother who made clever, constant jokes, an adoring sister with Shirley Temple ringlets, the possibility of a Christmas special or a spot on the Jerry Lewis telethon cooing over maimed children, how easy life would have been.

"What about sex?" Ellis asks.

"What about it?"

"Well, it hasn't been so great, you know. I mean, it's always a privilege to make love with you, Lace, and I love just being in the same bed with you, but I know you haven't been into it for a while, and, I don't know." He looks up at the rearview mirror as if for an answer. "I think

168

we should agree to make love only when we both want to. I guess it's part of the honesty thing. I know you do it sometimes just because you know I want to, and maybe all women do that, but I'm just telling you that I don't want you to do that anymore."

"All women do it," I say.

"Why?"

"Because it's easier than saying no. Because we're trained by our mothers to accommodate men. Because you get into a relationship and the sex is great at first and then when it starts to fade you just keep fucking, hoping for a glimpse of what was there before, and you just can't figure out where it went when the guy is the same, maybe nicer even than when you first met him, and it's not like his dick has changed size or he's started to smell bad or something, and you even know him better and he's maybe sweeter to you than when you first met him because you're not playing all those little beginning-of-the-relationship games, but all of a sudden you'd rather read a book or do the dishes than fuck him, but you just fuck anyway because you're trying to understand what happened, and when." I take a deep breath. "Best effort," I add, and I'm tired from speaking one paragraph of truth so I move the cooler full of Shiner to the backseat and put my head in Ellis's lap and he strokes my hair until I fall asleep.

I dream of Number 41 on my list: Our government puts birth control in the water, along with a vaccine that protects against all sexually transmitted diseases. People begin fucking with great joy.

We stop in Johnson City for gas and I say, "I'll drive, El," and I resist the temptation to call Eva from the pay phone. We trade places and Ellis scribbles on the list for a while.

"Lace," he says, "I don't mean that we can't have secrets from each other, because we need our own lives, I mean we don't need to be totally enmeshed with each other and dependent on each other, you know? I just mean, when we do communicate, let's attempt to be honest."

"I hear you."

"What about monogamy?"

"I think we should try it again," I say. "But if either one of us wants to fuck someone else, then we should discuss it with the other one first."

"So, monogamy with a loophole." He holds the pen tentatively against the paper.

"Do you have a better idea?"

"No. It just seems like all of our conditions here are sort of pointing back to the honesty thing. I mean, do you really think if you want to fuck someone that you'll be able to come to me and say, 'Ellis, there's this guy I want to fuck?' when you have a hard time being honest with me about when you want to fuck *me* and when you don't?"

"What are you saying, Ellis? You don't think I can be honest? I told you I'm going to make my best effort, and I'll get better with practice. Or is my best effort not good enough for you? I'm in *therapy*, for Chrissakes."

"Hey, check it out!" Ellis points to the left side of the road where a soft hill rises because we are in the hill country now, the soft, sweet, heart of Texas, the part of the state where you can come to when you're dried up by the relentless West Texas sun, when you're lonesome from the desolation of the panhandle, when you've been frightened away from the Rio Grande Valley by the stories of people who come up from Mexico to steal your internal organs, when you can't get a breath or stand up straight because East Texas is so humid it's like trying to breathe velvet, the hill country is where you can come to be renewed. The deer that cluster on the grassy hillside, looking with startled eyes at the roaring Cutlass, pausing mid-chew, are a joyful shock to me. When Ellis touches my hand where it grips the steering wheel, the space between my flesh and his is alive.

"Oh," is all I can whisper, and as I turn my eyes back to the road the front of the Cutlass slams into another deer and devours it, and the car swerves and shudders. I slow and pull onto the shoulder and Ellis says, "Fuck!" and I know that I am dragging the animal with my car. I hear the scrape of hooves against pavement in the final moment before I turn off the ignition.

"Oh, Ellis," I say. "Damn."

We get out and walk together to the front of the car where a doe is mangled in the caved-in grill, her hind legs and one foreleg stuck up deep inside the engine, the other foreleg dragging beneath the bumper. Her rump softly perspires blood, a moss of blood rising like sweat from her honey-colored fur. Her eyelids are still fluttering.

Ellis gets a T-shirt from his pack, wraps it around the doe's free foreleg, and drags her from the car. She falls heavily in the dirt, straining to breathe. Tufts of blooded hair frame the hole in the car.

"Do you think she'll die?" I whisper, as if I'm already speaking over the dead. "Should we kill her somehow?"

"I don't know, Lace."

Ellis looks tired, holding the bloody T-shirt. Grateful Dead. Summer Tour, 1986. I don't know how to kill an animal, and neither does Ellis. It's one of the things I like about him. But the man I married, the man who grew up in Boston and has never held a gun in his life, who, when he first came to Texas, laughed out loud every time he saw a truck with a "Protected by Smith and Wesson" sticker, this man kneels next to the doe, crooks his arm around her neck, and strangles her in the bend of his elbow. When he stands up, a long, tawny deer hair trails across one lens of his glasses. I brush it away. We don't say anything. We stand in silence on the side of 290 with the sun blazing and a mangled doe at our feet, when we should be past Fredericksburg by now, hurling at eighty miles an hour toward the Guadalupe Mountains. We should be heading to a grateful sleep on the yielding floor of Dog Canyon, an ancient flood plain coated in soft grasses, grasses tamped down by wind and white-tailed deer so that they point uniformly toward the river. I should be kneeling soon to touch the muddy trickle of this river whose violent flash floods and long dry spells remind me of my life, water and desert, water and desert and you finally end up with a mixture of both, a dry cracking place in your heart with a sweet band of moisture running underneath, or sometimes it's the other way around.

"It's hot out here," I say.

"Here comes a cop," Ellis says.

A state patrol car pulls up behind the maimed Cutlass and an officer gets out and walks toward us. He wears a wonderfully large cowboy hat. As he approaches us, I grow enormous in his mirrored sunglasses.

"Hit a deer, didja?" he greets us.

"It just came out of nowhere," Ellis says. "There was nothing we could do."

I hand him my license and papers before he asks. "Looks fine, little lady," he says, handing them back to me. "Let's take a look at your car, here," and he moves the doe aside with his foot and I pop the hood for him. He starts laughing. "All this hair gonna be smellin pretty damn bad for about fifty miles or so, but looks like you still got your radiator. That's what the fuckers usually take out," he says to Ellis, then to me, "Pardon my French, ma'am." He closes the hood and looks under the car for leaks. "This thing's a damn tank," he says. "What year is it?"

"Seventy-one," I say.

"You're damn lucky," he says. "I seen cars totaled by a

goddamn deer. If these environmentalists had their way, there'd be so many deer on the damn highway you couldn't drive straight."

"What about this one?" Ellis asks, pointing to the quiet doe.

"You gonna dress her out?" The trooper hitches both his thumbs inside his belt and waits.

"What do you mean?" I say.

"You gonna dress her out for the meat? You got a good fat one here, didn't even have to waste a bullet."

"Oh, no," I say. "We don't even eat meat."

"I got a daughter like that," he says. "I got six children, all saved but one, and she don't eat meat, neither. Well, if you don't want her I ain't lettin her go to waste. You mind backin your car up a bit, and I'll just pull right in here, make it a little easier on my ol back?"

We get in the car and Ellis starts it and the engine sounds rich and strong like it always has. The officer takes off his big hat and we see the ring of tamped-down hair where he's been sweating. He lifts the doe with a grunt and rolls her into his open trunk. He's smiling, excited. "Buckle up, folks," he calls, giving us a brief salute. "It's the law," and he drives away with his prize.

"Texas," Ellis says. "Never stops surprising me."

"Me neither," I say. "And I'm a goddamn native."

"Should we keep going?" he says. "I think he's right about the car. We just need a new grill."

"I can't do this, Ellis," I say. "I'm not ready." As I speak this I know it as the truth. I know my truth is that I'm going out to do this ceremony with Ellis almost as foolishly as I went to perform our wedding ceremony, knowing even as Irene buttoned the thirty pearl buttons down the back of my wedding dress that each button was a different mistake, a different lie, that each would bind me into my sorrowful and deceitful way of life even as they trapped me into those yards and yards of ivory silk. I know that I am not prepared to do the things we've talked about for the last two hundred miles, the honesty, the monogamy with a loophole, that I am not ready to give it my best effort. I know that beautiful doe is part of the feminine force of this universe that guides and protects me. I know that she put herself in front of my 1971 Oldsmobile Cutlass to say to me, *Sister, do not do this thing. Turn around and go home and cleanse and heal yourself some more and you'll know when you're ready.* I'm sure Eva would agree.

"What do you mean, you can't do this?" Ellis says. He turns the motor off.

"I mean I'm not ready to promise you all these things. I'm not ready to commit to you again, and I'm trying to be honest with you and not make the same mistake I did with the wedding."

"God *damn*, Lacy!" He hits the steering wheel with his open palms.

"Don't hit my car, please," I say.

"What's your story, Lacy? Going back to your black musician lover?"

He's too angry to hear me tell him that is not my story. This is not the story of a black man. It's the story of a white woman.

"You have been jerking me around for I don't know how long, *Oh, I want to fuck a musician and I'll just marry you even though I'm in the middle of an affair and let's not be married but pretend like we are.* Let's not and say we did, Lacy."

"Ellis, I know you're mad, but —"

"Just shut up, Lacy. Just shut the fuck up. I'm gonna drive you back to Houston and you can move out of our fucking house and fuck whoever you want and just forget I love you cause I'm not doing this anymore."

"Do you still love me?" I whisper, looking at my lap.

"Don't ask me that," he says. "Just don't talk to me."

"How much?" I say.

"Shut the fuck up, Lacy!"

"More than you did yesterday, and less —"

"Shut up!" He rips his glasses off his face and slams them against the windshield. They break without much sound. I want to take Ellis in my arms but when I look up at him his face tells me I've given up that right, that Ellis is not my partner anymore and I am left with what I am: a woman, a Texan, a survivor of sexual abuse, a wayward Jesus freak, a soon to be divorced not very hirable Ph.D., a redhead, an ex-teacher with a misdemeanor conviction on my record, a person with no place to live and $7,000 left in my bank account and Mama in control of the money my grandma left me, someone who alternates between lying and battering people with the truth, someone who has hurt a good man, deeply, and can't do a damn thing about it.

"Ellis," I say, "I'm asking for a year. I'd like that much time to figure things out, and then I'd like to meet you on top of McKittrick Ridge and we'll see if we love each other or what. Will you meet me there, one year from today?"

"You've watched *An Affair to Remember* one too many times, Lacy. I mean, I knew you were nuts, but I guess I thought it was kind of charming or something. I'm stupid, I'm just stupid."

"Will you be there or not?"

"I'm not promising you, Lacy. I might be there and I might not."

"I'm promising you," I say. "I'll be there. In the first clearing at the top of the trail."

"You have to drive, I guess," he says, looking at his broken glasses.

We get out of the car and change places. I start the car, pull a U-turn, and we drive without speaking. After fifty miles of silence I turn on the radio. It's my favorite show besides the prison show — *America Asks Bruce*. People call and confess to Bruce their terrible financial problems — the tax blunders, the misguided purchases of time-share condos, the horror when their houses are appraised for less than their purchase prices, when the attorney tells them personal bankruptcy is the best option, when they realize the bluebook value of their cars. Bruce is blessed with a deep, soothing voice, and ends every call by saying, "I do wish you well." He sounds as if he means it. While I drive too fast and Ellis stares out the window fermenting his deep love for me into hatred, I hope this is the beginning of the show. I hope I will have the maximum number of chances to hear Bruce say, "I do wish you well."

HOW MANY FLOWERS
DOES IT TAKE TO STUFF A
MATTRESS?

Dear Mama,

Please find enclosed your vet bill and dog psychiatrist bill. I would not pay them if I were a millionaire. You should not have brought Presley to the Ritz Carlton in the first place. I'm sure he'll be fine in a few days. Also, please quit telling people that my "brother" has passed away. The dog is still alive, as you told me yourself. Plus, I have never considered your pets my kin, and I am not about to start now. I hope you are clear on that. I ran into Georgia O'Hare in the organic wines section of Whole Foods — she was a year ahead of me at Hockaday, with all that pretty, dark hair and a beauty mark like Marilyn Monroe's, only real, remember? — and she said, "Lacy, I heard you lost your brother. Was he at St. Marks? I swear I can't remember him and I feel so awful." Mama, I just couldn't stand getting into the whole dog story with her, so I told her "my brother" had gone to boarding school in Virginia and that's why she couldn't recall him. Isn't that awful? Georgia even cried a little bit, and by the end of the conversation I was starting to feel so bad that I'd lost my only brother, and I don't even have a brother! Now I feel awful that I lied to Georgia O'Hare, and they'll probably write it up in the alumnae magazine and everything. I'm trying to stop lying, you know.

I know you expect me to apologize for what I did, but to tell you the truth, I'm not a bit sorry. So I'm not going to say I am. Are you sorry that you've always treated your dogs better than your children? Are you sorry for the sugar-sweet voice you use to talk to your pets, when you've so often spoken to your daughters through a rage? Are you sorry that the hands you used to slap us have petted and soothed your dogs? It's no wonder I've always envied Presley, and before Presley, Marcella. They got the best part of you, Mama, and we got the worst. Nacho gave me his best, which is why I get so upset when you talk nasty about him, upset enough to slam Presley's face into a bowl of hot oatmeal. I know you think Nacho was inferior to us, Mama, because he was black and uneducated and chewed tobacco instead of smoking expensive French cigarettes like you do, but he wasn't inferior at all. He knew a lot of things, and he tried to teach me what he could. He was a man who didn't try to fuck me. He was a Christian who didn't tell me I was going to hell or getting leprosy. He was family who didn't torture me.

Remember the day you took away my mirror? You paced back and forth across my room, stepping all over the pieces of broken glass and china. You ground them into the hard-wood floor with the heels of your shoes, muttering, "Tooth-paste will get it out." What were you talking about? Nacho came upstairs and tried to pick up all the broken things, the china cat and the glass bluebird with the garnet eye. You got tired of his hands darting between your feet to snatch up pieces of things, so you told him to go out and buy you two dozen of the Flower Used to Stuff Princess

Grace's Mattress. "Take Lacy with you," you said. You pulled a fifty-dollar bill from your bra while Nacho looked away.

"How many flowers does it take to stuff a mattress?" I asked Nacho when we got in the car.

"More than we gonna find," he said.

I could tell he was tired from the mirror episode, the yelling and crying, the hot, dry summer that was burning up our yard faster than he could water it. He didn't much want to talk — maybe he didn't even want me riding along with him. But when we stopped at the first stoplight, the one at Forest and Inwood, he said, "Lacy girl, you want to see somethin pretty?"

"Yes," I said, and he twisted the rearview mirror down so it showed my face. I looked at the tear stains, the blue bump on my lip where I'd bitten it, then the light turned green and he wrenched the mirror back up again. Then we drove out to Arlington Stadium so we could see the lights of the baseball game and hear the crowd yelling over something awful or wonderful, who knew which. In every block of bright stadium lights I saw my own face, I heard Nacho's voice saying, "Somethin pretty." Then we drove all the way out to Oak Cliff so I could make wishes going over the railroad tracks. I don't know what I wished for. I don't know what Nacho wished for, either. I probably wished that my earlobes wouldn't fall off from leprosy, because I knew I was bad for looking in the mirror too much. But I had to look, Mama. I had to look for the leprosy blisters I knew I was bound to get. I had to tug on my ears sometimes to make sure they were still attached.

In the years after that night, when I'd get scared some part of me was about to darken and fall off, I could always count on Nacho to drive me around Dallas, find a long stoplight, and say, "You want to see somethin pretty?" He'd say it at every light if I needed him to, and sometimes I did. He was not perfect, Mama, but he was as essential to my life as oxygen. Please don't talk trash about him. He worked hard a lot of years making our yard nice and making sure Irene and I didn't grow up any crazier than we had to. Let him rest in peace, Mama, if you can.

Love,

Lacy

I FEEL BAD ABOUT
ALL THAT SHIT THAT
HAPPENED

Ellis stays out of the house while I wander through each room collecting my things, whatever I can fit into my car. I choose items randomly, not knowing exactly what I will need in my new life. I stand for an hour in front of our CD collection. I pull out one CD after another without a single song coming into my head. I finally leave Ellis everything but the Black Jesus. I stare at the jumble of our kitchen drawers for a long time. I decide to take the garlic press. I adore garlic. So does Ellis. I put the garlic press back and close the drawer. I ignore the rest of the kitchen. I pack Ellis's letters without looking at his handwriting. I pretend not to notice the furniture, some of it my grandmother's. I take the leftovers from the fridge: cold spaghetti, a paper carton of crispy tofu with lemon grass from the Thai restaurant. I open the paper carton while my car warms up. I notice that our lawn needs mowing. It's full of dandelions. I start picking the tofu out with my fingers before I get to the first stoplight. I'm supposed to go to Eva's. She's expecting me. But I'm thinking of Black Jesus,

of how his dick feels inside me, of how sometimes he bites
me so hard that tears rush up in my eyes, of how the next
day I like to stroke the marks he made and remember what
it felt like when he made them. I'm thinking of the field
of electricity between us when he pressed me up against
the hot metal of the van outside the Catfish Palace, of the
life dancing in his eyes. I'm thinking of how I don't have
to sneak away from Ellis anymore, of Black Jesus's dark
body and the brightness of my thighs next to his. I stop at
a 7-Eleven and call the hotline for his band. No shows
scheduled this week. I call his apartment in New Orleans
and get his machine. I don't leave a message. Finally I
reach him at his father's house, site of the slaughtered pig,
the dead buck, and Marcy's shattered hand.

"Hey my baby," he says. "Where are you?"

"I'm just drivin around."

"Around Louisiana or around Texas?"

"So far I'm still in Texas."

A woman in a blue truck pulls into the handicapped
parking space by the pay phone where I'm talking. She
gets out of the truck and goes into the store. I can't tell
what her handicap is.

"Listen, baby," Black Jesus says, " I feel bad about all
that shit that happened on the road between you and me.
That's how the road is, nothin but everybody gettin pissed
off all the time."

"I didn't notice anyone pissed off except you," I say.

"And you," he says. "You want to come over?"

"Who's there?" I say.

"Nobody but me and Karl's dog, baby."

"Where's Karl?"

"Baton Rouge. Gone off with a woman and left the
damn dog here for me to fool with."

The supposedly handicapped woman comes out holding
a Big Gulp.

"Where's your daddy?"

"Gone to New Orleans to see my sisters. You remember how to get here?"

"You remember how to fuck me till I come?"

"You know I do, baby. Come on over, now."

I hang up, get in the Cutlass, and start driving, out of the Houston city limits and through East Texas with its moss-hung trees and billboards advertising Jesus Christ, with its many roadside vegetable stands and heat so thick it makes the highways look wet, it makes you think of rain. I'm good and sweaty by the time I get over the Texas border. Black Jesus's daddy's house is about an hour west of New Orleans. Driving down the country road, I wonder what I would do if I got a flat tire, how far I would have to walk. Ellis was supposed to teach me how to change a flat, sometime.

I get to Black Jesus's daddy's house with all my tires intact. The front yard is mostly garden, explosive with lettuce, tomatoes green and hard on the vine, corn as tall as a child. On the front porch, Black Jesus leans back in a rocker. I walk slowly up the steps, watching his face. A double-barreled shotgun is propped against the porch railing. I stop at the top of the steps.

"What's this for?" I say, touching the shotgun lightly.

"That's to run off all the crazy white women that follow me around."

"What would a crazy white woman want with a crazy black man?"

"What would a crazy white woman want with a crazy white man?"

"I don't have a white man anymore," I say.

"No? You want a black one?"

"You got something for me?" I ask. Purple martins swoop in and out of the birdhouse hung from one end of the porch.

"Yeah, I got somethin goin on for you." He barely smiles.

I don't know what's going on. My body becomes porous. I turn my gaze from Black Jesus to the garden. I stare at the tender lettuce growing in moist, tight bunches. The afternoon light brings a blush to the young tomatoes. I see Karl's pretty border collie racing up the driveway. She takes the porch steps in one leap and thrusts her head under my skirt. I push her away, then sit on the top step to let her lick my face and neck. Black Jesus is pulling me up. "Come on, girl. I told you I had somethin for you, and it wasn't this damn dog. Stay, Soph," he calls over his shoulder as the screen door slams behind us. I look back and see her face through the dark mesh of screen. Black Jesus leads me upstairs to a bedroom I've never seen. Tiny yellow flowers cover the walls. A weathered Bible sits on the night table.

"Do you want to fuck me, Lacy?" Black Jesus says, unbuttoning my skirt. He doesn't listen to my answer. He doesn't care if it's yes or no. Sometimes I love this about him. We both try to keep from smiling. "I said, do you want me, bitch?" He lifts my T-shirt, puts his lips around one of my nipples and sucks it softly, then a shot of iron goes through me as he bites down.

"Yes," I say. "I said yes, dammit. Can't you fuckin hear me?" I start to laugh.

He runs his tongue around and around the ring of teeth marks on my breast, the meanness gone from his face. "You gorgeous, you know that? Just pretty damn beautiful. You know I'm crazy about you."

"Show me," I say.

He puts his mouth all over my sex while those tiny yellow flowers pulse on the walls, while the gold-edged pages of the Bible shimmer on the night table. Sophie barks at something out in the yard. I imagine the tomatoes in the garden ripening with miraculous speed, I imagine that every pulse of blood and muscle that Black Jesus gathers from the far ends of my body to the flesh that touches his lips is somehow connected to those vegetables. I picture a tornado of ripe tomatoes, green peas, and okra whirling around the confused dog, and I come against Black Jesus's mouth. I laugh as he kisses me, my taste all over his face.

"You think that's funny?" he says.

"No, I think I'm happy," I say. "I think I'm real damn happy."

We fuck until the light changes to late afternoon.

I stand up and wrap myself in the quilt folded at the end of the bed. The quilt is embroidered with the names of Black Jesus's ancestors, one square for each family. "Let's go downstairs and sit on the porch," I say, tugging on his foot. He is falling asleep. I am filled with life. I want to watch the garden. I want to see how it's changed since we've been up here in the bedroom.

"Girl, lemme rest," he says.

"Let's sit on the porch and pretend like we're old people," I say. I stand in front of the dresser mirror and read the reflected names from the quilt: Harmon Sharp m. Ellen Connor, Frederick Sharp m. Alice Williams.

"You gonna make me old," Jesus says, but he gets up and pulls his pants on and we walk downstairs to sit in the rockers in the hot summer evening. "I'm so glad to be off the road for a week, you don't even know."

"You're tired of it?" I say.

"Tired of the damn club circuit. Tired of people comin up to me askin if I know any George Strait songs. I guess I'd just like to know when all this work is gonna pay off."

"But you're doing what you want to do," I say. "A lot of people would trade places with you in a minute. I mean, have you ever worked in an office or a restaurant? Have you ever worked some job that a robot could have done?"

"No, my baby, I ain't. All I done is play gigs, long as I

can remember. I hear you. I just get tired of the road. It makes me act crazy sometimes, makes me forget where I came from. My kin say Nana would be so proud if she could see me now. But sometimes I think she'd want to take me over her knee if she could see me carryin on."

"I bet she would sometimes," I say. I watch Sophie chasing something at the end of the yard.

"You somethin else," he says. "You speak your mind, don't you."

"Not always," I say. "But I'm working on it. What do you think she's after down there?"

"Don't know," Jesus says. "Lizard maybe." Sophie furiously circles something on the ground. Suddenly she leaps the chicken wire that encloses the garden and crashes through a row of corn. "Goddamn! Get the fuck outta there!" Jesus yells. Sophie is barking and digging at the base of a cornstalk. Jesus picks up the shotgun that leans against the porch railing.

"Don't shoot at her, Jesus," I say.

"Nothin but birdshot in this thing," he says. "It ain't gonna hurt her. Just gonna scare her outta there. Put a little sting in her ass."

He rocks forward in the chair and levels the shotgun.

"Don't!" I yell.

"You gonna run out there and get her out?"

"I'm naked," I say. "What if someone drives up?" I pull the quilt tighter around me, although it's hot on the porch.

"Well, my daddy gonna drop dead if he come back to a torn-up garden. I'm sick of chasin the bitch outta there."

Sophie kicks up dirt all around her, still barking. The barking and the shine of sunlight on the gun are making me panic.

"Don't!" I plead again as Jesus closes one eye to aim. "Jesus!" I hear the noise of the shot and see Sophie tumble twice and lay still among the soft lettuce.

"Motherfucker!" Jesus says.

"You said it was just birdshot," I say. "You said it wouldn't hurt her. Karl's gonna freak out! That's Karl's fucking dog!"

"Shut the fuck up," he says.

He walks out into the yard, still holding the shotgun, and steps over the chicken wire. I see his foot prodding the dead dog. He walks back after a minute or two and sits in the rocker next to me.

We stare at each other for a long time. The porch is almost dark. I trace my fingers over the letters embroidered on the quilt, an "H" then a "J," but it is too dark to read them. The blushing tomatoes, the vibrant lettuce, the delicate yellow flowered wallpaper and my lover's smile all disappeared with the shot. I think of Nacho. I think, *Something terrible has happened. Where are the grownups?* I wait for Nacho to come and pick up the dead dog and dig a hole to bury her in. Then I think, *We are the grownups*. I walk up the stairs, fold the quilt in thirds, and arrange it on the bed just like it was before. I pick up my scattered clothes, pull them on, and walk back downstairs. Jesus is still rocking, the shotgun across his knees.

"Let's go get some catfish," he says. "I'm hungry."

Black Jesus gets his shoes and we drive out to a little joint where the waitresses wear pantyhose under their tight polyester shorts and people smoke cigarettes and eat at the same time. I order a basket of fried catfish but I don't eat a bite of it. Black Jesus eats all of his and then all of mine. Instead of eating I stand by the jukebox and feed quarters into it. I play all the George Strait songs. As I punch in the numbers, I think about how I will lie with my eyes open in Black Jesus's arms all night long. I will tell myself over and over, while I listen to his breathing, that this is the last night I will sleep next to him. In the dark room with the yellow flowered wallpaper, I will plan a trip to the place where Nacho died in Mama's backyard. This will help make me a grownup. This will help make me a woman who won't fuck men who hit women and shoot dogs. While Black Jesus covers the catfish in hot sauce, I tell myself I could have walked out into the garden with the family tree quilt wrapped around my shoulders and made Sophie come to me. The soil would have felt warm under my bare feet. If a neighbor had driven up in his pickup truck, he would have seen my pale calves, my red hair loose over the embroidered names of Jesus's kin. He would have seen Black Jesus sitting up on the porch with a shotgun in one hand, humming a blues tune or maybe laughing at my nakedness. He would have seen Sophie running toward me like a good dog.

THAT'S NICE ABOUT
THE BLUEBONNETS

The next morning I slip out of bed while Jesus sleeps. I stand by the edge of the bed buttoning my skirt and memorizing his face, the close-cropped beard and the dimples that show through it when he smiles big enough. I stare for a few minutes at the family tree quilt, trying to find Jesus's name. I don't see it anywhere. I even lift one edge of the quilt to look at the other side, but Jesus moves his foot and I put the quilt back and stand perfectly still until his breathing is deep and even again. I find my purse and walk out of the bedroom slowly, my shoes in one hand. I walk barefoot down the stairs, out the front door, past the garden bright with dew. I don't look at the spot where the birdshot sent Sophie tumbling. Black Jesus went out last night after I got in bed and did something with her body. I didn't ask him what. I pretended to be asleep when he came to bed and pulled me up against him. His hands felt hot on my stomach, and I hoped he had washed them. I hoped he hadn't touched Sophie. I sit in my car for a minute and look up at the window of the bedroom where he's sleeping. I think about Karl and the way he shakes his head slowly when he doesn't like something, as if to say *no, no, no. That's not the way it's gonna be.* I start my car and hate how loud it is.

"Shhhh," I say stupidly.

I pull out of the driveway, hoping Black Jesus will sleep a while longer, hoping he is deep in a sweet dream. I start trying to think about what I will tell Eva about why I didn't show up at her house when I was supposed to, why I came to Louisiana instead. The three-hour drive back to Houston yields this excuse: "Sorry I'm late."

"Lacy," Eva says, twisting the doorknob of her front door back and forth, "that would be an appropriate thing to say if you were ten or fifteen minutes late. You're twenty-four hours late."

"I'm really sorry, Eva. I had a lapse. What can I say? Did you call Ellis?"

"No, I'm happy to say I refrained from calling Ellis. I assumed you had gone to fuck Mr. Jesus. Am I correct?"

"Can I come in, Eva? It's really hot out here."

She turns without a word and I follow her up the stairs into the cool garage apartment. She turns on the kitchen faucet, pulls on a pair of yellow rubber gloves, and starts washing dishes.

"Eva?" I say. "Hello?"

I turn off the water. She turns it back on. She grabs a bottle from the edge of the sink and squeezes out more soap than necessary, long, green strands of it.

"Should I leave?"

"Maybe you should," she says.

"Okay," I say. "Maybe I'll go up to Dallas. I've been thinking I need to go to there. I need to do some kind of closure on Nacho's death. I don't think I've ever really grieved him, and something that happened yesterday with Black Jesus made me realize how much I miss him, how much I depended on him to protect me in my childhood, to make everything all right. I was hoping you would go with me, but I understand why you're mad. It was really rude of me to not come over when I was supposed to and to not even call. I just had this burst of irresponsibility. It's been getting worse and worse since I quit my teaching job. I don't know what's up with that."

"Oh, Lacy," Eva says. She turns off the water and throws her arms around me. "I'm so proud of you for wanting to do closure on Nacho. You sweet thing," she says, hugging me tight. The gloves are wet against the back of my T-shirt. "I was just so worried about you, that's all. I'm not really mad."

"You're not? You should be."

"Let's just put it behind us. I'd love to go to Dallas with you. I'm honored that you would include me." She pulls back from me and I notice her hair.

"Where's your turban?" I say.

"Oh, I don't usually wear it at home," she says. She pulls the yellow gloves off and flings them into the sink, smiling. She touches her short red hair at the temples.

"You look good like that. You should go out that way sometimes."

"Most people think I look like a dyke with this haircut," she says.

"Are you a dyke?"

"Well, sort of."

"What do you mean, sort of?"

"I mean," she says, twisting the hot water on and off, "that I don't love penises or vaginas. I love people. So I've been in love with men and I've been in love with women." She looks me in the eyes, but her hand is tight over the faucet.

"What's it like being with a woman?"

"Really, Lacy. What's it like being with a man?"

"Pretty fucking fun sometimes. But you know that. I'm asking you something I don't know."

"Well, my dear," she says, "I find a woman's shape inherently beautiful. It stirs something very old and primitive in me. I find it wonderful to marvel over a woman's body and then to look at my own body and know that she and I are traveling the same mysterious path, the woman's path. It's comforting, it's exciting. It's like driving out to the hill country to look at the bluebonnets in the spring. You look at those masses of blue flowers all day, and you have that stamp of blue in your vision for a long time afterward. You're tired," she says. "I can tell."

"Yeah, I am," I say. "I didn't sleep much last night. I stayed awake all night telling myself I wouldn't see Black Jesus anymore."

She loans me a nightgown with tiny ladybugs printed all over it. I get in her bed, although it is the middle of the day, and she sits beside me and strokes my forehead.

"Tell me the thing you liked the most about Nacho," she says. "And you will have a sweet dream."

"He was the only person in my life with a dick who didn't try to fuck me," I say. "That was nice about the bluebonnets," I add.

Eva stays beside me until I fall asleep. I don't have any dreams at all.

LAMB OF GOD

By the time Eva and I take our trip to Dallas, the bluebonnets along I-45 are faded husks, the kids from Tyler are selling their tight, fragrant roses along the dime-bright shoulder of the road, and it is the beginning of a long summer in Texas. We buy four bunches of roses between Houston and Huntsville because Eva thinks it's important to encourage children, and I do, too, come to think of it. Eva drives like she's at a tea party, her feet delicately crossed over the gas pedal.

"Eva, no animal rights stuff this time, okay? I'm just not up for it."

"Okay, you dog killer," she says, "Don't you worry. I have something else in mind, anyway. I'd like to talk with you about your spiritual roots."

"I didn't kill the dog, Eva! Jesus did it! I know I could have stopped the whole thing if I hadn't been so lazy from fucking all afternoon, but *he's* the stupid motherfucker who said birdshot wouldn't hurt her."

"Dearest, forgive me. I wouldn't tease you about that. I

know how terrible you feel. I was referring to your mother's dog, actually."

"Oh," I say. "Well, I didn't kill it, either. I only burned it a little. Besides, that's not even a dog, it's a rat. So I scalded a rat. Big deal."

"Now about your roots."

"Eva, you know what my spiritual roots are and I don't want anything to do with them," I say. "It's all just hellfire and damnation and having to hold your arms up for an hour waiting for God to zoom down through your fingertips. Except he never comes down — all that ever happens is the men look at your raised-up tits while they're supposed to be praying and your arms get tired and everything you ever do in your whole life is another step on the path to Hell. If it's something fun then it's a shortcut to Hell. I don't want to talk about it."

"Dear Lacy," she says, "you cannot cut your spiritual plant off at the roots. If there was a lack of spirituality in your childhood religious tradition, you will simply take that emptiness into whatever new tradition you choose. If you deny your spiritual roots and cut off your plant at ground level, the plant will simply die. You must acknowledge the tradition from which you come and use it to form a new tradition. Tell me, dear, was there anything positive or nourishing in the religious ceremonies of your childhood? Think hard, now."

"Watch the road, Eva!" A huge armadillo barely makes it to the shoulder. Eva's very big on eye contact, even at the expense of her driving.

"Okay, okay," she says. "Now answer my question. Or do you need some time to think about it?"

"I don't know, Eva. I liked some of the singing. You know I love to sing, and some of the songs didn't have scary words, and when we'd do one of those and everyone would get to singing and it would go on long enough so even the people who didn't have great voices would forget themselves and really get into it, that was good. And I liked the silent prayers, because then I could just quiet down and get into my own mind and pray for the things that I really wanted."

"And what were those?"

"Love. My daddy. A ten-speed. That Donny would get run over by the ice-cream truck and all the push-ups and Popsicles and Eskimo pies would spill out and every kid in the neighborhood would trample over his dead body getting the free ice cream."

We both start laughing, and the sound of my voice with hers is nice, like the singing used to be.

"So, even in that threatening environment, you found comfort in singing and silent prayer."

"I guess, but there was so much that was bad. So much, Eva," and I am thinking of Reverend Greever and the abundance of fat that clings to his jawbones. It is the fat I concentrate on, holding it in my mind like a constant prayer, and its mass moves rhythmically from his chin to his ears, quivering obediently with the violent movements of his head as he begs the sinners to come forward, to leave their filthy ways in the leather seats of their Jaguars, in the cushioned velvet of the pews, in the fragrant hands of their lovers, and come forward to be sanctified.

"Sinners, come home," he bellows, and one by one they are drawn by the jiggling beacon of fat down the blue carpeted center aisle to be blessed and cleansed by the soft, moist hands of Reverend Greever. First comes Mrs. Stewart, who co-chairs the Junior Symphony League ball with Mama and gets saved all the time, then Sandra Courtney, Mama's arch-rival for the top slot on the ladies' tennis ladder, and God knows she needs saving because she fucks Mrs. Stewart's epileptic husband. If Mrs. Courtney's maid hadn't known what to do to keep him from swallowing his own tongue the day he had a fit right on the hand-painted tiles of the Courtneys' kitchen floor, he could have died right there in the throes of his own sin. Now the front of the aisle is clogging with well-dressed sinners, women who smooth their silk dresses as they kneel and men wearing just the right amount of Polo cologne, and suddenly Mama is poking her sharp fingernails into my ribs saying, "Get up there, Lacy." I shake my head and stare hard at the swirling flowered pattern of my dress. She puts her arm around my shoulders and leans close to me so that anyone watching would think she's telling me how much she loves me, but the words seep from her in an angry hiss: "Get up there and get saved, you little bitch, or you'll be sorry you were ever born," and I shuffle down the length of the pew in my white patent leather shoes. The old ladies whisper, "Oh, isn't she sweet, lamb of God." I am terrified of ending up a leper. I touch my earlobes to make sure they're still there. And when Reverend Greever finishes casting the demons from the seersucker-suited man next to me, he stoops down to slightly above my height, and he leans over so I am shaded by his swaying chins. He asks solemnly, "Child, what is your sin?" He is ready to hear the worst, his fat cells can absorb the most gory detail, the most scintillating account of one's liaison with Satan. He is most disappointed when I whisper, "I don't know."

"Do you know," Eva says, "I think it is time you did some gardening. I think you have root rot."

I start laughing. "Damn right I do. The worst case of root rot in modern agriculture."

"I mean it," Eva says, but she is laughing, too, and we let the good laughter chemicals flow through us and make us high as we speed past Texas Burger, a collection of chain-saw art staggered along the guardrail (bears in cowboy hats and jagged armadillos), and a boarded-up shack called "Freedom Tattoos." We're almost there.

THE EXIT WOUND

Eva sleeps while I drive the last stretch into Dallas, and instead of going to one of the Motel 6's off the highway I take the downtown Elm Street exit and park in a 24-hour lot near the Kennedy Memorial.

"Guess where we are, Eva." I reach over and straighten her turban where it's slipped to one side.

"Dallas," she says, then opens her eyes, looks up, and recognizes the Texas Schoolbook Depository Building. "Oh, Lacy! You sweet thing!" She leans over and gives me a quick hug. "I've never been!"

"I know," I say.

"How did you know?"

"Because if you'd been here you would have told me about some profound experience you had or something. I know you."

"Well, let's go have one, girlfriend."

We take the roses we bought along the highway and walk in the Dallas twilight through the bleached white walls of the Kennedy Memorial. We circle the stone slab that's covered in plastic flowers and votive candles and taped-on cards.

"Should we read them?" I ask Eva.

"Oh, no," she whispers reverently, laying one bunch of roses at each corner of the stone, "that's so invasive. They're meant for the president, not for us."

"You're right," I say.

"Let's write one, though," she says, and we sit on the warm concrete ground and rummage through our purses for pens and paper. I have my memo pad with one piece of paper left on it, but the closest thing to a pen we can find is a half-used tube of lipstick. Sheerly Sangria.

"I think he'll like it," Eva says.

"What should we say? I mean, what is it you like so much about him?"

"I like it," she says, "that after the Bay of Pigs he went on TV and said he'd made a mistake. He actually used the word 'mistake.' I don't think I've ever heard a man, certainly not a president, use that word in reference to himself."

I think hard about all the men I've known, Nacho and Donny, Mama's string of boyfriends who brought good bottles of Merlot and whose fingernails never had cuticles, and Ellis, who said such romantic things to me, who once said, "Everything that is Europe is in your face," and Black Jesus and the band. I cannot remember ever hearing these men say anything like what John F. Kennedy said on national television in front of his wife, enemies, close friends, and lovers.

"You know what I like about him?" I say, and it's hard to think about much because it feels so good to sit cross-legged next to Eva on the ground that holds all the heat of this long summer day.

"What's that?" Eva says.

"I like him because you like him. That's kind of stupid, isn't it?"

"I love you dearly," Eva says.

Dear President Kennedy, she draws in fat, lipstick letters.

"Oh, damn," she says. "I've used up the whole page. Do you have any more paper?"

"I have a Visa receipt," I say, "but it's got my card number on it. I don't want to leave that here for anyone to see. What about the other side?"

"Grocery list, it looks like," she says, turning the paper over.

"I think it's fine like it is. The president will understand." Eva blows on the paper to dry the lipstick and after a while we anchor it with one of the votive candles and stand back to admire our work.

"It's important to celebrate the good men," Eva says, "and to ask in that celebration that some of their goodness be put back into the universe."

She links her arm through mine and we walk over to the grassy knoll and we stare for a long time up at the window where Oswald is said to have stood. I imagine the motorcade must have looked lovely from above, women's hats like bright, bobbing targets.

"There had to be a second shooter," Eva says. "I can feel it."

"Damn straight there was," says an older black man who walks up from the curb stabbing bits of garbage with a long, pointed pole. He waves the shish kebab of garbage at us. "Ain't no fuckin Warren Commission gonna tell me Oswald could hit a movin target at that angle from that window. No sir, no sir."

"I agree completely," Eva says. "Oswald was a poor shot. It would be a difficult feat even for an excellent marksman."

"Speak it, woman," he says. He stabs his pole of garbage into the soft grass and stands at attention beside it. He lifts his right arm in a salute to nothing in particular.

"Every description," Eva says, "every description given by the doctors and nurses describes the back wound as significantly larger than the anterior throat wound. The back wound was an *exit* wound, not an entrance wound, and therefore could not have been made by Oswald. You don't ignore *nurses*," she says, clutching her pink-turbaned head with both hands. "They are the caretakers of our society. They see our urine, our feces, our blood, they are the first to hold our babies, wet and dark from the womb. They are the mothers of us all — they are not to be ignored."

"You ladies got your heads on straight," the man says. He relaxes his salute and tips his dirty baseball cap to us. "You see this?" he says, gesturing to the stick of punctured Marlboro packages and unreadable patches of newspaper. "Warren Report ain't no better than this garbage. Ain't no better." He spits on the ground between him and us. "Me?" he says. "I'd rather read the likes of this!" He tears something from the pole and offers it to us. Eva hesitates, then takes the dirty paper. I look over her shoulder and read, "The decision to use a tampon is, as it has always been, a personal decision." Eva hands it back to the man. He drops it on the ground and stabs it vigorously with the tip of the pole.

"How right you are," Eva says. "And do you know what the worst thing about it is?" she says, her face reddening slightly under the shrimp-colored turban.

"What's that, ma'am?"

"The lie about our president's death is a great scar on the American consciousness. We will never do closure on that death. We will never be able to grieve it properly as long as the truth remains hidden. And that great collective lie has spawned a society of liars, a society of concealers. I am no exception. I live in a society that lies to itself about its own president, and I, too, am a liar." She moves suddenly to grip the garbage man's hand where it rests on top of the pole.

"Amen, sister," he says, "God bless you," and he continues on his way up and over the grassy knoll, collecting debris as he goes.

We're so excited over our dead president that we go up to Reunion Tower, the restaurant that slowly rotates inside a mesh of lights, and drink gin and tonics until it's late enough to sneak over to Mama's. The motion of the restaurant and the gin make me slightly dizzy.

"Lacy, it was a wonderful intuition to go to the Memorial," Eva says as we watch the lights of Dallas far below us. "For while we cannot do closure on our dearly departed president, we can grieve fully for Nacho, your protector and father figure."

"I feel like I've been grieving him all my life," I say. "Even when he was alive, I hid how much I loved him, because as soon as Mama saw we loved something, nothing could stop her from taking it away."

"So you are in the last phase of your grief, my dear. Of this grief, anyway. Are you ready?" and we finish our drinks and take the long elevator ride down with all the tourists. We drive north up Central Expressway and then Forest Lane to Inwood. We park a block away and walk quietly to my mother's backyard and the pond where Nacho shot himself so many years ago. I take Eva's hand and guide her through the maze of stepping stones, cast-iron frogs, and the rosebushes heavy with blooms. Not twenty yards away the kitchen windows glimmer dark black against the gray brick house. We kneel at the edge of the pond, and I watch the reflection of the live oak stretch across the smooth water, water too smooth to understand the jagged grief that led Nacho to kill himself. Eva dips her cupped hands in the water and lets it flow through her open fingers.

"Water is the lowest thing on earth, yet it is stronger even than the rocks," she whispers. "Touch it, my dear.

Your friend chose the strongest of the elements in which to die."

I skim my fingers across the water's surface, then let it come up over my wrists, then I lean over until it covers my elbows. I sit up and pull my T-shirt over my head. I'm sweating, suffocating. I cannot get my sandals and jeans off fast enough. When I am naked I roll into that warm, mossy water and float on my back across the pond, only a sliver of moon lighting my body. I see the sky and the roof of the house and the trees as Nacho must have seen them on that last swim. I understand that from where he floated he could not see the things that needed tending in the yard: the roses wanting eggshells crushed around their bases, the tomatoes needing cardboard collars to keep the cutworms away, the carrots ripe for thinning, the dark upstairs window of a seventeen-year-old girl who needed to hear Nacho saying, "Lacy girl, we gonna be all right," and "You want to see somethin pretty?" I understand how he could leave us, seeing only the sky filtered through the meshed leaves of the live oak. I see that it must have been easy to float and to keep on floating.

"Lacy," Eva says, then an explosion comes from the house and something crashes into the water and the voice that screams, "You marijuana-smoking bastards! Think you'll rob me again, do you?" is my mother's voice and the mass floating toward me is Eva. I grab her with one arm and swim with the other to the edge of the pond, her turban slowly unfurling, and I scream, "Mama, it's Irene, don't shoot," but she has already done enough with her SuperMag revolver because Eva is heavy in my arms. I push her up onto the soft, muddy ground with her feet still dangling in the water and I breathe into her mouth like I've seen on *Cops* and *Real Stories of the Highway Patrol.* Eva's lips are soft and slippery and her pulse is fluttering wildly. When I look up, I see Mama standing there in her black silk robe with the white gardenia pattern all over it, the gun straining at the flimsy pocket.

"Mama, call a fucking ambulance!" I yell.

"I thought I told you not to swim right after you eat. You'll get cramps, Lacy," she says quietly. She walks back into the house and closes the door. I run after her and bang on the door but it's locked. "Call an ambulance, Mama!" I yell, but the house stays dark so I run past Eva and through the hedges to the Garretts' house behind Mama's backyard.

Joel Garrett answers the door, Joel the math genius who went all the way to the National Finals in Washington, D.C. with the St. Marks Whiz Quiz team. Now he stands in the doorway in a Phish T-shirt while a guy comes up from behind him and says, "Joel, man, is this the girl?" Joel's friend holds a water pipe decorated with a crude painting of a marijuana leaf.

"I need to call an ambulance," I say. "Please help me, Joel."

"Dude, call nine-one-one," he says to the stoner friend.

The boy turns too slowly to pick up the hall telephone. "Dude, what should I tell them?" he says.

I run past Joel and grab the phone. My voice cranks out the bare necessities: Mama's address, a gunshot wound. I, too, am moving in slow motion. When I hang up the phone Joel says, "Is that you, Lacy Springs? Fuck, I didn't even recognize you until you said your address. Jesus, what's up?" and I look down and see that I am still naked, my body flecked with bits of moss and mud. Joel takes off his T-shirt and helps me pull it down over my head.

"Find her some pants, man," he says to his friend. The friend doesn't move, but stands there with his gaze fixed on my breasts.

I know I am wasting precious seconds. I know I need to get back to Eva.

The stoner snaps his gaze from my breasts and says, "Where's the shot person?"

"In our backyard, by the pond."

I watch his friend set the water pipe on the floor and run out the front door and across to Mama's backyard.

"Dwight took this EMT course last summer," Joel says, hugging his arms across his bare chest. "He learned a lot of cool shit. Maybe he can do something. Is it your mom?"

"No," I say.

"Want to go back over there?"

"Yeah," I say. "Come with me?"

"Sure," he says. "Let's get you some jeans first. Or you want a skirt? My mom's got closets full of stuff up there — you want to look?"

"Anything's fine," I say.

He runs up the stairs, two at a time, and comes back with a blue silk skirt.

"How's this one?" he says, offering it to me.

I pull it on and button it around my waist. It fits perfectly. The silk is cool and soft.

"You look good," he says.

"Thanks, Joel."

"It kinda goes with the shirt."

"Yeah, I guess it does," I say, looking down at the T-shirt.

"I guess we should go," he says.

He puts his arm around me and guides me out the door. I glance up at him as we pause at the top of the porch steps. I notice how his little goatee, the size of a postage stamp, sharpens his chin. We start down the steps, and I'm careful of Mrs. Garrett's beautiful silk skirt. I lift the hem a bit like it's a prom dress. I try to use my good posture, my best smile.

SOMETIMES I
IMAGINED THE MOST
HORRIBLE THINGS

Dear Irene,

I know you are probably too busy being an important attorney to listen to me. But I am writing this letter for me as well as for you, so I guess I don't care if you listen or not. I am learning how to express myself, Irene. I don't speak in blues verses too much anymore. I know it annoyed you to death when I'd do that. Maybe next time I see you I'll do it again, for old time's sake. No. I don't think I will do that. Instead, I will look you in the eyes and talk like a regular person.

Do you remember that we were not allowed to roll our eyes or talk much when we were little girls? Do you remember that we were forbidden to look in a mirror? Couldn't look in a mirror! So we looked at each other. You became my mirror, Irene. We looked at each other so much, parting each other's hair with the yellow comb, brushing the sleep from each other's eyes, that sometimes now when I look in the mirror (I look as much as I want, Irene) I'm surprised I'm not you. My red hair shocks me, and my green eyes are like two lakes from a travel brochure. Sometimes I really expect to see your dark hair and your pretty pale skin that you have always been so vain about, and your black eyes that get darker when you're mad. I know these things about you, Irene. And you know them about me.

If I ever get as rich as Mama, I'm going to build a house that's nothing but mirrors. I'll walk around in it naked all day long. I'll make love with who I want and I'll see every angle of his body, maybe a few he doesn't know about. Do you think that's nasty? I suppose you think I am a whore, and selfish, too. Well, I will tell you what I think of you, Irene.

I think you are wrong to represent Mama when she shot down my best friend and therapist like a dog and would have shot me, too, if I hadn't yelled out, "Don't shoot, Mama! It's Irene!" It was my survival instinct, sister, that made me tell Mama I was you. I believe she might have shot me if she'd known I was me. I think you are mean, Irene, to go to the *Dallas Morning News* and tell them Eva and I were performing a "cult ritual" in the backyard when Mama mistook us for robbers. Irene, you are not a hick. How can you get so absorbed in the religious right and all that Republican silliness? Remember, just say no to sex with pro-lifers. Ha, ha. There are too many unwanted babies in the world, Irene, and I think you and I are two examples. But about Eva and me: you made us out to the newspapers like we are a few sandwiches short of a picnic. You made us sound like those crazies out in Waco. Yet you know damn well we didn't have a thing to do with any cult. And even if we were part of the most ridiculous cult, does that make it right for Mama to go around shooting people out in the yard? With all the damage she has done, that woman does not have the right to shoot a mosquito. And now you have gone and convinced the police that she was right to do it! Do you believe that in your heart, Irene, or is it part of being a lawyer? If it had been me, and not Eva, who'd fallen into the pond with a punctured lung and a bullet through my spinal cord, would you still stand up next to Mama in court and swear she is innocent? I believe you would! I believe you'd be glad, because if I were dead you wouldn't have anyone to remind you where you came from. Without me, you could pretend it was all just debutante balls and getting our pictures taken for the Social Register and all the mirrors you could ever want to look in. You could even pretend we had a father!

Sometimes I looked, Irene. In the big armoire mirror in the living room. Sometimes when you and Mama were asleep, I'd crawl out of my room and sit on the top step, then scoot down the stairs on my bottom, step by step. Even Marcella couldn't hear me, I was so quiet. When I'd slid off the last step, I'd lie on the hardwood floor, my white nightgown spread around me like pale butterfly wings. I was too scared to stand up. But I'd roll onto my stomach and push myself across the smooth oak floor, an inch at a time, all the time imagining what I would see in the mirror when I got there. Sometimes I imagined the most horrible things! A little girl with leprosy sores blistering all over her face, nose already gone, skin and tissue falling away with every sin she committed. The opposite of Pinocchio, I guess. And my little leprosy girl would have to stare very hard in the mirror to keep her body parts stuck together, to keep her ears on her head and her head on her neck, but she knew she'd waste away eventually and a shimmer in the mirror would be the only thing left of her. Or sometimes I'd imagine Mama's face looking back at me, saying something crazy like, "I told you not to wear white shoes until the old witch woman has pressed and dried the petals of the Last Gardenia to Bloom Before the Korean War." Or I'd see a little black girl looking out at me, I wanted so much for Nacho to be my daddy. So I'd push my way to the Oriental rug, which itched me like crazy. You'd think such an expensive rug would be nice to lie around on, wouldn't you? It's not. So many things are not what you think. Then I'd roll, three turns from the start of the rug to the armoire. I'd put one hand on each of those sturdy feet and pull myself up until my own face surprised me like a ghost. My own face, Irene. I don't think I even thought of it as my own, all those freckles and the thick stalk of red hair that Mama called whorish. Now tell me, Irene — how can something be whorish when you're born with it? When I think of whorish, I think of the ladies in the ads in stock car racing magazines, or the girls who answer the 1-900 numbers. But even they are probably not whorish. They're probably bored silly with talking dirty on the telephone and wearing those uncomfortable G-strings. But I think I had to find something to think of as whorish besides my own head of hair, so I started thinking of those women. Maybe I will get to the place where the word *whorish* won't mean anything to me, any more than a word in a language I don't understand. I'd like that, because I don't like thinking badly of women. We have been called whores long enough and I don't want to do any of the calling from now on. I guess that's why I felt sad when I tried to tell you about my friendship with Eva and you said, "Oh, spare me your new age women's crap!" I just felt like putting down the phone and crying myself to sleep, to tell you the truth. You are a woman, too, Irene, and you are a woman who is also my sister. I know you like to pretend that our lives have been normal and even dull. Maybe that's what you have to do so you can go to your Junior League meetings and keep a serene smile on your face. So you can stand up in court in your lovely Donna Karan suits — you have always had wonderful taste in clothes — and help rich people get divorced and defend executives who hit their wives. So you can get Mama off scot-free so that now she thinks she's some kind of neighborhood hero! Go ahead and forget our past, Irene, because I will remember for you, and I will remember the part of you that is womanly, the goddess in you that you've stabbed to death with your spike heels and buried in your business suits.

I remember once, before Mama took away the mirrors, when you and I leaned our heads together in front of the blue dresser in my room. We took one strand of my hair and two strands of yours and we braided them together. Remember how pretty that piece of red hair looked running through the dark braid? And how we laughed as we tried to walk around the room with our heads stuck together? We were little then, my sister, and so many of the bad things had not happened to us, yet. We wore our hair like precious crowns. That was fun, wasn't it?

I'm not writing to criticize you, Irene. I'm writing to ask you a favor. I would like to find Donny and talk to him. I'm not going to sue him or anything messy like that. But I want to see his face. I want him to see that I grew up whole. Then it will be over. I am asking for your help because I know you have many friends in law enforcement and that you have access to programs that track people's whereabouts. Please get me an address, Irene. It's all I'm asking. I have a feeling he's still in Dallas, but I can't imagine what he would be doing. Probably head of Boy Scouts. Ha ha.

Irene, do you still have your season tickets to the Cowboys? Who's winning, who's fighting, like Nacho used to say. I've thought a lot about how much I used to love football, back when I thought the Dallas Cowboys hung the moon. I just adored those big silver stars on their helmets and the way Tom Landry stood on the sidelines with his arms crossed and his face cold and expressionless, but you knew he would never do anything mean or embarrassing because he was such a *Christian.* Please! I bet he's done all kinds of mean and nasty things, although I can't think of what they might have been. Can you? Donny taught me that a football is made from a pig. He taught me that artificial turf burns when you slide across it. He told me about the brief phase of tear-away jerseys, what it means to face third and long. He told me all about the Monday night games I couldn't watch because they were past my bedtime. He showed me how to look for the pink patches on a player's skin that mean steroids. So when he fucked me the first time, and all the times after that, I didn't completely hate him. I still looked up to him a little bit. I still wanted him to tell me how a zone defense works and why Landry never called fancy plays like the flea flicker. I wanted with all my heart to see a flea flicker. It would be easier for me now, I think, if I had been able to hate him back then. If I'd never spoken to him again, if I'd never answered when he said, "Who's number 56, Lace?" When we were old enough to stay by ourselves and Donny didn't come over anymore, Nacho taught me about baseball and I didn't watch football much after that. Baseball seemed more peaceful, and I liked the way you can see the players' faces. I didn't know anybody's numbers after a while. But I'm still a little bit interested in football, in spite of myself. I sneak a look at the sports page now and then. I cheer inside when the Cowboys are winning. And I guess that's how I feel about you, Irene. I love you in spite of everything, and I still look up to you a little and I'm proud of you for getting through law school and looking so professional all the time and getting your hair stuck up in that nice French roll every day. My French rolls always fall out the minute I move my head. You'll have to show me how you make them stay, sometime.

Your sister,

Lacy

THERE'S THIS
MATTER OF THE
DEPOSIT

After Eva stabilized, her family had her airlifted from Park-
land Hospital to some fancy place in Yankee land. I had to
talk to Eva's mother on the phone about it a number of
times. She spoke to me like I was a criminal. I've had to
talk to a lot of people about Eva lately, including the police,
Irene, Dr. Troy, and most recently Eva's landlady. The
landlady is so thankful to have me take over the apartment that she brings me a batch of beef stew. We stand in
the open doorway and talk without really looking at each
other.

"I don't know what our cities are comin to," she says,
squeezing the Tupperware to her chest. "Course Dallas is a
sight worse than Houston, from what I hear."

"You think so?"

"Just look at our Eva, shot down in cold blood." She
offers the vat of stew. "This here's comfort food, dearie."

"Thank you," I say.

Her gray, curled hair puffs over the top of a transparent
green visor. "Now dearie, are you planning to take over

poor Eva's lease, or are you just kind of house-sitting until she gets back?"

"I'm taking over," I say. "If that's all right with you. I don't think she'll be back. Her family asked me to clean out her things and ship them to New York." I can't bring myself to say that Eva is still unconscious.

"Of course, there's the matter of Eva's deposit," she says, lifting the visor slightly so I can see the color of her eyes, gray. "I could just keep it and call it your deposit, seeing as you're doing the work of cleaning out her things. With her kin so far away I'd probably have to do it otherwise."

"That's fine with me," I say. "I'm sure it will be okay with Eva."

I don't tell her that I don't intend to clean out Eva's things right away but that I will live among them for a while, in flagrant violation of Eva's mother's instructions. I will wear her lavender paisley seventies dresses, burn her vanilla-scented votive candles and sage sticks, bathe with her chamomile bath oil, let her white cat wind around my ankles, write with her fountain pens, wash with her Body Shop soaps, cry into her pink, flowered pillowcases. I don't tell the squint-eyed landlady that I will smooth Eva's makeup over my own face. I hold the container of beef stew against my chest. I don't tell her that I don't eat meat.

I spend a couple of days sitting around Eva's apartment, reading the classifieds and trying to imagine going back to teaching, maybe at a community college. I'm completely out of touch with the academic scene. I don't know who's criticizing what these days. I had promised myself, when I finished grad school, that I'd keep up with that shit, but I've ended up reading the sports pages and Ann Landers a lot more than I thought I would.

After a while Eva's things start to annoy me, the incense ashes and the stickers all over the fridge: Get a Feel for Fur — Slam Your Hand in a Door, No Grapes, Practice

Random Acts of Kindness and Senseless Beauty. I decide to blow twenty bucks to hear Branford Marsalis play at Rockefeller's. I consider inviting someone, because that's what people do, right? You call a friend and invite them out to hear a band and you order drinks and talk and laugh. If it's a male friend you think about fucking each other, and maybe you do fuck, later. If the friend is a woman you talk about who you're both fucking, the irritating things they do, the size of their dicks. If you're gay or bisexual, I guess some of this is different, but the fucking is in there somewhere. I don't have time for the foolishness of the human experience right now. Jazz is music you pay attention to, and that's what I feel like doing.

On the way to the club I pass a little brown Nova with a bumper sticker that reads: Kiss Random Ass, You Sad and Senseless Hippie.

"Are you expecting anyone?" says the ticket taker who escorts me to a table at the edge of the balcony.

"No," I say.

"Mind if I take this?" He picks up the chair from the other side of my table.

"Not at all," I say. He moves it to an empty table at the opposite end of the balcony.

"Have a good time," he says when he passes by me again.

"I will," I say.

I order a gin and tonic when the waitress comes. I watch the people talking and checking each other out. The couple at the table next to me appears to be on a first date. They look at each other a lot. Their faces are not familiar to one another.

"I do yoga for the stretches," the woman is saying. "I don't get into the religious part of it, the vegetarian stuff."

"Is yoga vegetarian? I thought that was yogurt," the man says. I decide he's far too good for her.

"Yeah, I think yoga, well, I think if you really get into it you're not supposed to eat meat. I mean, yoga comes from India, right, and don't they have some kind of thing about cows?"

"They don't eat them," the man says.

"They keep them as pets," she says. "I heard they've got so many cows over there you can hardly walk down the streets. Every place you go is jammed with cows. They've got more cows than cars in India."

"They've got more cows than people in Vermont," he says.

"Really? I wouldn't want to live in Vermont then."

She keeps talking, nervously, even when Branford comes out and the lights dim.

"Shhh," her date says.

Branford Marsalis holding his tenor saxophone is the most beautiful man I've ever seen. He wears a dark suit and a tie that should be in the Museum of Modern Art. His face is sweet and boyish. His hands are full of talent. His mouth is strong with the wisdom of his sax. I love him purely; I am religious and he is a god. It's a trio tonight. They open with a hard-swinging blues, a burst of conversation between Branford, the bassist, and the drummer, like they haven't seen each other in a long time and have a lot to say.

"He looks different on the Leno show," the woman says.

"Listen to how the drummer varies his cymbal stroke in relation to the bass pulse," her date says. "Can you hear that?"

Above the foolish conversation happening all over the room, Branford begins the slow work of building his solo, developing one idea after another, elaborating on the themes handed to him by the bass and the drums. His smile at the end of the tune is a final, perfect note to the song.

"Did you notice how the drummer hardly uses the toms, just for coloring, really," the date says. The woman looks confused.

"Beautiful, really beautiful," she says.

The next song is "The Nearness of You," a spiritual, melodic ballad that could make me believe in love again, if I listened to it closely enough. Instead I listen to the people talking next to me.

"He really has the melodic diversity of a Charlie Parker," the date says.

"I was just thinking that," she says, toying with the straw in her drink. "I was just thinking about Charlie Parker."

The room is divided into people who are talking and people who are listening. I suppose the world is divided that way, too. I am a listener. When I become a talker, everything will be different.

At the set break, the female part of the date gets up to go to the ladies' room and returns with a fresh gloss of red on her lips.

"Miss me?" she says as she sits down.

I move my chair around so I can see her better. The man is younger than I imagined, perhaps even college age. He wears little round glasses. He is drinking something milky.

"Of course I missed you," he says. "What were you thinking about in the bathroom?"

"Charlie Parker," she says.

I feel a hand on my shoulder. From the strength of the grip, its slow, insistent pulse, I know before I look up that it's Black Jesus.

"Hey my baby," he says. His silver bracelet is cold against my bare shoulder.

"Hey Jesus."

He lets go of my shoulder and leans against the railing

by my chair. The woman with the newly red lips stills her chatter to stare at him.

"Excuse me," the male part of the date says, standing up. "Could I have your autograph?" He already has a pen and a little snatch of paper out.

"Sure," Black Jesus says. "What's your name?" He leans over their table to sign.

"Preston. I love *Solitaire Blues*, I mean, it's one of my favorite CDs. I play it all the time." The boy adjusts his glasses every few seconds.

"Thanks," Jesus says. "I appreciate that."

"Thank *you*," the boy says, sitting back down at the table. He passes the slip of paper to his date. She looks at it blankly and passes it back to him.

Jesus turns away from them and talks to me in his quietest voice.

"Why'd you leave like you did?" A strange blues starts pulsing in my ears.

"I was ready to go."

"What's that mean, Lacy, you was ready to go. All I know is I fell asleep next to you and woke up by myself. You lookin good," he says.

"Thanks."

"He really swings the eighth notes on that one," Preston says to his girl, still holding his autograph. He is trying hard not to look at Black Jesus.

My head fills with the clinking of glasses and the phrase *swing the eighth note*. I stare at Black Jesus's clothes. He wears a white silk shirt with a black linen jacket and black linen pants. I imagine how that white silk would feel against my skin, how quickly I could wrinkle that black linen suit. The volume cranks up on the blues in my head. *Don't make me do your laundry/ Don't make me cook your food/ Don't ask me to pretend that your friends ain't rude.*

"What are you doing in Houston?" I say.

"Came over with Marsalis," he says. "We known each other from back in our raisin up."

"He's really good," I say. "He's blessed."

"Brother can play," Jesus nods. "You want to meet him? I been hangin backstage but I came out to take a piss and saw you up here."

Yes yes yes yes yes I want to meet him.

"No, thanks," I say. I hope he will leave before I change my mind, before my willpower softens and I follow Black Jesus downstairs and past the guard and the cluster of hopeful women at the backstage door, before every woman in the club looks at me like, *What'd she do to deserve him,* before Black Jesus introduces me to the beautiful Branford Marsalis and I see his instrument resting in the open case, just to see it would be enough.

"Why not?" Jesus says. He leans easily against the rail, his hands in his pockets, his head thrown back. "You just said you dig the brother music."

I know he's getting angry by the way he said *brother* instead of *brother's.*

"Jesus," I say, trying to keep my voice low. "I just can't. I can't hang out with you anymore. I don't want to see you anymore."

"You didn't have no problems with me the last time you saw me. You seemed real damn happy, if I'm rememberin right."

"I shouldn't have gone there. I shouldn't have gone to Louisiana. I need to move on, you know?"

"We ain't in Louisiana now."

"No, we're not."

"You don't want to be in a relationship, that it?"

"I don't want to be with someone who hits women and shoots dogs, I guess that's it."

He puts his hand on the edge of my table and leans

down until his mouth is almost over my ear. I can feel his breath in my ear, and if he started kissing it, gently, I might take back everything I just said.

"I don't want to be with a fuckin ho," he whispers, then walks away.

Don't be callin me a bitch/ Don't tell me I'm a ho/ What I am is a woman who don't want you anymore/ What I am is a woman who don't want your ass no more.

I stare at my hands, white and ringless in my lap. I know when I look up, everyone on the balcony will be watching me. If I look over the railing, I will see Black Jesus inviting one of the stray women near the stage door to go back with him. I know I have said what I needed to say. I know if I wait long enough, Branford Marsalis will walk out and begin to play his sax. The sounds of his jazz will scatter all of this foolishness to the far corners of the club and I will be a listener again, pure, intent, holy with expectation of the melody to come.

STOP

Sometimes I miss Ellis, and sometimes I get ecstatic over sleeping diagonally across the bed. We haven't spoken since I left. I spend a lot of time driving my Cutlass around the Houston freeways: Hwy. 59 with its sad terrain of potholes and run-down apartments fronted by billboards that say, "If You Lived Here, You'd Be Home by Now," and 610, the wonderful loop that circles the core of the city, that gives us all a reference point, a boundary. You live either inside the loop or outside the loop. I don't often go outside the loop. But when I drive around it, making the whole circle two or three times in an evening, I love to watch the outer-loop sprawl racing by, the strip malls and the Astrodome with its oppressive air conditioning, the discount liquor stores and the occasional police cars that are the same pale blue as the Houston Oilers' uniforms. Is there a connection? *Everything is connected,* Eva tells me as I speed past the Galleria. Tears run into the collar of my T-shirt. *Everything is tacky as Florida, everything is honest and elegant.*

Between making these ritual loops around the city, I start teaching a class for illiterate adults as part of my community service hours, and I put a notice on the appropriate university bulletin boards offering my services as a tutor. All this gas is costing me.

The first night I meet with my illiterate adults, I'm amazed at how they stay in their seats. They don't throw things at each other. Who gives a damn if they can't read — they are in control of their own bodies and voices. I love them all — the men still in their work clothes darkened with grease, the women with proud faces who have somehow raised children and earned paychecks and gone grocery shopping without knowing how to read the labels of the food they bought for their families. They can all read one word, though: STOP. And maybe instead of having signs all over the streets of America that say "Stop," we should locate some taxpayer dollars to install signs with more inspirational words: "Joy," perhaps. If everyone in the country is going to know how to read one word, and one word only, shouldn't it be something more interesting than "Stop"?

Our class meets in an old church on lower Montrose, across from a Stop 'n Go. We decide that the last ten minutes of every class we'll all hang out on the balcony and practice reading people's T-shirts. Oilers shirts don't count. The first night a man stands out in front of the store like a sacrifice to our class. He wears black cowboy boots with real spurs, black jeans with black leather chaps strapped over them, although it's at least a hundred degrees out. His belt is fake barbed wire wrapped loosely three times around his waist, and he stands in front of the store looking up at us like he's ready for a shoot-out.

"Tell me what the letters are," I say to the man standing next to me, the man who confessed at the beginning of the class that he's been buying a newspaper and pretending to read it every morning for ten years, because he didn't want his wife to know he couldn't read.

"*Chronicle* or *Post?*" someone asked him.

"I don't know," he said.

Now he spells out the letters of the man's shirt, everything except "W," and we slowly put them together. By the time we remember the sounds of each letter and merge them all together into words, another man comes out of the store with a jumbo-size soft drink and a pack of Marlboros, and he and the man with the "Queer Cowboy" shirt start up their truck and drive away.

Some weeks it's raining and no one stays outside long enough for us to look at their shirts, but throughout the long summer and fall, my adult illiterates gradually learn to read. During their in-class presentations they read Dear Abby, they chronicle the devastating last-minute losses of the Oilers, they howl over books of Aggie jokes. One day Marilyn Taylor reads from a review of Black Jesus's new album: "Black Jesus fans will undoubtedly be pleased with the gritty, ambitious vocals and soul-searing guitar of the Louisiana legend's second album, *Straight Edge Blues*. An excellent follow-up to the seminal *Solitaire Blues*, *Straight Edge Blues* is likely to confirm Black Jesus's position as the premiere spokesman for his generation of bluesmen, and as one of the most innovative southern bluesmen we've seen."

"Oh, he's so fine," Marilyn sighs.

"Does it say that?" someone asks.

"No," Marilyn says. "It's my personal commentary."

"Very good, Marilyn," I say. "Nice, smooth reading. You didn't stumble once. I'm proud of you," and I'm thinking of the CD Jesus sent me with his autograph that said, "I think of you every time I sing 'Storebought Bread.' " And I think of him every time someone mentions domestic violence.

Our last class before Christmas we go on a field trip to

Brentano's bookstore so everyone can pick out a book. I'm using the Christmas money I would have spent on Mama and Irene, had Mama not shot my best friend and had Irene not been mean and spiteful to me my whole life.

"I've never been in a bookstore before," Marilyn whispers reverently as we walk through the electric doors.

"Well you lucky thing," I tease her. "Have fun," and I watch her head straight for the Music Personalities section. I decide to check out the fiction. Halfway down the aisle is Ellis's book, *Nothing to See Here, Move Along.* I had no idea he'd sold it. I pull it out slowly and look at his picture on the back cover. It's a shot I took of him out in the Guads. He has a great tan. His glasses are a little bent, and behind him the wall of West Dog Canyon rises violently. The front cover is a painting of Faith, clothed only in her mosaic of tattoos. I see a few I don't recognize from the book. I want to read the last page to see how it ends, but I resist the temptation and turn instead to the beginning. The first page reads:

FOR LACY

give entirely each Forever its freedom
e. e. cummings

I remember reading Ellis a lot of Cummings, on the same Spring Break trip to the Guads when I took the photograph. I didn't think he was paying a bit of attention, but I think Ellis secretly pays attention to about everything I do and say. And I think that by putting that in the front of his book he was wanting to tell me that he understands something about me, maybe why I have a hard time promising anything forever or even for a little while. Standing in the brightly lit bookstore waiting for my eleven semi-illiterate students to pick out the first books they will ever own, I hug my ex-husband's novel to my chest and feel his love and forgiveness flooding over me. I can't wait to read it to see what happens to Faith. I can't wait to see what happens to me.

YOU'RE SO BEAUTIFUL
AND I CAN'T WAIT TO BE
WITH YOU LATER

Dear Ellis,

I saw your book at Brentano's the other day, and of course I bought it and started reading it right away. I like the changes you've made since the draft I read in jail, particularly the mayonnaise scene and the part about Faith's encounter with the Catholic lesbian. Are Catholics allowed to do that? And how do you know all that stuff about women doing it with women? Have you been renting lesbian porno movies?

I also like the Eva-type character. See, Ellis, as much as you criticized and ridiculed Eva, you got something out of her — and I think you should admit that if she's interesting enough to be a character in your novel, she can't be all bad. And don't go trying to tell me that character isn't based on Eva, because how many shrinks do you know who run around Houston with New York accents and big turbans on their heads?

Anyway, I think your book is wonderful so far, and I will let you know when I am finished with it. Maybe you could autograph it for me sometime, ha ha. I'm reading it slowly, the same way I tried to eat that box of Godiva chocolate you gave me that Valentine's Day before you went to Mexico to do research. I ate one piece every night after dinner, wasn't I good? Every night for three weeks, the chocolate on my tongue reminded me that you loved me. That was nice. So I'm reading the book bit by bit, the way I should have gotten to know you when we first met, instead of rushing into love like I did. The first time we kissed and you said, "You have a beautiful body," I should have kissed you one more time and walked away. Then I would have come back another day to kiss you some more. Bit by bit. Lips, then tongue. Then maybe some teeth. Instead I said, "You want to see all of it?" and that was that. I have always done things too fast. I need to taste everything slowly, the way I tasted that Godiva chocolate. But that is not what I wanted to write you about. I'm writing because I'm upset about some of the things you put in your book. In the last draft I read, Faith's lover was a Hispanic man, a flamenco musician. Now I see you've gone and changed him to a black man, and a blues musician. Really, Ellis! Do you think you could be a little more obvious? The Hispanic lover was just fine. I suppose you thought I wouldn't mind your writing something like, "Faith had had as many lovers as she had tattoos, and of as many different colors and types. She was hardly present when she fucked them; she became a colorful shell, an engraved tapestry of skin with her soul rattling around inside like a broken toy." First of all, I think you're overdoing it on the metaphors. Also, you make me sound like I've fucked every nationality in the United Nations. And don't try to tell me you're not writing about me — just because you disguise Faith with all those tattoos doesn't mean I can't recognize what you're doing. And how dare you compare my soul to a broken toy? Fuck you, Ellis. I've never insulted your soul like that. I know I wasn't always present when we fucked, but it's not because I've had so many lovers that my soul somehow got broken or erased. It's because I learned to leave my body when Donny fucked me as a child, and it's a hard habit to break. I *want* to be in my body, Ellis. I want to feel every cell of it. I do have a soul, you know, and I hope you will clarify that point if you write a sequel. I am not the whore you think I am. Whores fuck for money. I fuck for fun, and when I'm fortunate, for love. Maybe you think I've fucked too much, but I've been trying to get it right, you know. I think I got it right with you a few times, as you may or may not recall. I think it was right the time we drove to that restaurant way out in the country — can you remember the name of it? — and we had the upstairs table that looked out over a field of bluebonnets. And you leaned across your plate of salmon and whispered in my ear, "You're so beautiful and I can't wait to be with you later." I couldn't eat much after that. You were wearing that wonderful linen shirt that's the color of coffee with an obscene amount of cream, and white linen pants. I adore you in linen. On the way home I asked you to pull over so I could look at the stars, and you held me in your arms while we leaned against the Cutlass and watched the sky. I saw a falling star and made a wish. I didn't tell you what I wished for. I don't think I'll tell you now, either. Then you kneeled in the grass on the side of that country road, lifted my blue silk skirt and pressed your face against my sex. You breathed me in, softly at first, like you'd sniff a good wine before you tell the waiter it will do. Then you took a deep, long breath like I was something you hadn't smelled in a good while, like I was the ocean and you'd been living in the desert. Then you tilted your face upward, your tongue found my center, and I came against your lips. Your face smelled like me afterward, when you stood up and held me some more.

Maybe you could put something like that in your sequel,

instead of making me out to be such a heartless slut. Whatever the case, I want you to know that I certainly have not
had as many lovers as Faith has tattoos. I don't see how
you would know, anyway. If you've been talking to Irene,
she doesn't know anything. By the way, thanks for dedicat-
ing the book to me. It made me very happy when I saw it,
and even later when I got mad over the part about the
black lover, I still felt a little pleased. I'm sorry I was unfaithful to you, Ellis. I've been so much more unfaithful to
myself.

I had a boyfriend in high school who was a musician,
and I used to run all over Dallas to hear him play. I always
hoped he would dedicate a song to me, and I spent huge
chunks of time imagining how the dedication would go.
"This song is for someone I love so much," he might have
said. Or, "I'd like to dedicate this song to someone very
special," or even a simple, "This is for Lacy." I envisioned
his hands resting gently on his red Les Paul guitar while
he spoke the tender words of the dedication. I imagined
how, when he started playing, I would know each note was
meant for me. He never said anything about me, though.
He played his gigs and packed up his equipment like it was
just a job, which I think is why he's a music producer now
instead of a musician. I didn't know then that you can't
dedicate a job to someone. You can only dedicate something
that comes out of your heart. I know your book came out
of your heart, and I'm thankful that you thought of me. If
you ever get famous enough to go on Oprah, can I come
with you? I would just love to meet Oprah. And don't forget
about possibly meeting me on McKittrick Ridge. Maybe
we'll see some falling stars out there. I just can't stand to
think about all the stars that fall without my seeing them,
so many wishes unmade.

Lacy

GRACE PERIOD

"Lacy," Mama says over the phone, "I'm just calling to let you know that you're out of my will. My attorneys will be sending you a waiver to sign. Please do it and don't put up a fuss. I don't want my estate bogged down with lawsuits when I'm gone. Those goddamn estate taxes are bad enough."

"Fine, Mama," I say. "Anything else?" I'm stirring a big pot of gumbo with one hand, holding the phone up with the other.

"All those good Scudder stocks. The Memphis Housing Authority bonds — of course they don't yield that much but they're steady — and all that wonderful AT&T stock your father had the foresight to buy. And the house — did you know I bought this house for thirty thousand dollars? And Caralee McKee, she's made God only knows how much money selling with Prudential, she says she could sell it tomorrow for half a million. Oh hush, sugar," she says to her dog. "There, Mama will give her baby a treat. Irene's getting everything. And my jewelry, too. Don't go thinking you'll get my diamond dinner ring, because it's on your sister's finger this very minute."

"Mama, I don't want your diamond dinner ring. You've been an abusive bitch to me my whole life, and as far as I'm concerned your ring could only bring me bad luck. Please don't call me again."

Perfect, Eva says.

"Your father's going to hear about this, young lady. I'm going to contact him in the afterworld as soon as we hang up and tell him to make sure you get leprosy. Everything will fall off, Lacy. You'll have nothing left but your bones, and you won't be able to find a thing that will fit you properly. Not even petites!"

"I'll manage, Mama. Goodbye."

I hang up the phone and turn the ringer off. As I stir the slippery okra into my gumbo and watch its greens brighten, I wonder what my father would think of me. I'm not like Mama and I'm not like Irene, so I must be something like Daddy. I wonder if he'd be proud of me, if he'd like it that I've taught some people how to read. I think he liked to read. I think he was romantic. Once Mama and Irene and I watched the old version of *Wuthering Heights* on TV. We had all the lights off and we couldn't see each other's faces so I let myself go and cried at all the sad parts. And when Cathy is desperate with sorrow and says to Nellie, "If I were in heaven, Nellie, I should be extremely miserable," because she would rather be on earth with Heathcliff, Mama burst out laughing and said, "Your father loved this part. He was such a sap," and she and Irene made fun of the whole movie after that and said the scenery looked fake. I wonder about my father's supposed sappiness, I wonder what kind of person he would have been, if he had lived. He could have been any number of awful things: a sexual harasser, a used-car salesman, an avid fan of pornography, a ditto-head, a tongue-speaking Jesus freak, a racist, a child beater, an eater of pork rinds. But I imagine he was something like me, trapped in Mama's web of horror, and, unlike me, he didn't have growing up to look forward to. He could not say, as I could, *I will turn eighteen and go to college and Mama will be miles away from me, miles and miles and miles.* He could not stretch out that distance before him as I could, unfurling it in my mind like a satin hair ribbon you wear only on your birthday.

If my father and I can ever manage to be alive at the same time again, I'd like to tell him about all the things Eva has taught me: how to stand up for myself, how to speak my truth and look people in the eye while I'm doing it, how to scream out my anger in the privacy of my own home so I won't get cancer, and how to be in relationship with women — that there are many women in this world who are not Mama or Irene. I'd like to tell him about the things Ellis taught me: how to blacken catfish, that a deep, patient love layered over friendship is better than doing it standing up in the back of a nightclub with cigarette butts all around your feet, that when you're hiking up a steep trail, keep your center of gravity over your feet and remember that you have a fraction of a second of friction everywhere you step, a grace period in which to get to the next step before you fall. I'd like to ask my daddy what it was in Mama that made him love her, and maybe I could think back over the years and find a glimmer of that thing. But I'm not fooling myself. I know who my mother is. I know I have to rebuild my idea of the feminine from women who are strong and kind, like Eva and Vaughan Sharp as I imagine her in her big hat with her hair stuffed up in it, women who are something I want to be.

SOMEONE OUT THERE
GOT THE BLUES

When I've calmed down from Mama saying she's disowned me, I walk downstairs to get my mail. Among the bills and catalogs is an envelope from Karl. In it is an interview with Black Jesus from the New Orleans paper entitled "Hometown Star Brings New Life to Blues." At the top of the page Karl has written in neat, square letters: "Just lookin' out for you. Karl."

One of the most exciting developments in the blues world today is the increasing number of young African American artists dedicated to honoring the blues idiom while incorporating into its traditional themes the salient issues of our times: unwed mothers, drive-by shootings, substance abuse, and related problems typical of American urban decay. On the forefront of this movement is twenty-eight-year-old New Orleans native Black Jesus, whose unique brand of blues is drawing praise from all sectors of the music industry. Last weekend Black Jesus and the Down Brothers thrilled the hometown crowd at Tipitina's, and

Black Jesus took a few moments after his set to give the following interview.

TP: Industry-watchers are saying your music will set a high-water mark for future generations of blues artists. How do you feel about this kind of attention, and who were your influences?

BJ: Well, first of all, I don't feel like I'm getting any more attention than I've ever gotten. Maybe people are saying this or that about me, but it don't feel different to me. If people are listening to my music and it's speaking to them in some way, then I'm doing what I set out to do. Making the connection. Getting the feeling of the blues across to my audience. Maybe when the royalty checks start coming in, I'll feel different {laughs}. But like tonight, playing to a full house at Tip's don't feel much different from when I used to sit on my mama's front steps and mess around with my brothers, just picking out tunes. I probably sound a lot better now, but you know, the feeling is the same. Making music. As far as my influences, about every one of my kin when I was coming up was some kind of influence. Everyone in my family except my mama either played the blues or listened to blues and appreciated it. All kinds, too, country blues, urban blues. My mama was a religious woman, thought the blues was nothing but the devil speaking. She'd say to me, "You quit trying to be B. B. King and sing something for the Lord!" I didn't want to be B. B. King, although I got nothing but respect for B.B. and his music. I wanted to play my own music my own way and I couldn't find nothing sinful about that.

TP: Part of what's attracted so much attention to your style is your ability to talk about modern-day problems

using traditional blues rhythms, yet your sets also include such standbys as Robert Johnson's "Come On In
My Kitchen." Do you feel torn between the old and new?

BJ: No, I don't feel torn. The old blues singers sang about
what they knew: plantations, growing cotton, plowing
mules and all that. I got some of that stuff from the
older folks in my family telling me about it, but cows,
corn, and mules are not part of my own experience. I
grew up in New Orleans. My daddy lives out in the
country now, but he doesn't have cows or mules, and he
does not grow cotton. I don't have any plantation boss
making me plow his fields, but I know what it feels like
to walk into a restaurant in New Orleans, and I won't
say which ones, and have the waiters look at me like
I'm gonna hold up the place. Some of the things them
old guys were singing about weren't so different. We
don't have slavery anymore, but people still can't get
together, still can't see past black and white, rich and
poor. If you can get the feeling of the blues, you can get
past some of those lines we draw between ourselves.
When I sing an old tune like a Robert Johnson, or a
Lightnin' Hopkins, I'm just giving what's due, I'm saying I know I ain't the first person to sing the blues, a
lot of people done it before me.

TP: Yet "Storebought Bread," perhaps the most widely
played cut off your new album, is anything but urban.

BJ: Yeah it is urban, in a way. It's about a man falling
for a woman who bakes her own bread, and that's something most women don't have time to do nowadays cause
they got to be working jobs and working at home, cleaning, taking the kids here and there. It's about a woman
who still has a lot of country ways about her, and that's

something a man don't run across every day. When's the last time you made a loaf of bread with your own two hands?

TP: I have a bread machine.

BJ: Yeah, well.

TP: Have you had any formal musical training?

BJ: Didn't need it with my family. My grandmama taught me most of what I know by putting my fingers on the right spot on the guitar and saying, that's it. Do it that way. She taught me to play by ear. Now it's hard for a child to really get the feeling of the blues because when you're just a child you ain't been through much. You don't learn how much something can hurt till later on. But I heard this kind of pain and sadness in the songs my grandmama and my daddy and uncles used to sing, so when it came along in my own life it was like, yeah, I know that.

TP: You seem to be riding on top of the world right now. Your second CD is selling well, you've become a sort of hometown hero in New Orleans, and I understand you have a wedding planned this fall. With things going so smoothly, is it hard to tap into that "low-down" feeling you describe as essential to a blues artist?

BJ: No, because no matter how happy I am or how well my music may be going, I can't forget about the people all over the place who are on hard times, hungry people, people with no homes, brothers who can't get out of the inner cities, can't get clean. Don't need white people to kill us anymore, we're doing a pretty good job killing each other with crack and guns. No matter how happy you or I might be, there's always someone out there got the blues, and got it bad. I don't have to look too far to find something to sing the blues about.

I stare at the line that reads "I understand you have a wedding planned." I wonder if the interviewer really understands. I wonder if Jocelyn will wear white, how long it has been since Jesus last hit her, what kind of music they'll have at the wedding. I wonder how Black Jesus can seem so thoughtful, so humble, so concerned about the homeless, the hungry, the state of America's inner cities. I wonder why he didn't say motherfucker fifty times, how he could talk so long without a pulse of anger tinting his voice. I try to remember how I thought about him before I met him, when I knew only his music, and I guess it was something like nice young black man using music to examine race and gender issues. I tear Karl's address off the envelope, tuck it into my address book, and toss the rest into the trash.

DAMN, YOU ARE
STRANGE

I forget about Mama disowning me until I sit down to pay my rent and utilities and realize how broke I am. Not that inheriting money years from now would help with my immediate bills, but it's all related somehow. I love my work teaching adults to read, but I'm going to have to find something that pays good American dollars pretty soon.

I shove the bills back in the desk drawer, grab my purse, and drive aimlessly around the city for a while, wasting valuable resources with my big, gas-sucking car. I drive around downtown and watch the people hurrying in and out of buildings in their nice work clothes. I hope their professional hair, their scuffed briefcases, and the cut of their business suits will inspire me. It doesn't. When I've had enough of that I drive by Rockefeller's to see what bands are playing. I'm such a slacker these days. I try to keep driving past the Rockefeller's marquee that reads "Black Jesus and the Down Brothers, Fri-Sat," but instead I pull into the first parking place I see and sit in the hot car for a minute.

"You can't go," I tell myself, out loud. "You absolutely cannot go."

I walk inside the dark lobby and wait for the boy in the ticket booth to notice me. His short, black hair is spiky and stiff. His face is unnaturally pale.

"Yeah?" he says.

"The Black Jesus shows are sold out, right?"

"Definitely," he says. "Been sold out for days. I got the Derailers, I got Stanley Jordan, I got Ani Difranco, I got Buddy Guy. Black Jesus I do not got."

"Okay," I say. "Thanks anyway."

"Definitely," he says.

I drive to the ice house on White Oak where Taylor Robbins, one of my students, works as a bartender. The ice house is empty except for an old man playing solitaire at a wooden table. He lays the cards down slowly, snapping them against the table with a small, satisfying sound. Taylor's watching the old man, too, but he looks up when I sit down at the bar.

"Miss Springs!" he says. "I'm sorry I wasn't at class last week. It's like this, see — my wife had this baby shower she had to go to for a lady at her work, and the kid had some kinda thing at school, and we only got the one car right now cause —"

"Don't worry about it," I say. "You think I'm chasing you down because you missed class?"

"I guess not," he says, smiling. He has bright blue eyes and violently crooked teeth. "What can I do for you?"

"You told me one time that you make a few bucks here and there selling tickets to otherwise sold-out events," I say.

"I told you that?"

"You did."

"What otherwise sold-out event would you be wanting to attend?" he says, offering me a Shiner.

"Thanks," I say. "Black Jesus and the Down Brothers. Friday night at Rockefeller's."

"That's right, I knew you were a blues fan," he says.

"I am."

"I can help you out," he says. "You stay right here."

I watch him walk out to his car and open the trunk. He comes back holding a thick envelope.

"Two?" he says, ducking back behind the bar.

"Just one."

He raises his eyebrows slightly. I ignore his look, but I wonder for the millionth time what is so damn weird about going places alone? If we all liked ourselves alone, maybe we'd like each other a little better when we get together. He hands me one ticket.

"How much?" I say.

"It's on the house, lady."

"Oh no," I say. "At least let me pay you what it cost you."

"Listen," he says. "if it weren't for you I'd still be asking my kid to read those tickets for me. He's in the third grade, can read like I don't know what. I wouldn't know if that said Black Jesus or the goddamn Houston Ballet if it weren't for you."

"It's not me," I say. "It's you. Anyone could have taught you to read. You had to make the decision to do it."

"I don't know about that," he says. "but you have yourself a good time Friday night. Sure you don't want another ticket?"

"Yeah," I say. "I'm sure. Listen, thanks a lot for the ticket, Taylor. I'm kind of broke right now."

"See you in class," he says.

I glance at the old man's game of solitaire as I pass him. I can't tell if he's winning or losing, but the shiny cards look cool and clean on the battered wooden table.

I drive home and try to call Eva at the hospital in New

York so she can talk me out of going to the show. I heard from Dr. Troy, Eva's dissertation adviser, that she regained consciousness, just opened her eyes one day and said, "Yes, please." According to Dr. Troy, Eva is expected to recover fully, with all her faculties intact. I've been waiting to call her. Waiting for what, I'm not sure.

A nurse answers the phone in Eva's hospital room. "Are you family?" she asks.

"No," I say. "But I'm sure she'll want to talk to me."

"She's still very weak," the nurse says. "She's not taking phone calls yet. If you want to call back during visiting hours, you can talk to someone in the family."

"That's okay," I say.

I hang up and stare at my precious ticket to Black Jesus's show. I slip it in the medicine cabinet behind a bottle of multivitamins and tell myself I might or might not use it. I promise myself I'll spend every minute between now and the time when I might or might not use this ticket working on my résumé. It's the most responsible thing I can think up to do.

By Friday afternoon, my résumé is perfect. Someone, I don't know who, will freak out when they see it and hire me immediately. I decide that I'm only going to Black Jesus's show to hear some blues. No fucking. I'm a music fan, right? I shouldn't miss hearing a musician I like just because he's a woman-beating animal killer. I decide that I will wear a disguise, something so hideous that Black Jesus will never recognize me. Eva's closet is full of weird clothes I'm supposed to be packing up and sending to her mother. I pick out a horribly ugly dress, a purple contraption splattered with yellow daisies. Its long bell sleeves dangle past my wrists. The buttons are the size of silver dollars. I find a length of purple silk and try to make a turban around my head, but I can't keep all my hair in it. How did Eva do it? Finally I twist my hair into a long braid and tie the cloth around my head so that the excess material hides most of the braid. I find a huge pair of sunglasses that change color with the light, like a mood ring. I look like a fortune teller, or like someone who might kidnap your child and sell its internal organs.

When I walk into the dark club I can hardly see a thing through the sunglasses, but I leave them on anyway. The ticket taker directs me upstairs to a seat by the soundboard. The club is filling up quickly with excited white women and their bored boyfriends. I don't see anyone from the band, but after a while I notice Jocelyn walking out from the backstage door and up to the bar. She's wearing a wonderful thing: a red and black sequined pillbox hat, a red silk tank top and black silk pants that are baggy until a few inches above the ankle, then all of sudden get very tight around the ankles with a band of red and black sequins that match her hat. I feel ugly in my seventies disguise. I watch Jocelyn order a drink. A lot of people are looking at her — she's pretty damn beautiful and she's one of only a few black women in the club. I wish I could go say something nice to her, I can't think what. She returns to the back with her drink and after a while the band comes out and plays an instrumental without Black Jesus. That's something new. He comes out for the second song, and the crowd gives him a standing ovation before he even opens his mouth or picks his guitar up from its stand.

"I love you, Jesus!" a woman with poodle hair near the front yells. She jumps up and down, waving, in case he didn't hear her.

I've never seen a crowd so fervent about him. I want to quiet them, to yell over the balcony, "Shut up! His ego is huge already! You'll ruin him!" Black Jesus nods, grabs the mike like he's snatching it away from someone, and starts into "Storebought Bread." He sings a slower, more teasingly powerful version than the one I'm used to. He makes bread sound like a very sexy thing. I feel shaky hearing Jesus's voice. Everything about him is slightly different. His shoes are new. His guitar looks shinier. He stands a little closer to Henry John instead of exactly in the center, where he usually stays. He seems so sincere about what he's playing, he lets his guitar hang on the strap and his mouth searches the length of his harmonica, like if he could find exactly the right spot, he could blow his sorrows on out. The band falls into a groove right behind him. I wonder if they have always been this good, or if I've been too busy thinking about Black Jesus to listen to their playing. I've always thought Wells, the drummer, was the weak link in the band, not Marcy like some people think, Black Jesus included. Usually Wells sits back there behind his drums like he's glad to be sitting down, like the drum set's in his way somehow and if it weren't there he could put his feet up and really relax. He spends most of the time scanning the audience, looking for women he might want to fuck. But tonight he's different, and he even keeps his eyes on Marcy during his bass solos. Something has changed in Wells and I'm glad, even though I never got to know him much and he probably thinks of me only as something that took up space in their touring van. The funny thing is, when Wells used to spend the whole set checking out the women in the audience, they never paid much attention to him. I mean, he always got *someone*, because he's a musician, after all, but he got the leftovers — the women who really wanted to fuck Black Jesus or Marcy but settled for Wells instead. But tonight, when he's tending to his drums like *they're* his lover, when he's listening more closely to Marcy's bass lines than to the ladies squealing in the front row, I notice all kinds of women watching Wells. I get up to go to the ladies' room during "Cadillac Assembly Line," but I stop halfway down the stairs to listen to Wells's drum solo. Another woman coming up the stairs is doing the same thing. We look at each other when the solo is over and smile. She leans toward me so I can hear her over the music.

"Have you ever had a drummer?" she says. "They can do, like, five things at once."

"No," I say, laughing. "I haven't."

My reflection in the bathroom mirror scares me. The lenses of my sunglasses change from cherry red to rose under the bright track lighting. The woman in line ahead of me wears sunglasses, too. I wonder who she's hiding from.

"It's really bright in here, isn't it?" she says.

"Yeah," I say. "It's way too bright."

As I walk back to my seat, Black Jesus's guitar sounds so sweet I have to remind myself that making good music doesn't mean you're a good person. Musicians are great fakers, better than I would have imagined. A few minutes after I sit down again, Jesus leans into the mike and says in his sexiest voice, "We gonna take a short break, so y'all just stay where you are and we'll be right back with you." I relax behind the safety of my costume and watch everything changing color through the sunglasses. I see Karl coming up the stairs to talk to the sound man, and he gives me a smile.

"Jesus says he can't hear nothin off his front monitor," he says to the sound guy.

"I'm working on it," the sound man says.

I look the other way and I hope Karl will go back downstairs without recognizing me. Instead he taps me on the shoulder and says, "Excuse me. Can I buy you a drink?"

"No, thanks," I say.

"I don't mean no harm," he says. "I just noticed your glass was empty and we got a pretty good tab here and I just thought —"

Suddenly I miss Karl and how sweet he was to me, so I say, "Sure, okay, I'd love a gin and tonic. But only if you'll have one with me."

"Done," he says, although I know for a fact that he does not like gin.

He walks downstairs and comes back up after a few minutes with two drinks.

"Thanks," I say.

"You like blues?" he says, and I start laughing. I make my laugh harsher than the one of mine that Karl knows.

"I wouldn't be here if I didn't," I say. "You think there's anyone in this room doesn't like the blues some?"

"Maybe," he says, and I know what he's thinking — that there are always a few women at every gig, or maybe more than a few, who don't give a damn about the music, who come to look at Black Jesus with his fine ass and his long hair and his hands that can play a woman's body so as to coax a song out of it. "What's your name?" he says.

"Rose," I say. "Do you work with the band?"

"Yeah, I'm their road manager," he tells me. "Right now I'm tryin to get everyone ready for our European tour."

"Really?" I say, although I don't believe for one minute that they're going to Europe.

"That's right," he says. "France, Spain, Italy . . . all over the place. Then after that we got a tour of Asia."

This seems particularly bizarre, because Black Jesus is so prejudiced against the Asian races I don't think he could play a show over there with a straight face. But I guess it's true what they say — that money can buy anything. Or is it that money can't buy everything?

"I hear they eat dogs," I tell him.

"What the hell?" he says. Karl is such a dog person. I wish I could tell him how sorry I am about Sophie.

"They eat dogs just like we eat chicken," I say. "Fried, sautéed, baked, shredded up in soup. You can get dog burgers, dog enchiladas, refried puppy. I'm sure you'll love it."

"Yeah, well, I'll have to talk to our agent about that. I ain't about to eat no dog, I'll tell you what."

"Oh, you can't avoid it," I say. "They put dog in everything. They use dog like we use salt. When they had the Olympics in Seoul, you know? They moved all the dog markets off the main streets because of the press and all, but they're right back out in the open, now. You just wait and see."

"Girl, you givin me a stomachache," he says.

"So, what's it like working with Black Jesus?" I ask.

"It's work."

"Is he cool, though? I mean, are you friends?"

"I known Jesus all my life. We came up together in New Orleans. You ain't friends with people like that — you family. You don't think about bein friends."

"Who are his friends, then?"

"Oh, he got people all over the country he'd probably call his friends. But we in one place one day, one place the next. You can't get too close with nobody. Anybody want to hang with Jesus got to go on tour with him, follow him around like a puppy."

"Is there anybody who does that?"

"Nah. He had a woman for a while followed us around some, a good woman if you ask me. But she was a white woman and Jesus don't never get too close with white women."

"Why not?" I say. "I thought he was so into improving race relations. That's what his songs seem to say."

"That's just business, girl. Just business."

"Do you?" I ask.

"Do I what?"

"Ever get close with a white woman."

"Girl, you a reporter or somethin? What you want to know all this stuff for?"

"Just passing the time," I say.

"So, what do you do in town?" he says.

"I'm a fortune teller."

"Yeah? You kinda got the look, you know."

I see Jesus walk out the backstage door and wave at Karl to come down.

"What's he want?" I say.

"I gotta get to work," Karl says. "Probably wants me to sign some posters for him."

"He doesn't sign his own autographs?"

"Nobody does, girl. Could I come back up and sit with you after the set starts?"

"Sure," I tell him.

"You want to come down with me? You want to meet Jesus and the band?"

"No," I say. "You go on."

I wonder if Elvis signed his own autographs. Probably not.

The woman who asked me if I've ever had a drummer squeezes her way to the front row for the start of the second set. She stands up on her toes so Wells can see her from behind his drums. Karl comes back up and sits next to me after the first song of the set, but we don't talk much because the music is so loud. After the show he says, "I gotta break down the equipment, but after that you want to do somethin? You want to come have somethin to eat that ain't dog?"

"Well, I don't know," I say. "I'm kinda craving Labrador."

"Get outta here, girl," he says. "We got someone bringin some Cajun food over to the hotel, be better than the best damn dog in China."

"Okay," I say.

I wait around while Karl gets everything packed up and then I follow the van to their hotel. I feel terrible all dressed up in a lie. I'm afraid it will cancel out all the times I've been honest. I almost turn around to drive back to my place, but soon I'm handing my keys to the valet at the Ritz Carlton, which means the new album must be selling like crazy because we never stayed anywhere nearly that nice when I was hanging around with Jesus.

"Nice digs," I say to Karl as we walk through the lobby.

"Yeah, we don't usually have it this good. I don't know what got into Jesus this time. You want to meet him?"

"Sure," I say.

We go into Jesus's suite, which has a nice sitting area with shelves and some leather-bound books that might or might not be fake. Karl introduces me to everyone, Jesus and Jocelyn, Marcy, Bill, Wells and Henry John.

"Y'all this is Rose," he says.

"I like your headpiece," Jocelyn says of my purple turban, "but isn't it hot?"

"Oh no," I say. "It's very comfortable." I notice her engagement ring, a solitaire diamond in a distressed gold band.

"What a beautiful ring," I say. She holds her hand out so I can look at it more closely.

"I'm still not used to it," she says.

Jesus doesn't even look at me. He's sorting the seeds from a bag of pot.

A delivery boy brings a raft of food from Ragin Cajun, a restaurant Ellis and I used to go to after the Astros games sometimes. We all start stuffing ourselves with crawfish and boiled shrimp and fried oysters, and it's just like it used to be, everyone talking at once. Karl tries to smooth over the rough moments, Jocelyn sits there in her sequined get-up smoking cigarettes, Bill and Wells talk about all the women they could have had if they wanted, Henry John stares at the television without saying a word, and a violent tension stretches underneath everything Marcy and Black

Jesus say to each other. Excessive talk about Michael Jordan.

"I'm sick of hearin y'all talk about Jordan," Jocelyn says, lighting a new cigarette. "Don't you hate that?" she says, looking at me. "Jordan this, Jordan that, I don't give a damn how many points Michael Jordan scores, what kind of shoes he wears, what he eats, drinks, says, when he takes a piss and how many dollars he makes every minute. Y'all wish you was him but you ain't so get used to it."

"Yeah," I say. "It gets old."

"Get your own room, bitch, if you don't like the conversation," Black Jesus says to Jocelyn.

"Maybe I will," she says. "Maybe I'll find me a man can talk for more than ten minutes without havin to bring up Michael Fuckin Jordan."

"Good luck," Marcy says.

After a while Jesus says, "Y'all get on outta here, now. I gotta get me some sleep before we get on the road again," so everyone except Jocelyn leaves and goes to their own rooms and I go to Karl's.

As soon as we're in the door Karl starts rubbing on my shoulders. He's standing behind me saying all kinds of foolish things, such as, "I'd like to see what you got, baby." Then he leans down and starts kissing my neck. I pull the piece of purple silk off my head and yank the elastic off the end of my braid and let my hair start to uncoil. He can see some of it out of the corner of his eye, but when he lifts his face up from my neck to kiss my ear I guess something looks a little too familiar to him, and he turns me around to face him. He slides the sunglasses off my face.

"Hey, Karl," I say.

He starts to blush.

"Tex! What the hell you doin?"

"Just passing the time," I say.

"Damn, you are strange," he says, but he's smiling and

then he gives me a big hug. "I'm glad to see you, girl. I don't think I want to kiss you no more, though. You too much of a sister."

"Same here," I say. "I was just fooling with you."

"Good thing you didn't fool any farther than you did."

"I'm really sorry about Sophie," I tell him. "It was partly my fault. I could just die telling you that, but it's the truth. I'm so sorry."

"It ain't nothin," he says.

"Yeah it is," I say. "You lost your good dog. That's something."

"Yeah," he says. "She was a good dog, that's for damn sure. But you ain't got nothin to be sorry about, that's what I'm sayin. I know Jesus was responsible for the whole motherfucker. It was his finger pullin the trigger, not yours, and man, he shouldn't a been shootin at my dog. You just don't go around shootin at your friend's dog, you know what I mean?"

"I hear you," I say.

"I couldn't give Sophie no kinda life anyhow," he says, "with me always on the road and Jesus never lettin me bring her nowhere. Poor girl got shuffled around like nobody's business."

"Jesus is a jerk," I say. "I don't care if he's your cousin or whatever. You got all the sweetness in that family."

Then we hug some more and we sit up for a long time talking.

"Did you get my letter?" he asks.

"Yeah, I did. Thanks, Karl."

"Just thought you should know."

"I didn't want him anyway. But what about Jocelyn? Is Jesus beating her up or what?"

"Girl," he says, "that's somethin you don't even want to get into."

"So the answer is yes."

"Tex, the answer is that if I hear Jocelyn carryin on I go over to their room and knock on the door, and I walk Jesus up and down the hall till he ain't clenchin his fists no more. The answer is that I've taken that girl to the doctor more times than I can count, but I can't look out for her every minute. She gonna have to start doin it herself."

"I just want to know, that's all."

"Lacy, you the only woman that's ever said no to Jesus. You know how many women want to be gettin on a man makes the kind of money he does playin music? I mean to tell you, when you walked away from him, that's when I wanted to kiss you and dance you around the parking lot of the airport cause I was so proud of you. I know you seen him a couple of times after that, but it was pretty much over between y'all back then, far as I can tell. Somethin better's waitin for you, girl."

"Thanks, Karl," I say. "I'm gonna go on home now. You take care. Are y'all really going to Asia or was that just a line?"

"You take me for a liar, Tex? We got twenty shows scheduled over there already, and the office is workin on some more."

"Well, don't let anyone be slipping any dog into your food, now."

"Don't you let em, either," he says.

For the first few steps down the hall I can hear his sweet laughter.

YOU'D REMEMBER
ME BETTER IF
I WERE NAKED

I pull over at the rest stop outside Dallas to look again at the letter Irene sent me.

> *Dear Lacy,*
> *Enclosed is the address you asked for. Please don't do anything foolish.*
>
> *Love,*
>
> *Irene*

Underneath is Donny's address at a law firm in Northpark Towers in Dallas. So he is not president of Boy Scouts after all. He's an attorney. At the rest stop I crumple and uncrumple the paper while the man parked beside me changes a flat tire. People go in and out of the brick restrooms. Some get married, some get shot in quiet Dallas backyards, some become attorneys. The tire man's lips form mute swear words. The August heat fills my car and my mind stills in the heavy summer day. I start my car and drive down the ramp to merge with the Houston-Dallas traffic. When I get into Dallas I drive to Northpark, the shopping mall across from Donny's office. I park in a space designated for large cars. I walk around in the crisply air-conditioned stores until my sweat evaporates. In the Gap I see myself in a full-length mirror and think for an instant that it's someone else, I don't know who. My long hair is full of heat.

"Are you looking for anything special?" the teenage salesgirl says. She is undernourished and wears all black. An ID bracelet with nothing engraved on it encloses her wrist. Tiny silver rings pierce the peaks of each eyebrow.

"Not really," I say.

"All our minis are on sale," she says. Her feet in Doc Marten's look like two loaves of dark bread.

"Thanks," I say.

"They're in the back."

"Okay."

After I touch each on-sale mini I leave the Gap and drive across the highway to the Towers. A brass-lettered directory by the bank of elevators tells me the floor of the law firm Branham & Hall. A vase of daisies stands on the reception-ist's desk, but the chair is empty. From the front door I see Donny's office. He sits in a leather chair talking on the phone. He is looking out the huge window while he talks. The window has a view of the mall. If he wished, Donny could use his lunch break to take advantage of the Gap's sale on minis. A gold-plated football sits on his desk. I can-not read the engraving on its base. I stand in his doorway until he looks up. He has lost the baby fat he had as a teenager; he has somehow grown a jawline.

"Hold on a second, Al," he says into the phone. He presses the red hold button on the black telephone. "Can I help you?" he asks.

"I don't know," I say. "Can you?"

"I'm sorry," he says. "Do I know you?" One hand strokes his silk tie.

"Oh, come on, Donny," I say. "Do I look so different?"

"I don't know," he says.

"Maybe you'd remember me better if I were seven years old, naked, and sitting on your dick," I say.

I start to unbutton my blouse, one, two, three buttons.

"Stop it," he whispers.

A blush begins to rise from his collar, up and over the newly formed jawline.

"So you can blush," I observe. "Does that mean you're human?"

He hangs up the phone.

A man walks out of the next office and nods at me as he puts one hand on the door frame. He glances at my partially unbuttoned blouse.

"Don," he says, "we need to get that motion to continue filed today on Dalpez. Are you swamped?"

"Yeah," Donny says. "Course I'm swamped. But it's no problem. I'll get it in."

"Great," he says. He raps on the doorframe, inexplicably, then goes back into his own office.

"Lacy Springs," Donny says, as if we've just been introduced. "How are you? Do you still like football?" He gestures toward the gold-plated football trophy on one corner of his desk.

"Do you still like little girls?"

He comes from behind the desk, pulls me into his office, and closes the door. He is not as tall as I remembered.

"I don't know what you're talking about," he says. He lowers the blinds on the huge window. The phone starts ringing. He picks up the receiver and sets it back down again.

"Yes, you do."

"I actually don't. It's been really great seeing you, Lacy,

and I'd love to chat with you some more, but I've got this ..." He stares at his desk, his eyes darting back and forth over its surface. He toys with the string that controls the venetian blinds.

"Tell me you know what I'm talking about," I say.

"I really don't ..."

"Tell me you know what I'm talking about. I won't leave until you tell me."

"Okay. I know what you're talking about," he says.

"Yes, you do. But I'm not leaving yet."

"What do you want?" he says. "Do you want money?"

"Do you have a wife, Donny? Or do you go by Donald, now that you're a grown-up attorney?"

"Don or Donald is fine."

"Do you have a wife, Donald?"

"Yes, I do. I have a wife. We've been married four years." He picks up a silver frame from one corner of the desk and offers it to me. "My wife," he says. I hardly look at the photo. I don't really want to know what she looks like. I set it back on the corner of the desk. Donny backs away from me. He jerks the venetian blinds up a couple of inches, then down again.

"What's your wife's name?" I say.

"Marianne," he says.

"Does Marianne know she married a child molester?"

"I don't think so, no."

"Do you and Marianne have children?"

Up, down, sunlight and dust. The light slanting through the quivering blinds bounces off the football trophy on the edge of the desk.

"No, no children," he says.

"Don't have any," I say.

"What?"

"You heard me," I say. "I want you to know that I'm watching you," I say. "I want you to know that if I ever see you near a child, I'll spend the rest of my life putting you in jail."

He moves away from the window and picks up the golden football. He shifts it from one hand to the other.

"Okay," he says. "Well, it was nice seeing you. You've made yourself very clear."

I don't speak or move until his blush congeals into sweat, then I walk out of his office, past the secretary's vase of daisies, the brass-lettered directory in the lobby, the miniature palm trees planted along the building's walkway. Dallas is too cold for palm trees. I don't know what they were thinking.

MINE

I don't realize until I start packing for my trip to the Guadalupe Mountains that I left Ellis with most of our camping
stuff: the MSR stove, the tent, the horrible tin dishes that
are supposed to be so lightweight. I have my backpack, a
decent sleeping bag, and a few topo maps. I resist the temptation to call Ellis. I just want to drive out to West Texas
and hike up McKittrick Ridge as fast as I can and see if
he's there waiting for me. Or maybe it'll be me who waits
for him. I borrow a tent from Marilyn, one of my formerly
illiterate students, and buy a little propane stove. Marilyn
brings her tent over and we set it up in the living room.

"It's pretty comfortable," she says. "even for two people.
Are you going with someone?"

"I don't know," I say. "I might be meeting someone
there. A guy I used to be married to."

"Oh, Lord," Marilyn says. "Me and my ex, we were married twice. First time didn't teach us a damn thing. Neither
did the second time, come to think of it."

I crawl into the tent and look up at its tight blue ceiling.

"Come on in, Marilyn," I say, and she crawls through the flap and we sit in the artificial blue light and laugh.

"Playin house," she says. "That's what it always felt like when I was married. Then when the game's no fun anymore or you're losin so bad you'll never catch up, well, that's that. I'm sure you'll have a good time, though," she adds. "I'm sure it'll be different for you. You're so smart. Anyway, this ol thing could use a workout," she says, patting the nylon floor of the tent. "No fuckin been done in here for a long time."

"I can't promise you anything," I say.

"What do you mean, girl? You'll get out there away from this stinkin city and you'll start to feel all peaceful and horny and the next thing you know — wham bam thank you ma'am. Then when you get the first fuck out of the way you can do it nice and slow, like you got all the time in the world. Which you will, because what else is there to do in West Texas besides fuck?"

"I hear you," I say. "It's just hard to imagine right now. But maybe when I get out there I'll feel exactly like you say." I don't think I'm ready to make love with Ellis. I'm definitely ready to sit down with him on a warm stretch of rock and tell him some of my stories, and listen to some of his.

"You wanna go out for a beer?" she says. "I know a good place."

A six-inch-high Jesus statue is glued to the dashboard of Marilyn's old Cadillac. The sloppy plastic seam runs straight down his forehead, over his diminutive nose, down his collarbone, and the length of his blooded robe.

"Marilyn, you a Jesus-head?"

"Nah," she says. "That's just in case."

"Just in case what?"

"In case he's the real motherfucker, you know?"

"Yeah, I guess."

"Did I tell you I'm gettin me a real short haircut?" she says. She runs her hand through her long hair of an unidentifiable color. "It's all comin off, baby. Y'all are gonna think I'm a damn dyke."

"Yeah?" I say.

"Yeah," she says. "I gotta get some of this weight off my brain, open up some room for some new stuff to come in."

She drives us to a bar called the Tall Texan. I drink a beer so cold I can't taste it and contemplate Marilyn's future haircut.

"You sure about this hair thing?" I ask her.

"Yeah, I'm sure," she says. "It has somethin to do with you teachin me how to read. Watch, Lacy," and she reads the Surgeon General's warning off the side of her Shiner label.

"Show-off," I say.

"Anyway, the hair thing, it has somethin to do with that. All those years I couldn't read a damn thing, I just tortured my hair. Perms, all different colors. I been a redhead, a blond, I been dark as a Mexican. Lemme tell you."

"What's your real color?"

"I don't even know, girl. I couldn't tell you. Some shade of brown, I guess, but it's been so long since I seen it, I can't even picture it."

"I know what you mean," I say, and I do because I've done this with my own body — lived in it and fucked with it and let it carry me around without ever looking at it or stopping to know it.

"So, I'm gonna chop it off as short as I can stand it and let it grow back my own color, and I'm gonna read so many books — by the time my hair's long again, I'll be a goddamned genius."

"Hey, girl," I hear someone say from behind me, and

when I turn it's Laverna, my cellmate from county jail. She's got her hair in tiny dreadlocks, each the size of a pinky finger.

"Hey, Laverna," I say. "We're both free! Great hair," I add.

"She was my roommate in jail," I say to Marilyn.

"You still got that good-for-nothing husband?" I ask her.

"Yeah, I got him," she says. "Just barely. You still got that Elvis-hatin genius?"

"No," I say. "I sure don't."

"That's a shame," Laverna says. "This girl's only in county for two days," she tells Marilyn, "and her damn husband's callin her up on the prison radio show straight off. That's too bad, girl. It sounded like he had a good heart, you know what I mean?"

"I think the problem was more my heart than his."

"Yeah?"

"I guess so."

"You got a new job?" she says.

"Oh yeah," I say. "I had just quit, or been fired, I guess, when I met you in county."

"Has she got a job?" Marilyn says. "Listen, the girl rocks. She's the goddamn head of the city's illiteracy program. She teaches hundreds of dumb-asses like me how to read."

"I'm not the *head*, Marilyn."

"Well, you're next to the head — close enough."

"No way," Laverna says. "After all that kidnapping bull-shit?"

"Check this, Laverna — when I was trying to get this job, they called up my old school and my boss said I was one of the best teachers she'd ever had the pleasure of working with."

"Well, goddamn. You like it?"

"I love it," I say. "I love teaching grown-ups."

"Come in the bathroom with me," she says. "I gotta show you somethin," so I follow her through the door with a bow-legged cowgirl painted on it.

"What is it?" I ask. The bright bathroom reminds me of our cell in the county jail.

She grins at me, then unzips her tight jeans and tugs them down over her shiny green underwear. She pulls down the underwear, and across one side of her ass in solid, block letters is tattooed "MINE." The letters are maroon colored, a dark glow against her black skin.

"Oh, Laverna," I say. "That is too cool." I get goose-bumps looking at it.

"You like it?" she says. "I knew you were wantin to see it back in county, but I didn't feel up to showin it then. My husband can't stand it. Says he gonna cut it outta me. But if he did, I'd get another one just like it. Bigger letters."

"Laverna, maybe you should, you know ... look for a man with a good heart."

"You gonna give me yours?"

"I might still want him," I say.

"Yeah, I thought so. You got no business givin up a man who says he loves you over the radio."

"What about you, though?"

"I'm workin on it, girl." She touches the tattoo, runs her index finger back and forth over it a couple of times, then pulls her pants back up and we go on out to finish our beers. She hugs me before she goes back to her table of girlfriends.

"What the hell were y'all doin in there?" Marilyn says. "Maybe you should be the one gettin a dyke haircut."

"Maybe I will," I say.

DESSERT

The morning I finally start up the trail to the top of McKit-trick Ridge, all I can think about are the two empty slots on my list of One Hundred Things I Want Out of Life. The first slot's been empty all this time, so I'm used to that, but the second one bothers me, especially what it used to be — my wish to hear Black Jesus say hey my baby to me over and over. Maybe I wouldn't mind being called baby by a man who knows without a doubt I am not his baby or anyone else's, who sees my power and knows he can't take it from me, but I don't want to hear it from Jesus. What an asshole. I'm through with gods. I'm going to work on the human aspect of things for a while.

I think about the end of Ellis's book, *Nothing to See Here, Move Along,* which I finished in the parking lot of a gas station outside Van Horn when I couldn't stand to drive another mile without knowing what happened. Things turned out pretty well for Faith. At the end of the book she has one space left on her body that's not tattooed. One morning she wakes up and drives to her favorite tattoo parlor to see Hubbard McGinley, the kind tattoo artist who started out branding cattle on his uncle's ranch up in the Texas panhandle. He's learned a lot since his cattle-branding days, enough to have done the fine rendition of Fenway Park that curves across Faith's lower back. Faith just couldn't stand the Red Sox losing the '86 Series in that awful way.

"Well hello, Faith," Hubbard McGinley says when she's hardly through the door. He's lounging in his Naugahyde tattoo chair, a Shiner in one hand, the other turning down the volume of some early season baseball game, some game that doesn't matter much. But Faith matters to Hubbard, he's loved her ever since she brought in her illustrated Hans Christian Andersen and had him etch the girl with the red shoes on her inner calf. Hubbard loves to work on Faith, loves touching her soft, colorful skin that is a quilt of tattoos, some brighter than others. But he can't stand the pain his needle causes her, and when he does her tattoos he gets so worked up that he shakes for an hour or so afterward, and has to drink more beer than usual and sometimes smoke a little dope to calm himself down, and if he has another customer right after Faith he has to keep reminding himself what it is they asked for, he has to keep asking questions like, "You wanted the wings black, right, with a yellow stripe on the diagonal?" So this day, the day at the end of the book when Faith walks through Hubbard McGinley's door in a solid black sundress, tattoos up to her jawline, Hubbard McGinley feels the shakes coming on before he ever touches his tools, before Faith even tells him what she wants. Faith looks great in the dress. She always wears solid colors — patterns clash too much with her tattoos.

"I've got one spot left, Hub," she tells him, and pulls up her skirt to show him the bare space in the middle of her right thigh, the space next to the rosary made from tiny

balls of flame. Faith, like me, has had her own conflicts
with organized religion.

"Well, you must be savin that for my name," Hubbard
McGinley teases her.

"I was saving it for mine, actually," Faith says, and they
share a smile.

Then she writes out her signature for him and he spends
a slow afternoon copying her lovely script onto the last bare
spot of her thigh. He gives her the coldest beer from his
small fridge and he's more nervous than usual because he's
said her name so many times in his mind, and once caught
himself scrawling it on the back of an old invoice. But Faith
doesn't pay much attention to Hubbard because she's come
a long way to make this decision, she's spent a lot of hours
in the tattoo chair learning to love her own name. She's
spent a fair amount of time learning to love various parts
of herself: voice, eyes, sex, soul, walk, and finally her name.
And that's the way it ends, Hubbard a bundle of desire and
Faith full up with power and love for her ownself, not even
feeling the needle against her thigh or the longing of the
man who touches her.

About a mile up the trail I feel so hot I can't think about
Faith or anything else. It's really too late to be out in these
mountains, it's so hot and dry. I should have come a month
earlier, at the beginning of May, but my timing with Ellis
has always been slightly off. We just have to go with it. I
stop and lift my hair off my neck and start to twist it into
a braid. The hair that was closest to my neck is wet
through, and I twist these strands in with the dry ones,
bending my head down to get it out of the way of my
backpack. Then my neck starts to stiffen and I look straight
up instead. I see a white-tailed hawk riding the updrafts,
tilting in a smooth upward spiral. His back is tawny and
mottled, his wings are tipped with black, and the single
stripe at the base of his tail gives me that breathless, about-

to-cry feeling I think people sometimes get when they remember some happy moment from childhood. But I'm not
remembering, I'm looking forward, and I slip the heavy
pack off my back so I can lie in the red Texas dirt and get
a decent look at that hawk. If Eva were here, she'd tell me
it's a good omen, she'd ask me what message I hear in the
soft slice of feather and bone through air. I'd tell her it's
the end of a few things that have happened to me, including my family, my first career, my marriage, Black Jesus
and my blues phase, and some other things I've already
forgotten. I'd ask her what message she hears. Who knows
what she'd say.

Maybe Ellis will be waiting for me at the end of this
trail. Maybe he'll see my red braid through the trees and
feel a deep swell of delicious love. I hope he'll be there,
because I'd like to take him in my arms and hold him so
hard that he'll know I'm strong now. If the clearing where
we're supposed to meet is empty, I'll make my own sleeping
place and cook a pot of rehydrated soup only I will know
the taste of. Either way, I'll be me, Lacy. That's a good
thing. Either way, I'd like to say to my sisters, my brothers,
and future lovers: the white belly of the hawk stretching
away from me is the first great happening of this day. I
don't know what fine thing will come next — do you?
Something always does.